AN UNCOMPROMISING TALE OF LOYALTY AND BETRAYAL THAT CHALLENGES OUR LONG-HELD BELIEFS ABOUT POWER AND TERRORISM.

Karla, a German terrorist, dreams of a free Palestine; Andrew Black, a renegade assassin, seeks order beyond disorder, and Jim Murphy an FBI agent is haunted by the memory of a daughter abandoned years earlier. After a hostage situation goes awry, Karla flees the scene with Murphy in pursuit. As the chase continues the three find themselves trapped in a world of shifting alliances, faceless informants and deceit. Torn between conflicting loyalties, each is drawn to a fateful rendezvous in Geneva.

A street hawker's cry pierced the air, the city alive now. The man bent down and unzipped the portfolio, letting the case flop open. He took up the surgical gloves and pulled them on, flexed his fingers and settled back in the chair.

Perspiration inched down his temples as he waited. A cockroach darted across the back of his hand. When it came to his wrist, the roach stopped, lifted its head as if to scent the air, then turned and wandered back down his hand. Down one finger, then the next. Cul-de-sacs.

The man didn't move.

An hour later when the Salvadorans' ancient Chevrolet coasted to the curb he stiffened as if awakened by a noise in the night. The man exhaled deliberately, the sound harsh at the back of his throat, then reached down and lifted the rifle from the case, his hands like porcelain in the early morning light, and eased the curtain sheer aside with the tip of the barrel.

i

Across the way sunlight glinted off the black paintwork of the Chevrolet. After a few moments three dark figures emerged. When the Salvadorans entered the bank, he rechecked everything, the angles and fields of fire, then lowered the rifle and propped it upright on his thigh.

"Dennis Medina's novel, *The Madness of the Brave*, is a wonderfully high strung telling of professional assassins and of a woman who is ducking their crosshairs, set in the post-Viet Nam and Palestinian era of tensions... there are shades of John le Carré with the twists in plot, the international settings, and the utter duplicity of several of its characters... Medina has a fine ear for his characters."—*John Keeble, author of Broken Ground and The Shadows of Owls*

"In the world of international intrigue Dennis Medina proves once again that the most compelling espionage thrillers aren't necessarily about super spies. He crafts a thought-provoking story with vivid characters whose lives as cool operatives are complicated by deep stirrings of the human heart."—*Joanne Meschery, author of Home and Away*

"Dennis Medina has created an addictive, skillfully composed thriller about passion and power. A masterful blend of history and fiction. Uniquely plotted and filled with finely wrought, dedicated yet disturbing characters."—*K. Bartholomew, author of We didn't know any better: Poems. About life*

"Dennis Medina's novel follows Karla, a German woman abandoned as a child by her GI father, as she navigates the insular world of 1970s political terrorism...Through Medina's finally focused, tactile writing we experience the moment the trigger is pulled, the harshness of a comrade's death and the taste of betrayal. A brilliant work by a fine emerging writer."—*Raymond Hutson, author of Topeka, ma'shuge and Finding Sgt. Kent*

THE MADNESS OF THE BRAVE

D. P. Medina

Moonshine Cove Publishing, LLC

Abbeville, South Carolina U.S.A.

FIRST MOONSHINE COVE EDITION JUNE 2018

This book is a work of fiction. Names, characters, places and incidents are products of the author's imagination or are used fictitiously. Any resemblance to actual events, locales or persons, living or dead, is entirely coincidental.

ISBN: 978-1-945181-38-2
Library of Congress Control Number: 2017947276
Copyright © 2018 by D. P. Medina

Photo courtesy of Fancycrave, front cover design by Kenyon Sharp, back cover design by Moonshine Cove staff.

For two women: my mother, Margaret Mary (Peggy) Medina, and my wife and partner, Barbara London Medina.

About The Author

The author, a former international marketing executive, has contributed material to numerous mining industry magazines  and published fiction in SpokeWrite. He attended the University of Southern California and has a graduate degree from Eastern Washington University where for a time he was Fiction Editor of Willow Springs. As a graduate student he received a Weber-Riemcke-Schreiner Scholarship from the Washington chapter of the Daughters of the American Revolution. He loves the irony of that. In his younger years he worked as a clerk in a general store, a caregiver of autistic teens, an EMT/ambulance driver, and as a manager at Squaw Valley Ski Area. He is a trail runner, hiker and cyclist. He and his wife currently live in southwestern Colorado and travel extensively. They have two adult sons.

For news about the author and what he is working on now, visit his website: www.dpmedina.com

Acknowledgments

So many to thank for their tireless support. I am especially indebted to John Keeble, Joanne Meschery, Ursula Hegi and Tom Jenks for their encouragement over the years. Special thanks to Kaye Bartholomew and Raymond Hutson for their close reading of various drafts of the manuscript, Dylan Medina for his French translation and web-mastering, Gabriella for the Italian translation, Ted Wagner and Brett Smith for their bits of German, and Kenyon Sharp for the cover design. Thanks also to the many people who read various drafts of the manuscript and their spot-on but gentle criticism – Ed Adams, Rick Boal, Carrie Bucher, Debbie Cain, Anastasia Hilton, Pamela Kester, Christopher Newton, Sheryl Redding-Hutson, Mark Shrader and Dixie Zahniser as well as Gene Robinson for his astute editorial advice. And finally, my wife Barbara for her unwavering support.

The Eastern Washington University Creative Writing Program provided the freedom to focus on this novel during its early stages. As part of my research I made liberal use of information contained in the following texts: *Vietnam – A History: The First Complete Account of the Vietnam War* by Stanley Karnow, *A Bright Shining Lie: John Paul Vann and America in Vietnam* by Neil Sheehan, and *FBI: An Uncensored Look Behind the Walls* by Sanford J. Ungar.

In closing, this is a work of fiction written through the prism of memory.

The madness of the brave is the wisdom of life.

—Maxim Gorky

THE MADNESS
OF THE BRAVE

PROLOGUE
September 1979 — San Salvador

Shadows filled the room darkening the whitewashed walls. The man stepped to the French doors and peered through the gauzy curtain sheers. Just beyond was a small balcony, the ornate scrollwork of its wrought-iron railing painted black, and the boulevard one-story below. He had a clear view of the bank opposite and the angles were perfect. Exactly as they had said.

For a few moments the man considered the possibilities. Getting involved in the Salvadoran operation would complicate everything, he knew. He could still walk away, blow them off. Yet he was here as a favor to his friend Khalil. An obligation, he felt. A debt owed. And they told him to act only if necessary. Keep it clean, they'd said. He preferred it that way too.

The man eased the doors open without a sound, then retreated a step and settled himself in a straight-backed wooden chair, hidden, the art portfolio propped upright beside him. Across the way a gray-haired woman dressed in black dragged her broom across the sidewalk in front of the bank; farther down the block the tortilla man, the only other soul in sight, wobbled down the street astride his bicycle, straw hat flickering as he passed beneath a streetlamp. Humidity was thick in the air.

The man sat back.

Salvador, he thought. El Salvador.

***

The dark shadows had lightened to gray and the sound of a bus accelerating rose to the open doors. A street hawker's cry pierced the air, the city alive now. The man bent down and unzipped the portfolio, letting the case flop open. He took up the surgical gloves and pulled them on, flexed his fingers and settled back in the chair.

Perspiration inched down his temples as he waited. A cockroach darted across the back of his hand. When it came to his wrist, the roach stopped, lifted its head as if to scent the air, then turned and wandered back down his hand. Down one finger, then the next. Cul-de-sacs.

The man didn't move.

***

An hour later when the Salvadorans' ancient Chevrolet coasted to the curb he stiffened as if awakened by a noise in the night. The man exhaled deliberately, the sound harsh at the back of his throat, then reached down and lifted the rifle from the case, his hands like porcelain in the early morning light, and eased the curtain sheer aside with the tip of the barrel.

Across the way sunlight glinted off the black paintwork of the Chevrolet. After a few moments three dark figures emerged. When the Salvadorans entered the bank, he rechecked everything, the angles and fields of fire, then lowered the rifle and propped it upright on his thigh. Only a few more minutes. And if all went according to plan he could leave as he had come, uninvolved. Without complication — the thought a shimmer in his mind.

There was a gleam at the edge of his vision, a reflection where before there had been nothing. He swung the rifle and saw two guardias walking toward the bank, the high polish of their helmets catching the light. And a third — a U.S. military advisor, his jungle fatigues crisp, like a flag in a breeze.

He zoomed the scope to full magnification and the advisor's rosy features sharpened. Then dialed the power back down. No one had said anything about Americans.

The soldiers paused at an intersection one hundred yards up the block and chatted for a few moments. The advisor reached into his blouse pocket, took out a pack of cigarettes and offered it. The guardias slung their rifles over their shoulders; pedestrians eddied around them as they lit up.

All the while the man in the room kept the advisor centered in his scope. It was coincidence, he decided. A *faux* opportunity. They were out for a stroll.

He lifted his head and glanced back at the bank. One of the Salvadorans stood just inside the doorway, head swiveling, surveying the street, bird-like, the Chevrolet idling smoothly at the curb. After several moments the other two appeared. He looked back down the street; the soldiers hadn't moved. *Keep it clean.*

The doors flew open and the robbers burst from the bank, backpedaling across the sidewalk, pistols waving. The soldiers dropped their cigarettes. The man put his eye back to the scope, the moment fraught with possibility. With complication.

Keep it clean … keep it clean. A mantra now.

Then his mind cleared. Silence, the moment distilled. A moment beyond their bounds, beyond friendship, beyond all bounds.

He took the first *guardia* slightly high and away to the left, the side of the man's head coming away with the gleaming helmet. The second, after correcting, he took dead center. The street quiet as he swung the rifle — in cadence — on the advisor. But the advisor had moved.

He slid the rifle over the scene, saw the green fatigue cap peek from behind a parked car then drop from view. He was thinking, the gunman knew, trying to figure out where the shots had come from and how to get to the dead men's M16s.

The gunman waited, calm, breathing easily. The street remained quiet, no cries, no whispers, no screams. As if time had stopped. Then there was a long low keening wail and the screaming began …

People flashed across the scope; the dark shape of the robber's Chevrolet streaked past. Still he waited, patient, trigger at the limit. When the cap popped up, he squeezed off the shot and watched the bullet tear into the American, his head exploding in a fine red mist.

He withdrew the rifle and placed it back in the portfolio, replaying the shots in his mind. His SSG performed perfectly, absolutely perfectly. Except for the scope, he thought. Someone had fiddled with the windage and elevation adjustments in transit, someone who didn't know what he was doing. One of Raymond's people.

The gunman shook his head as he bent to retrieve the spent cartridges, tossing them into the case with the rifle. Just then the sound of a bus slowing rose from the street and for a moment he pictured the copper-skinned men clinging to the open windows, toeing its rippled skin. Then he zipped the art portfolio closed, picked it up and left, leaving the room as he had found it. Shadows everywhere.

***

He squinted in the sunlight as he stepped outside. People stumbled into him as they rushed past. Halfway down the block the bus had stopped, a black cloud of exhaust rising above it; the men he imagined only moments ago clinging to its metal bodywork joined the crowd gathering at the end of the block where the dead men lay.

Their bounds, the man thought. Not mine. And he turned and

walked away slowly.

After several blocks the gunman crossed the cobbled boulevard to a dented Volkswagen van and exchanged the art portfolio for the travel bag he left inside earlier. As he slid the side door shut, he noticed his hands were pale, white from the powdery residue of the latex gloves. He shucked his jacket, folded it neatly over one arm and signaled an approaching taxi.

"To where?" the driver asked.

"*Al aeropuerto*," he said, keeping his hands low behind the seat as he climbed in.

"*¿Usted no es de aquí?*"

"No," he agreed. "*Soy del Brasil.*" Which explained his accent and fair skin.

"*¿Va a Rio?*"

He ignored the question and when the driver's eyes sought his in the mirror he ignored them as well.

As the cab pulled from the curb the gunman settled back on the seat and closed his eyes. In the distance he could hear sirens screaming.

I

Chapter 1

Karla lay on the mattress, Sam asleep beside her. The city-heat close, palpable. Air conditioners hummed in the airshaft beyond the burglar's gate and locked window; thunder rumbled in the distance. From somewhere in the building came a sharp scream. Of pain? she wondered. Or of pleasure? She could no longer say for sure — two weeks cooped up in apartment house in New York had dulled her senses. And she hated the waiting, unable to relax, hovering just above sleep, dozing but never dreaming.

Karla rolled onto her side and took a deep breath, exhaled deliberately. The window was dirty, she noticed, smudged. The light outside gray, listless. Another day, she thought as she let her eyes wander from the window across the drab-white walls. They lingered for a moment on a spot near the door, pale where the plaster had been patched, then she tossed again, the clammy sheet sticking to her bare wet skin, and lifted her head and rolled her long blonde hair up and off her neck and lay upon it like a pillow.

It was the empty time before the action, Karla knew. *Zeit in der Vorhölle*. And she accepted her mood without question, without qualm. As she did her presence here.

Their mattress lay on the bedroom floor — cooler there, Sam told her before he went to sleep. The top of the sheet was tucked neatly at his waist and his belly rose gently with each breath. The desert had left him lean and taut, had turned his skin tea-brown; droplets of sweat lay gathered along his upper lip and Karla wanted to lick them off, to touch him, to feel his naked body against her own. But she didn't disturb Sam. Instead she wiped her fingers on the sodden sheet and when she did the air didn't move.

She envied Sam his sleep. His military service in Vietnam left him impervious to the jungle heat. The thought made Karla smile — New York City, the cultural center of the universe, and the climate was primitive.

The wet heat was as much to blame for her restlessness as was the waiting, she knew. In the dry air of the *hamad* she was content to wait, and came to love the quiet time between operations. Without effort she let her mind drift back to those times, to late afternoons in Saba' Byar when she would climb the rise behind the camp and sit cross-legged on the desert ridgetop. She remembered the heat all around, remembered staring into the distance waiting for the landscape to come alive. Remembered the breeze rustling through the brush, through her cotton blouse, remembered the dampness between her breasts. And the quiet, so quiet.

***

The sun filled the pale desert sky and late summer heat shimmered above the valley floor. Without shifting her gaze Karla loosened the kaffiyeh where it touched her face and let the scarf bag out so she could breathe more easily. A jackal cried in the distance, a yelp in reply. Before long a flock of sheep clambering down the dry wash that split the valley caught her eye, their keeper, a switch in hand, picking his way over the rocks behind them. Then she noticed the squad of new recruits weaving through the roan-colored boulders to the south, returning from the day's exercises, their weapons aimed haphazardly at the ground. Farther out, too far for her to make out the sound of its engine, a car approached. A swirl of dust funneling in its wake.

Hand to her brow, Karla tracked the car. It was a Mercedes

sedan, dust-faded and colorless, and she wondered if it carried more recruits. Sam came that way only six months ago though it seemed longer than that. Longer before they became lovers — shorter since. Their affair began two months ago in a flash of pure heat and had since cooled to an anticipatory glow. In her mind it simply happened.

When the car pulled among the tents below her, Akira, the Japanese man who oversaw camp activities, ran to greet it. Only one man — a trifle of a man — got out. He was swathed in a baggy djellaba and a red and white headdress not unlike the one she wore covered the lower half of his face. The two men embraced then held each other at arms' length, heads bobbing as they spoke, their words lost in the late afternoon breeze.

In time they retreated to Akira's tent. Thirty minutes later they sent for her and as she hastened down the hillside Karla scanned the valley of Saba' Byar one last time. The sun had dissolved behind the mountains to the west and the distant cliff faces glowed blood-red in the early evening light. Like ancient monuments, she thought. Sculpted by time.

When she pushed aside the flap on the tent, the two men looked up from behind the makeshift desk. Khalil al-Fasani — it hadn't occurred to her that he was the visitor — stood beside Akira.

A smile drifted across the Palestinian's face. "You look well, Karla. The desert agrees with you."

"As it should," Akira put in.

Karla smiled. She hadn't seen Khalil in more than a year. He had recruited her five years earlier — rescued her really — from the ruins of the Rote Armee Fraktion. The RAF's actions had become increasingly vicious, reactive, and Khalil had appeared among the flames, a vision. He spoke eloquently of the

Palestinian cause, how they were the great irony of the post-war world, how they had become the Jews of the late 20th century while the Israelis were the new National Socialists, and as he spoke she caught a glimpse of a new direction, a new life, a new dream.

And Karla smiled again, smiled as she had that day in Syria. Waiting even then.

Khalil removed his kaffiyeh and shuffled through some papers on the desk. Even in the shadows his dark coarse hair gleamed.

"We need several teams," he said as he continued to dig through the papers.

"You know I am ready, Khalil."

The Palestinian looked up. This time he didn't smile, his expression grave, somber. "You leave for New York tomorrow. You'll use the Ulrike Herger passport."

Karla nodded without a word. Khalil had given her a Swiss passport in that name when he recruited her. She used it to travel to Syria and during the Haifa operation, and kept it tucked among the few things she brought with her from Germany.

"You will be holding a hostage for the Red Path," he went on. "A man named Raymond will be your operational control."

"Sam Grossman is the other member of your team," Akira said, cutting in once again.

"How do you feel about him?" Khalil stared at her.

Karla met his gaze. She appreciated his directness — the whole camp knew about their affair — but she knew Khalil wasn't asking about her love life. He wanted to know if the relationship posed a problem. And more importantly if Sam, a new recruit, posed one.

She took her time with her answer. Sam was young, impulsive, resentful at times, but she had watched him these past few months, listened to him open up about his past, about *his* dream, and now for her questioning his commitment seemed almost an act of betrayal.

"He's too impatient," she said at last. "He's anxious to prove himself."

"His ardor could be a ploy."

"You know how Americans are, Khalil. They always have to prove themselves."

The Palestinian studied her face a moment longer. "Watch him, Karla. This first operation don't trust him any more than is necessary."

"You know I am always careful."

Khalil waved away her words as if her assurances went without saying then returned to the papers scattered on the desktop. He rifled through them until he came to a thick stack of American Express travelers' checks. He picked them up and tossed them onto the desk in front of her; the checks were unsigned in $100 denominations.

"That should be enough to carry you through the operation. Grossman will have money as well."

"The operation will take time," Akira said. "Like your American friend, you must be patient."

"The other teams have to be assembled," Khalil said. "And even once the operation begins it will go slowly."

Karla looked at the pile of travelers' checks — at least $20,000 U.S.

"Our cause won't evoke immediate sympathy," Khalil went on. "At times it may seem you are waiting for nothing. But you must wait, Karla. You must wait."

***

And so they waited, she and Sam, her American lover. For two weeks they waited for the contact's call, never venturing out of the apartment except for the occasional trip to the grocer's. Wasting time.

Karla rose onto an elbow and gazed at Sam. He was still sleeping peacefully beside her and it occurred to her that the waiting didn't bother him. It only bothered her.

A fly buzzed into the room spinning erratic circles in the air. When it settled on Sam's shoulder, she whisked it away. His eyelids fluttered for a moment and again she wanted to touch him, to run her fingers along his cheek, over his chest, to feel him.

She crawled closer and Sam stirred. He had an erection, she noticed, and she imagined him inside her, remembering the first time they made love, the sweet rhythm, their bodies smooth and slick in the desert heat.

Her breath caught when Sam bent to her breast. His tongue flicked her nipple, circling, seeking. She pressed her hand against the side of her breast to give him more; Sam drew her into his mouth as if breathing him in and she felt the heat again. Close — like a warm bath.

She touched his head, played with the ringlets in his hair as his fingers slid down her side, over her hip, between her thighs, caressing her. She spread her legs and Sam shifted his weight on top of her. He nuzzled her neck, nipped at her ear, then she guided him deep inside, feeling him fill her. And with each thrust she coaxed him deeper ... deeper. The heat making it so easy, so natural, so instinctive.

**

Sam was asleep again when the telephone rang. It jingled once and stopped. Karla sat up and put her hand on the receiver. At the airport in Damascus Khalil had taken her aside and explained the contact procedure. There would be a call, a single ring, and an immediate call back. Once again he reminded her not to trust Sam. *Your American lover* — those were his exact words.

The telephone danced in Karla's hand. She felt Sam wake beside her as she lifted the receiver. When he opened his mouth to speak, she put a finger to his lips.

"Hello."

"There is a drugstore at the corner of 63rd Street and Central Park West," a man's voice said.

Sam scooted closer trying to listen in, but Karla kept the receiver pressed tightly to her ear.

"In the back is a phone booth. You will receive a call in ten minutes."

Then the line went dead and she set the handset back in its cradle without having uttered another word.

She swung her legs off the mattress, hopped up and grabbed her khaki trousers, then took a handful of tissues from the box on the nightstand and wiped herself. She didn't bother with panties and left them lying on the floor.

"Where are you going?"

"Out," she said as she tugged the pants over her hips.

"I'll go with you."

Sam started to get up.

"No, stay here. There may be another call," she said, slipping into the lie with such ease that it startled her.

Sam slumped back onto the mattress.

Karla stood on her toes, pulled up her zipper. They were only words, she told herself. A harmless lie.

"Who was it anyway?"

"Our first contact," she said, reaching for her cotton tank top.

"What did he want?"

"I don't know." Only a partial lie this time.

"You sure you don't want me to come with you?"

Karla smiled. "I'm sure," she said, then turned back to Sam and caught him ogling her, staring at her breasts. His aqua eyes bright, alight. He seemed to take delight in her body, a body she had always thought flat and boyish.

"Close your eyes. Go back to sleep."

Sam's eyes held her a moment longer, then he did as he was told. He was hard again beneath the sheet; remembering the intensity of their lovemaking, the incandescence, Karla felt a shiver of desire but put it from her mind.

She pulled on her tank top, shook out her hair and slipped into her sandals. "I won't be long," she called softly.

Sam raised a hand without opening his eyes and let it fall back to the mattress. On her way out Karla grabbed a handful of cash and the Herger passport from the living room table and shoved them into her pocket. She closed the apartment door quietly behind her and took the lift to the ground floor.

* * *

Outside, the street was deserted, empty: the city's quiet time. A sultry wind swept Karla east, crumpled paper like autumn leaves sailing in the gray dawn. At the corner of 65th Street and Central Park West she paused for a few moments. Across the way, above the park wall, the leaves on the trees were turned up in the wind, their undersides pale green, as if faded. A cross-town bus lumbered past spewing exhaust into the air and she was reminded of Syria again, of the Bedouins' charcoal braziers, their judicious desert hospitality. Home.

Karla glanced at her watch — six more minutes — then set off again, hurrying south. Somehow she knew her contact would be precise. *Exakt.*

When she entered the drugstore, a bell tinkled overhead.

There was a round balding black man standing behind the front counter, a newspaper spread on the countertop before him. He looked up and Karla motioned toward the phone booth in the back, reluctant to speak, afraid her accent would give him something to remember her by.

The clerk gave her a brisk nod and returned to his reading. She kept a bank of shelving between them as she made her way to the back. The shop, like the street, was deserted. A bundle of newspapers, edges dented and torn, lay on the floor next to the phone booth. U.S. ADVISOR SLAIN IN EL SALVADOR proclaimed the headline. Beneath it in smaller typeface: *Assassin's Identity Unknown.*

At least someone's operation was running, Karla thought. She hadn't allowed herself to believe theirs had begun.

She stepped into the phone booth and unfolded the door, securing it behind her. Overhead a fluorescent light blinked then flashed on, ballast humming; someone had tagged the wall next to the phone — CK in radiant purple on the dark wood. Her pants clung to her thighs as she sat down. Karla plucked at the fabric, then pulled the phonebook from the shelf beneath the telephone and flipped through the pages pretending to look for a number.

When the phone rang, she grabbed it in mid-ring.

"Karla?" It was the same voice, the same American accent.

"Yes."

"This is Raymond."

Karla felt the listlessness of the past two weeks lift as if her body had sighed. *Endlich.*

"Hello? Are you there?"

"Yes, I'm here."

"I trust all is well."

"We've been waiting."

"You were told to wait."

Karla didn't say anything. She shifted on the seat, tugged at her trousers again. He'd spoken to her as if she were a child.

"Your friend knows nothing?"

The question startled Karla and for a moment she wondered if this was some kind of test, the constant doubts about Sam, Raymond's tone, the waiting, though there were better ways to test her loyalty — and Sam's.

"I have told him nothing."

"Good. You leave New York today." Her heart stirred. "Rent a car. Use your friend's papers. You can arrange that?"

Karla let the question hang for a moment, a hush like electricity on the line. As a new recruit Sam was the logical one to use as a cutout, but the matter-of-factness of Raymond's request, the ease with which he was doing it, with which she was letting him, made her feel dirty, sullied.

She remembered the way Sam looked at her only minutes ago, the hunger in his eyes, her own desire and shivering.

Karla closed her eyes — it's hypothetical, a remote possibility. And she always knew where her ultimate loyalty lay. The cause was more important than Sam or her, was more important than any of them.

Spirits buoyed, she opened her eyes and found the clerk watching her. She stared at him and he looked away.

"He will do as I ask."

"Good. Khalil said you could be trusted to do that."

She pictured their control at the other end of the line, smiling, smug, pleased with himself — and with her.

"In one hour a packet of maps and instructions will be delivered to you." Raymond's voice was flat, uninflected, as if he were reading a script for the first time. "You're going to Vermont.

There's a farmhouse. Your friend will know the way. The area is familiar to him. Wait there for my call."

Khalil's words came back to her. *At times it may seem you are waiting for nothing.*

"For how long?"

"Not long," Raymond said, his voice stroking her now. "The hostage will be brought to you in a few days. I'll contact you day after tomorrow with final details. Be ready, Karla. Your part is crucial to the success of the operation."

Then he paused as if waiting for further questions but Karla didn't have any questions, at least none she could ask. She knew what she needed to do.

"Go now," Raymond told her. "Rent the car. Get to Vermont. And Karla …"

Another pause, another hush. She could hear the faint squawk of voices on a crossed line.

"This man. If there is a problem … kill him."

Raymond hung up without waiting for a reply. Karla placed the handset back on its hook and stared straight ahead, eyes fixed on wall. In a kidnapping, executing was always the last option, the final option.

"Yes," she whispered.

Yes, yes, yes.

It had finally begun.

***

The shocks wheezed as the Datsun 210 rental car bumped down the country lane. At road's edge were wet green ferns, glistening. The Ompompanoosuc — Sam made her pronounce the name over and over until she got it right — roared in the distance. A late afternoon thundershower had just ended and she could smell the earthy scent in the air. Like freshly sliced mushrooms.

Karla cranked the passenger window the rest of the way down and let her arm dangle along the side of the car. After a few moments her skin prickled and she shivered. The humid air had a cool edge to it this far north — and this late in the day. And it was September, she reminded herself. Almost fall. Long shadows of between seasons lay along the road.

She watched Sam out of the corner of her eye as he drove. He seemed at home here, negotiating the country lane with ease, swinging around the potholes and speeding up whenever they came to a straightaway. He hadn't uttered a single word on the drive up except for the occasional grunt for the map and his pronunciation lesson. That was the only time he had laughed, and he was sulking now.

Karla had told him about the car — she thought it the right thing to do — and Sam rented it with grace. But he couldn't understand why she wouldn't tell him anything more though she had to admit there was little to tell, something she willingly accepted.

Yet they weren't so different — she and Sam. America had betrayed both of them: Sam, six years ago in Vietnam, and her much earlier in Germany. In 1946 an American GI deserted her mother, leaving her pregnant. Her father promised to return and her mother believed he would until the end. As a child, Karla believed it too. But as she grew older she came to accept that her father would never be back. In time she even came to think of his return as a joke, his "second coming."

She never learned to hate him though. How could she hate someone who, for her at least, wasn't even a memory? It was the impossibility of her mother's dream — false hope, a life wasted on a lie — that she hated. At times she even wondered if her father was an illusion, a fragment of an imagined past. But there were the pictures — always there were the pictures. Karla would never forget watching her mother, fingers all-gnarled, leaf through the box of photographs, of memories. Her mother would always pause on her personal favorite and, eyes alight, hold the photograph of her lover aloft. His uniform had appeared crisp even in black and white. Her mother never gave up hope.

Karla believed her own hopes were less illusory than her mother's. They were based on the possible, not denial. On truth, not lies. And *they* drove her to the Rote Armee and eventually to the camp in Syria and her own GI lover, and the irony didn't escape her.

Sunlight flickered through the trees as they continued down the narrow road. Thunderheads like piles of egg whites billowed in the sky. Directly ahead a smear of dead animal marked the blacktop; Karla looked away and saw the farmhouse beyond a stand of birch on the left, at the top of a rise exactly as described in the instructions. A hayfield fronted the farmhouse and at two hundred yards the house appeared to rise from the golden waves, the dirt road leading to it like a part in a person's hair.

"There," she said, raising her arm and pointing it out.

Sam nodded, then slowed and turned into the rutted drive. The rental car rattled as they bumped up the hill. The house windows were dark and the porch out front stood empty, the floorboards sprung and warped. The place appeared abandoned and listed to one side as if leaning into a breeze. Behind it was a stretch of pure azurite sky.

The tires crunched as they pulled into the gravel clearing in front of the house. Sam shut down the engine and sat for a few moments, hand on the key. Engine coolant sizzled as it dripped back into the radiator; the air buzzed with cicadas. And with tension, Karla thought.

Sam climbed out and whipped his door shut. Still sulking he trod to the back of the car. She could feel his eyes on the back of her head as he popped the trunk lid — only he wasn't ogling her now. He was taking all this personally. Which in a way, she imagined, he had a right to. But in another he didn't, and she hoped he would come to understand her reticence by the time they were finished here.

Karla pushed the passenger door open and got out. The field rolled unimpeded down the hillside below her. On the far side of the road was a flat area of scrub and brush, and beyond that a steep hillside thick with maple and birch. The river, out of sight but still roaring, cut a path between the two, and for a moment she pictured the water rushing over the rocks, tumbling, foaming.

Sam nudged her arm and held out her bag. They walked around the car together and up the front steps in silence, treads creaking beneath their feet. Sam reached up and located the key hidden above the window, unlocked the front door and held the screen open for her.

Karla eased past him and stepped inside. The house smelled of old newspapers and neglect. Faded wallpaper hung in strips from the dingy plaster walls; a tattered beige sofa leaned against the wall facing the front door. Through the doorway beside it she caught a glimpse of a hallway and kitchen, a chrome-legged table and two chairs.

Silky cobwebs clung to her face and hair as she made her way across the living room. She swiped at them and wiped her hands on her pants as she entered the hallway. On the right a staircase led to the upper floor. On the left was the kitchen. There were two doors down the hall on the right, another at the far end. Karla walked down the hall and opened the doors onto two bedrooms, each as shabby as the other, and a toilet. She flushed the rust-stained fixture, tried the faucet. A deep groan — nothing. Then went back down the hall and jogged up the stairs, Sam following, and found three more bedrooms.

"I'll see to the water," Sam said as he started back down the stairs. "This place must have a well."

"Fine," she called after him. "I could use a shower. We'll use the two bedrooms downstairs."

Sam stopped, hand on the banister, looked up at her. "Two bedrooms?"

She'd slipped, Karla realized. And such a simple slip.

Sam waited for a reply. But she wouldn't lie to him — lying was for Raymond. He would just have to accept her silence.

"You don't trust me, do you? Any of you?"

Sam was still looking up at her.

"I trust you," she said quietly.

"I'm just as committed as anyone."

"I know. But none of us is given more information than is necessary. Nothing is lost that way."

"Nothing but your faith in people." Sam looked away, disheartened.

Karla went down the stairs to him, looped her arm through his. He refused to look at her. She rubbed his back, his shirt damp beneath her hand.

"It's the same for me, Sam. Honest. The less we know, the less we have to worry about telling."

But Sam didn't want to hear that. "I'm new, right. So don't trust me."

"It isn't a matter of trust. It's a matter of what makes sense. And even if I knew something of importance I couldn't say. Why should I? To prove I trust you? I thought we were beyond that. Trust isn't something you prove. It's something you give."

"It's you who doesn't trust me."

Karla gave up. She let her hand slip from his back and continued down the stairs. "I'm sorry. I've done what I can."

"So have I."

She stopped and looked up at him. For a moment his eyes met hers, challenging her. Then they flitted away. And once again she realized how young he seemed, younger than twenty-five.

"Okay," he said finally. "We'll do it your way."

"Come," she said, beckoning him. "Let's get to work."

Sam came the rest of the way down the stairs and as he passed her said without animosity: "You're so fucking stubborn, Karla."

"I know."

"Just so you do."

I do, she thought, I honestly do. Then followed him in his search for the well.

***

Late that evening Karla stood on the front porch staring into the black night. The air smelled of hay and the river was somnolent now. A light breeze whispered through the field. *Swishing.* A country sound, a desert sound. A sound from the *hamad*. From home.

Her mind began to float and Saba' Byar came back to her, the faded sky, the wind rustling across the valley floor, the desolation.

Karla caught herself and dragged her thoughts back to the present, to Vermont, to the day after tomorrow, and she let the questions come now, questions she hadn't allowed Sam or herself. She couldn't help but wonder about the operation, its purpose. It was natural, she thought, curiosity if nothing else. Everyone wondered. The harm came when you couldn't give others your trust. That was what she tried to explain to Sam that afternoon: without trust you had nothing, you were all alone.

Karla rested her hands on the porch railing, the peeling paint prickly against her skin, and gazed out over the field. Across the way the hillside was dark; the star-washed sky shimmered above. Behind her, in the house, a broom swept methodically across the living room floor. She and Sam had spent what was left of the afternoon and the evening cleaning the house, moving from room to room, sharing the tasks as they went, and her clothes felt filthy and clung to her like greasy rags.

Karla unzipped her fly, walked her pants down her calves and kicked them aside, then stripped off her cotton top. Naked except for panties, she pictured herself backlit by the house and moved to the far end of the porch where it was darker. She closed her eyes, felt the warm lush breeze on her face, on her arms, on her breasts.

The screen door creaked open then banged shut, and after a few moments she felt Sam's warmth envelop her. His hands roved over her belly, down her thighs, caressing her. She leaned back and into him and rolled her head from side to side so that her hair brushed back and forth across his face; he loved her hair.

"Thanks for the help today," she said softly.

Sam nodded, his breath velvety on her neck. She felt him smile as she guided his hand up the inside of her thigh. When his hand slipped into her panties to fondle her, she pressed into him and felt his erection at the small of her back.

They moved together, swaying. A slow dance.

A light appeared in the distance. Their bodies stilled. They watched the light move among the trees and after several moments they heard the sound of an engine, saw the dark shape of a pickup truck traveling along the road, headlight beams plowing through the darkness.

Finally the truck emerged from the woods and without

slowing passed below the house and continued on. Together they watched it go around the bend, headlights washing over the hillside. And then it was gone. Dark once again.

"Some local," Sam said. "An unreconstructed freak most likely."

Karla nodded, listening to the sound of the engine fade.

"You ready for bed?" Sam's hand was exploring again.

"In a moment," she said, still listening. Then the sound was gone too. "Go ahead. I'll be right in."

Sam ground against her.

"Go." She laughed, twisting away.

Sam's hand lingered for a moment on her bare shoulder. Then it fell away and he shuffled across the porch. The screen door whined.

"Don't be long," he called.

"I won't." She turned and watched the screen door slap shut behind him.

Her clothes lay puddled in a splash of light streaming through the front window. When the light flicked off, she turned back to the field, to the breeze rustling through the unshorn hay. She remembered the first night Sam came to her tent. He spoke of Vietnam, his time there, how being "in-country" altered his perspective, how his love of country transformed into moral outrage, outrage they shared.

Karla glanced back at the dark house, felt the faint stirrings of betrayal.

He's new. Unproven.

Trust isn't something you prove.

Telling him is poor security, bad form.

She turned back to the field, heard water running in the house, Sam splashing in the shower. Her skin flushed.

A riff carried on the breeze, too far away for her to recognize the phrase. *Some local.*

Then she heard Khalil's voice. *Don't trust him anymore than is necessary.*

Karla set her hands back on the paint-blistered railing, peered into the empty night. "I can't work this way," she said quietly. If anything I'll desert him.

Just then a deer crashed from the woods on her left, startled. She watched the ghostly shape lope down the hillside and bound across the road to the river beyond. *The Om-pom-pa-noo-suc.* Remembering it made her smile and she knew what she must do.

She felt another flash of warmth, sensed the rightness of her decision. She would tell Sam about the hostage, their role. *Without trust you had nothing.* Righteous.

Karla scooped her clothes from the porch floorboards and went inside. Arms extended in front of her, she felt her way across the living room to the hallway and bedroom beyond. To Sam, her lover.

No — she thought — her comrade, her partner, her friend.

Chapter 2

At about the same time that evening Andrew Black slipped from the streets of New York into Riverside Park a full half hour early for his scheduled rendezvous with Khalil. He didn't use one of the park's many entrances. Instead he waited for traffic to clear on the block between 86th and 87th Streets and hopped over the stone wall that ran along the east side of the park and crouched in the shadows pooled beneath the trees.

Dark shapes surrounded him — rocks, shrubs, the haunted silhouette of trees. Finally, satisfied that he was alone, Andrew closed his eyes and relaxed, letting his body go slack, the tension ease. He breathed slowly, deeply, as if meditating. Yet all the while he listened to the sough of tires on the wet streets beyond the wall, half-expecting one of the cars to stop, waiting for the flurry of footsteps, the shouts in the night. Even though he knew no one had followed.

On his way uptown he watched for a tail. He'd walked most of the way taking a roundabout route and doubling back twice. At one point he even hopped on a bus and exited abruptly after several blocks, and as he did it occurred to him that for someone who didn't believe in rules he led a very disciplined life but Andrew knew he shouldn't confuse rules with discipline. One was personal, the other not. And it was always better to arrive early and check, even when tired. Especially when tired, he thought.

Andrew reached up and massaged his eyes with the backs of his hands, then scanned the area again. No one was out there, no one was waiting, the park a cove, quiet except for the patter of light rainfall among the leaves overhead. He turned up the collar of his raincoat, pulled it tight. High above him, lights in the apartment houses along Riverside Drive stared across the river. The lights on the far shore blinked back. The buildings distinct, like dark sentinels guarding the night sky.

Behind him, on the far side of the wall, he heard the murmur of voices, gentle laughter as a couple strolled past on Riverside Drive. He listened to the sound fade then set off again, keeping low, skirting the block wall until he came to a dirt path that led down and into the park. Drizzle had left the ground slick but Andrew negotiated the path with ease, his step light and precise after years of running mountain scree and aided by his recollection of the place. He had used the park in the past though never in the middle of the night; only six weeks ago he met Khalil here, in the clearing ahead. It was then that his friend talked him into working for Raymond and the Red Path.

He refused at first. He hadn't known Raymond, still didn't — they'd spoken only one time on the phone — and in the past he worked only for himself, not some shadowy political cause, and for Khalil when the target proved mutual. But he relented in the end and went as a favor to his friend. And it became more than that, much more.

The faces came back to Andrew in rapid succession as he continued down the root-strewn path, like slides projected in his mind. He held onto the image of the American for a moment, the moment when the fatigue cap popped into his scope, then like a slide that has been left in a projector too long the face disintegrated. Black everywhere.

The moment became his — not the Red Path's, not the Salvadorans', not even Khalil's. His alone.

Tonight's summons, unexpected and irregular, had to do with

that, Andrew suspected. He was supposed to fly out of New York in the morning without further contact, but the summons was waiting for him in the hotel. He could have ignored it, he could have packed up and run, but he couldn't run from them any more than he could run from himself, from who he was. And he knew they would have come for him in the end. Even if Khalil was his friend. It was the way their world worked; it was *their* discipline.

In the distance a barge horn moaned and traffic hummed. Night sounds of the sleeping city. Through the trees he could just make out the red tail of lights snaking down the Henry Hudson Parkway, and beyond that the barges creeping along the river in silhouette.

Something darted among the shadows ahead. Andrew froze, ears pricked, scented the air. His eyes swept the area slowly. Too slowly, he thought, the images seeming to travel across great distances in his brain before making a connection.

Then he fixed on it, a dark shape, human-like in form. He waited for movement, for more dark shapes scuttling in the night, then Andrew realized he was staring at a rock. He had imagined the movement as he imagined deer leaping into the glare of his headlights when he drove too late at night. Phantoms.

He tilted his head back and sighed, the rain misty on his face. A dull ache dug at the back of his eyes. He was tired, worn-out, weary. Like a package tourist, he thought, on the last night of a two-week tour. In the past four days he had been in four countries — six if he counted the ones he'd visited twice — and when he returned to the Madison Arms earlier that evening all he wanted to do was sleep.

But he hadn't. Instead he came here to the park ... where shadows scurried in the night.

The thought sent a chill shivering down Andrew's spine.

Careful, be careful.

Andrew took a long deep breath, exhaled slowly, soundlessly, heard the quiet hum of traffic again. He set off once more. Before long the clearing where he was to meet Khalil came into view. The clearing appeared without depth in the darkness; swirls of fog clung to the ground. Off to the right was a building, Andrew recalled, a lavatory, and at that moment as if to reassure him moonlight poured through a gap in the clouds and flooded the field. The building lay exactly where he remembered, fifty yards away, its nearside wall hidden in shadow.

When he came to the edge of the clearing, Andrew hung back for a few moments waiting for the clouds to shuttle back in front of the moon. The light rain had ended so he unbuttoned his coat, shoved his hands deep in his pockets. When the moon slipped behind the clouds, he hurried onto the field. Wet blades of grass slapped loudly at his shoes and the stink of urine struck him as he closed in on building, but he kept moving, hurrying. Moonlight caught him for a moment before he slipped into the shadows.

Rainwater dripped from the eave. Andrew sidestepped the puddle beneath it and huddled close to the wall, the stench, heavy and thick, threatening to overwhelm him. He breathed through his mouth and focused on the darkly wooded slope — his friend would come from there — trying to forget that people peed on the walls when the building was locked. He hated New York, the filth, the heat, the drizzle that never seemed to relieve the humidity.

Andrew thought of Portugal, the southern coast where he lived. It was six-thirty in the morning there, the sun just rising, and the Algarve was always best then. He pictured his house, alone on the hilltop, glistening lime-white in the soft dawn, the memory soothing as a salve. A narrow dirt lane led down the hillside, cutting through a grove of cork oak to the main coast road. The earth sunbaked the color of clay, with hard, dry furrows left by the plow beneath the compact trees; golden stubble poked from the broken ground, while in the distance, far beyond more rolling groves of oak, the Atlantic was a blue haze, bluer than the pale sky, and he imagined he could hear the whisper of the surf, the hush of the waves.

The sudden slap of footsteps interrupted his reverie. Andrew remained absolutely still, his eyes fixed on the dark slope. He heard voices then saw movement — *real movement* — among the trees. After several moments two dark figures emerged. The men appeared to float above the fog as they moved onto the field. One of them was Khalil. Andrew didn't recognize the other man who loomed a full head taller than his friend, though he suspected it was Raymond. That they both came didn't surprise him.

When they were halfway across the field, the two men stopped, circled, looked all around. Then Khalil called his name: "Andreeew," the second syllable drawn out like an echo.

Andrew didn't move, eyes still on the woods.

The two men spoke in hushed tones, the one he suspected was Raymond fidgeting all the while. The stranger broke away and scurried to the far end of the field. "Wit –" Wit was the name Khalil told him to use when he spoke with Raymond on the phone.

Then again: "Wit!" more insistently.

Still Andrew didn't move. There must be others.

Khalil turned and faced the woods. He seemed to be looking for someone there. Raymond was still at the far end of the field, standing by the fence that separated the park from the roadway, headlights flashing past, and Andrew realized this wasn't some sort of set up. Just more imagination, delusions of a weary mind.

Careful.

Andrew arched his back and pushed off the lavatory wall. "Khalil," he called softly.

His friend spun around. "Andrew?" Then smiled, his teeth sparking in the moonlight, and came toward him with open arms.

Andrew leaned forward to accept his friend's embrace, felt the Palestinian's lips brush his cheeks.

Khalil drew back, sniffed at the air. "You pick interesting places to wait."

"You picked the spot," he said, still cautious, wary. "What is it you want?"

Just then Raymond turned and spotted them. He called out and started back across the field, his gait hurried, all elbows and knees, like a race walker's.

"Raymond," Khalil said out of the corner of his mouth and Andrew nodded.

As the other man approached, moonlight illuminated his face and Andrew realized he had seen him before. Not him, his picture. It was in a newspaper or magazine and Raymond's intensity fairly leapt from the page. But the name beneath the photograph wasn't "Raymond." It was something else, sharper sounding, harsher, less fluid.

Andrew tried to remember the name, where he saw the photograph, but it wouldn't come back. Later, he promised himself, when you are less tired.

Raymond's handshake was firm, studied, and when he spoke Andrew didn't have any difficulty remembering the voice. As on the phone, his voice was flat and without sympathy.

"Where were you, Wit? We called."

For several moments Andrew gazed at the other man, as if to measure him, then turned pointedly to his friend.

"What is it you want?" he asked again.

"To talk." The answer was like his question, a dance of sorts.

Out of the corner of his eye he saw Raymond open his mouth to speak and close it again.

"The situation in San Salvador," Khalil said slowly. "The three soldiers. It seemed strange."

"You blew away an American advisor," Raymond cut in, unable to contain his frustration any longer.

Andrew looked at him again, studied his face, his eyes, which like his voice, were spoiled, without sympathy. All of it familiar.

"I know what I did."

"Jesus," Raymond said, incredulous. "You were supposed to provide covering fire for the FPL team only if absolutely required. Now the Agency is all over their people and Congress is talking about sending more hardware. Maybe even troops. It could prove fatal to our cause."

"I don't care about your cause."

"What do you think you were involved in down there? Who do you think you were working for? The U.S. government?"

"No," Andrew said, biting off the word. "I was working for myself."

Raymond wasn't listening. "What were you doing?"

"What I do best!" he shot back, suddenly angry.

"My friend," Khalil said, "you must be realistic."

Andrew swung around, then pulled back, remembered imagining the dark shape in the night. He took a breath.

"No one denies your ability," his friend went on.

"Three head shots at two hundred yards," Raymond said.

"It was one hundred yards," Andrew said, his dislike of the man visceral. "With the rifle and scope involved the shot was trivial. Now at five — six hundred yards, with a moving target

..."

"What's the difference?" Khalil laughed. "Let's not argue about matters of no significance."

"The matter of significance," Raymond said, "is the advisor." And with that he looked directly at Andrew and waited for a reply.

But Andrew didn't have a reply, at least not one that Raymond would understand or find satisfactory. He turned away. Up on Riverside Drive someone hooted. Then again — an echo.

"I'm tired, Khalil. I need some sleep."

"We'll give you the two guards," Raymond said. "But why the advisor? Why him? He didn't have a weapon and no one said anything about assassinating an American military advisor."

Andrew sighed. "No one said anything about anything so I followed my instincts."

"You nearly decapitate a U.S. military advisor and you say you were following instincts."

"*My* instincts." Then he caught himself and turned back to Raymond and met his gaze. He felt Khalil's eyes as well.

"Listen, you sent me down there. Both of you. Without a specific target. To cover some local terrorist operation. I don't work that way."

Raymond opened his mouth to speak but Andrew cut him off. "I did my part. Your people were away clean. The soldiers were something else. I saw an opportunity I couldn't resist."

"But why the American? He wasn't some flunky military advisor, you know. You blew away a CIA agent."

Andrew smiled — the retaliation would be endless, revelatory.

"Did you hear me? A fucking CIA agent!"

"So much the better."

Raymond threw his hands up in disgust. "Christ. The press is having a field day and this prick is talking some shit about opportunity. He's your man, Khalil. Talk some sense to him, will you."

Khalil put his hand on Andrew's shoulder. He shook it off.

"My friend, please. Be reasonable."

"What is this? I don't work for this guy."

"Take it easy," his friend said softly.

"Take it easy, shit."

So angry that further words escaped him, Andrew turned and walked away quickly. To his surprise they didn't call after him. No cries, no shouts, no men leaping from the woods. When he reached the edge of the clearing he broke into a slow jog. He didn't bother with the trail, using the paved walkway instead. He'd made a mistake letting them see his anger. He was too strung out, too close to the edge; he'd lost control.

Better to have accepted their criticism and acted penitent. Better to have gone along. Now what if they won't let me go? What if by taking the job in El Salvador I've become their man without even knowing it?

You can run.

Long ago Andrew accepted that possibility. Before the first hit he had placed escape documents — passports, drivers' licenses, credit cards and cash in multiple currencies — in his safe deposit box at the UBS bank in Geneva.

But what if they won't let me out of the park? What if they *are* out there? Waiting ... hiding in the shadows. Sensing their presence now. Raymond's men.

Andrew ran faster. Faster still, heart pounding, coattails dragging at his thighs. And suddenly he recognized the signs — they were unmistakable. His emotions were shot and his reserves had run dry and he was tottering at the very limits of exhaustion.

And beyond that, he knew, lurked paranoia.

He slowed to a walk, lungs surging. Headlights flashed across the break in the park wall, as if on the far side of some great chasm. The *whoosh* of tires on wet pavement. The orange glow of streetlamps. A false dawn.

Then, without a word, a man stepped from the darkness at the edge of the path and blocked the way. Andrew stopped. The man remained where he was, twenty feet away, face hidden in shadow. Then another man appeared farther up the walk, then another and another. And seeing them now, Andrew realized there was no escape, nowhere to run, no way out but back.

No one spoke. No one moved. Cars continued past the exit undeterred; several blocks away a siren howled. Finally the man closest to him motioned him back and Andrew turned and walked back down into the park, and as he did he told himself it was always better to appear to go along, to act tamely. Even if it was an act. And above all, no matter how tired he felt, he mustn't let them see his fear.

Khalil was waiting at the foot of the slope. Raymond had remained well out in the field, traffic streaming past on the parkway behind him.

"We should talk."

"It seems I have no choice."

The Palestinian smiled. "It seems not. And for that I apologize. Let's walk."

Andrew nodded silently, acquiescent, and let Khalil take his arm and guide him back up the walkway. Raymond's men ducked back into the shadows as they approached but not before Andrew caught a glimpse of the man who waved him back. He was only a boy, a teenager, compact and Arabic. And again he realized he had gotten it wrong. These weren't Raymond's men, they were his friend's bodyguards.

"I just wanted to talk," Khalil said as if reading his mind.

Chastened, Andrew let his friend continue leading him up the path. It had been undisciplined. Folly.

"Raymond is a difficult man," Khalil said.

"Raymond is a scumbag."

"I agree."

The remark surprised Andrew. "So why didn't you say something?"

"Because right now we need Raymond and the Red Path."

"I could always depend on you to keep things in perspective, Khalil."

The grip on his arm tightened; the men in the shadows stirred.

"Perspective is an important thing, my friend. You should remember that."

The warning was unmistakable. Everyone was tense. Himself included.

"I'm tired. I overreacted, I guess."

Khalil made a guttural sound at the back of his throat, an Arabic sound, and rasped, "Aren't we all." Then he laughed and after a few moments Andrew joined him, their laughter like glass shattering in the night.

They walked on in silence. A car alarm blared on Riverside Drive, punctuating the night.

"We should go to the mountains."

Again Andrew was taken by surprise — he hadn't expected his friend to remember. When they were students at Stanford he and Khalil ran in the mountains together, bolting down massive fans of scree, chasing away their youthful anger. Using the mountains as an outlet, a retreat. But now when Andrew ran in the mountains he ran alone.

"So what is it you want?"

"Another favor, I'm afraid."

"Look what the last one got me."

The Palestinian laughed again, a bark almost, and steered Andrew around as they approached the park exit.

"My colleague has problems," Khalil said as they continued down the walk. "He knows there is an informant in the Red Path and he sees bogeymen everywhere. In his mind he has reason to suspect your motives."

"My motives have nothing to with him."

"Yes, but unlike you our Red Path friend doesn't like chaos."

Andrew ignored the remark, where arguing the point would lead. It was the order beyond chaos that he sought.

"He'll feel better if he understands," Khalil went on — he signaled one of his guards to follow. "Explain what happened in San Salvador."

Andrew shook his head. "I can't believe you, Khalil. You get me out here in the middle of the night to explain myself to some asshole politician …"

He stopped, flashed on the photo again, felt a rush of discovery. He held onto the image as he had the military advisor's earlier — Raymond was some sort of government official — then the image began to fade and was gone. Vanished.

"I've seen him before, Khalil. I just can't remember where."

"It's better you don't."

Again the warning was unmistakable, but this time the warning intrigued Andrew as if knowing the Red Path leader's true identity would give him an edge somehow. He tried to summon up the photo again; his head ached.

Khalil took his arm. "It would help me greatly if you could ease his mind."

"He doesn't want to listen."

"What could it hurt?"

Nothing, Andrew thought. Nothing at all. And he owed his friend. Six years earlier, shortly after he moved to the Algarve, Khalil came to him with the first hit. The other American. It was a difficult time for him, a time when a general malaise, dissatisfaction and disgust with life, threatened to overwhelm him, and his friend offered him a way out, a reason to exist.

He sighed. "All right, let's get this over with."

They found Raymond where they had left him, in the middle of the field, seemingly impervious to the damp air. Andrew told him everything: about the flight to Guatemala, the hotel he used, how he entered El Salvador and left the same day, where he found the Volkswagen van, and about his SSG rifle, how someone tweaked the adjustments on the scope — one of your people, he told Raymond, parceling the blame without criticism. How his absence at the hotel in New York went unnoticed and even what he did with the altered passport the Red Path supplied.

Then he explained his reason for the shootings. Society's rules meant nothing to him. He believed in the individual, not political groups or causes, in order beyond disorder, in natural order. He was an anarchist. "A shooter," he said, "pure and simple." The thought making him smile. He hadn't wanted to take out the guardias. Killing them had accomplished nothing — he would have let them walk if they had been without weapons. But the advisor was different. He was a symbol, an icon to the world as it existed, a world of moral ambiguity, of creative selfishness, a world where children were napalmed in the name of freedom. A world without honor. A world he wished to see destroyed.

So he came to believe in the act, the solitary act, the shocking act. The act of revelation. The response to the advisor's death, the retaliation, would so far outweigh what he did that people would see. They would understand.

It had been the right thing to do, Andrew insisted. And even as he spoke the irony didn't escape him, killing being the right thing. It was madness, pure madness. Yet at the same time it was perfectly sane. Beyond sane.

When he finished, Raymond stared at him for several moments as if he were some delirious sidewalk preacher, then turned to Khalil. "Maybe we can turn this mess to our advantage. I have a plan."

Khalil shot Andrew a look as if to say: what's one to do?

Andrew shook his head and walked away, trudging slowly across the field.

"Wait," Khalil called.

He stopped.

"I want to speak with you."

Andrew remained where he was, back to them, and gazed longingly at the dark outline of the trees along Riverside Drive, at the lights in apartment buildings above. It seemed hours since he entered the park and he thought of his room at the Madison Arms, the fresh dry air, the crisp white sheets …

His body twitched.

Andrew drew himself erect, forced his eyes open, felt the sodden air on his face. Heard the murmur of voices behind him.

"We can revive the CIA scheme we discussed," Raymond was saying.

"We dismissed that plan several months ago."

Andrew closed his eyes, tried not to listen.

"We can tie it to the advisor. It will look like part of something larger."

Remembering the cadence of Raymond's voice on the

telephone, his curt tone. Asshole.

"How many teams will you need?"

"Three."

"We can do that."

"Good. Maybe we can use Wit here. He seems to have a taste for Company men."

Andrew spun around. Both men were looking at him and for a moment he had the sensation of meeting two sets of eyes at the same time.

"No," Khalil said, shaking his head. "This one isn't my friend's style."

Andrew felt a surge of relief, noticed a slight tremor in his hands; he wondered if he would have had the energy to argue.

Then Raymond was shaking Khalil's hand and without a word to Andrew he left, scurrying across the field once more. Khalil's men had moved down to the edge of the clearing; they let the Red Path leader pass and he vanished into the tree line.

Andrew felt a nudge at his elbow, smelled the musky scent of his friend's cologne. "What is it you want?" Tonight the question resonated.

"I may have something for you."

The shipping lane on the Hudson had cleared. The river dark as ink, silent.

"I'm tired, Khalil."

"It won't be for a few months."

"Then ask me in a few months."

"The target will interest you. He is an influential man."

Andrew turned and looked at his friend. "I said in a few months."

"There won't be time."

"Then get someone else."

"You may not have to take him."

The remark confused Andrew and for a moment he wondered if he'd lost track of the conversation. "What are you talking about?"

"Others may take him first."

And with that Andrew understood. Tonight's summons had nothing to do with explanations or motives. It had to do with insurance.

"I'm not a back up man, Khalil."

"It won't be like last time. You will have a specific target and will be working for me personally. On the fringes where you like it."

"Raymond's involved, isn't he?"

Khalil looked away, his silence answer enough.

"I'm sorry. I can't help you. These people are just too devious."

The Palestinian looked back at him, his eyes glowing in the moonlight. "I understand. I'll get someone from the camp though I'd rather have you. After all you are the best, my friend."

"Don't stroke me, Khalil."

His friend grinned. "You know me too well. Perhaps another time."

"Another time."

Khalil embraced him then walked slowly across the field to join his men, and as he watched them depart Andrew couldn't help but wonder about the target, "the influential man." Then, too tired to think, he put it from his mind.

Five minutes later he left the park and walked to West End in search of a cab. Traffic was light and the wet streets looked shiny and clean beneath the glow of the streetlamps. Once again it started to rain.

Chapter 3

Use the automatic if necessary …

The words playing over and over in her head, Karla made her way across the living room to the screen door. Raymond's instructions were precise, his words curt and formal. He insisted on the automatic, a Browning 9mm Hi-Power, a handgun she knew well. Sam knew it even better.

She could see him beyond the shadowy screen, in the sunlight on the far side of the drive. He was working in the back of the Datsun, his torso half-buried there, the trunk lid extended above him like a wing in flight. Yesterday he noticed one of the rear turn signals wasn't operating properly and he worked at repairing it now. He was that way at the camp, Karla remembered. *Ein Tüftler.*

Hand flat on the screen, she watched Sam work a moment longer. The long muscles in his lower back flexed whenever he moved and she felt a flutter in her chest as she pressed the door open.

"Sam."

"What?" he said, continuing to work on the taillight.

"They telephoned. It's on for today."

Sam ducked from the back of the car. "When?"

"At half past seven."

He squinted up at her for a moment. "What time is it now?"

"Just past noon."

Another pause. Then he nodded as if that sounded about right and drew a rag from his back pocket and wiped his hands, seemingly at ease.

Karla stepped onto the front porch letting the screen door bang shut behind her. Immediately the sun's intensity enveloped her and she flashed on the desert, the bone-dry heat, home, but put it from her mind.

Sam was still standing by the car, rag in hand.

"Can you get the torch?"

He gave her a quizzical look.

"The flashlight," she said. "It's in the glove box."

"Sure, no problem."

She watched Sam walk briskly around the car to the passenger door and duck inside. Behind him stands of maple and birch rose sharply above the fog-shrouded river, climbing all the way to the top of the ridge, the leaves wet and shiny, bright green in the midday light. Earlier in the day a thundershower had brought fifteen minutes of hard rain, and Karla was struck by how much the place reminded her of her childhood home.

Fog clung to the Neckar the same way after it had rained, the same misty haze lacing the air, and on days like this she and her mother would tramp through the woods, sloshing in their yellow rubber boots along the narrow muddy paths. They would take an early morning train to Eberbach, or to Kailbach or Beerfelden, the train leaving shortly after dawn, and as they walked they would collect things, sometimes leaves and pinecones, sometimes wildflowers gone to seed — this when she was seven, eight, nine years old. And in her mind the walks always took place at this time of year, early fall before the leaves changed.

Karla shivered at the memory. It had been years since she thought of that, years since she trudged through the woods with her mother, since she thought of the Oldenwald as home. But that was all past, part of a previous life. And she and Sam wouldn't be collecting leaves or pinecones.

The car door snapped shut and she looked up.

Sam was holding up the flashlight. "What's this for?"

"Come," she said, crossing the gravel drive and taking his arm. "I'll show you."

She led him around to the back of the house and into the field. The unharvested hay slashed at their legs as they went down the shallow rise, soaking their trousers almost to the knee; tiny black gnats — no-see-ums, Sam called them — swarming in their path.

As they walked they angled to the southeast, toward the far edge of the field where the golden waves of hay washed up against the dark wall of woods. Even at midday the woods appeared dark, impenetrable.

Karla pointed toward the trees. "It's down there."

"What's down there?"

"The cellar," she said, "you can't see it from the road."

Still walking beside her, Sam cocked his head. "I thought we were keeping our man in the house."

"We are. Raymond said the weapons we'll need are there."

Sam didn't say anything. He just kept walking which disappointed her. She thought he would be pleased, excited at least. At the camp his best times had always come when weapons were involved, the others deferring to his obvious expertise, if not to him; Raymond had even mentioned it on the phone though she still wondered why he had waited until today to mention the cellar.

They trudged on in silence, the uncut hay whipping at their legs. The day grew warmer as they walked and a grainy smell rose from the field; wispy clouds whitened the sky. Karla plucked her sodden blouse from her breasts and glanced back over her shoulder. The wooded ridge loomed above the house and appeared distant now, more distant than it was. A trick, she knew, of the lingering mist — and it occurred to her that if anyone came for them they would take advantage of its greater height.

As they continued down the rise she imagined the *pop-pop* of the rifle shots, pictured the white puffs of smoke rising among the trees.

If there is a problem … kill him.

Fragments of the night operation in Haifa came back to her then, the lights sweeping the harbor, the oily slick of water, the phosphorescence. She heard the explosions — *crump, crump, crump* — building on one another like echoes. People had died that night, dozens of them; she was responsible and she had accepted responsibility with equanimity, even now she bore it well. But that was different. Those who died were crewmembers on a supply ship delivering Lance missiles to Israel, and she didn't have to put a gun to their heads, didn't look into their eyes.

For an instant, a shadow of a moment, she saw the hostage, imagined him — his face, his mouth, his eyes. He looked at her in a way that was openly frank, as if he had just lifted his head to gaze at her for the first time. Guileless. Then he was gone. Vanished.

She didn't know if she could do it. She didn't know if she was strong enough — or cold enough. She wasn't a shooter. Then Karla pictured the men firing from the far hillside, swarming up the rise below the house and knew that under those circumstances she could. *If necessary.*

"His name is Bacchetti," she heard herself say. "Luigi Bacchetti."

"Whose name?" Sam had fallen in behind her. His shoes snapped at her heels.

"The man we're holding," she went on though Raymond instructed her to give Sam only the barest details. But that she knew she couldn't do.

"They're bringing him here?"

Several farms away a chainsaw clattered to life, revving at first, then settled into a steady drone.

"No," Karla said, "we are to meet them."

"Where?"

"The Interstate."

"The Interstate?"

"Yes." Even she found the location strange, too exposed. "The exchange will take place elsewhere. Raymond said we are to pick the spot. They'll follow us."

As earlier Sam was silent for several moments. In the distance the chainsaw revved again, then bit into a tree, singing.

"How will we recognize them?"

"They'll be in a Volkswagen van. A camper."

Karla told him the color, recited the plate number.

"So who is he?"

She shook her head. "Raymond didn't say. He's Italian, I guess."

"What is he, a diplomat or something?"

Again Karla shook her head — Raymond didn't tell her. Then she shrugged. "We'll know soon enough." And it occurred to her that Sam with all his questions wasn't as relaxed as he seemed.

They kept moving, plowing through the field.

"He's Italian though, huh?"

Karla felt herself smile. "Not Italian-Italian. I meant his name sounds Italian."

"And that's all Raymond told you? His name?"

"Yes," she said, still smiling. "Only his name."

Sam grabbed her arm, startling her, and spun her around. His eyes flashed. "I don't know how you can work in the dark like this."

"I try not to think about it." She met his gaze, resolute.

Sam shook his head, ruefully almost, and she understood now why Khalil and the others didn't trust Sam. He lacked faith and discipline, which in their eyes left his commitment open to question.

She reached out and took his arm. "Come," she said quietly and Sam followed. As she knew he would.

They moved faster, and with more determination it seemed. Soon they came to the root cellar. It lay near the edge of the field as Raymond promised, a small mound not twenty yards from the woods. Twin doors were set in the side of the mound, the doors gray and logy beneath a tangle of weeds and dead leaves. Over the years dark stains had gathered around the hinges and all but a few screws holding them to the weathered wood were gone. Black wormholes remained in their place.

Without a word Sam slipped from her side and climbed the mound. Together they lifted one of the doors with care, easing it open, and the debris fell away. Cool air like a faint breeze rose from the depths of the cellar. There was a rustling in the darkness.

Karla shuddered. "Rats."

Sam grinned. "Probably just a cat," he said. "Farm country's full of strays." Then skidded back down the mound.

He switched on the flashlight. "I'll go first."

"No, I'll go."

"Come on, Karla."

"No," she insisted, taking the light.

"You sure?"

"Absolutely." And she remembered the rats — the size of cats — scuttling through the streets of Beirut. At night they came to the room where she slept and darted along base of the walls, their paws clicking on the concrete floor. Sometimes they even scurried across her mattress — across her legs. Her skin crawling with the memory, the fear exquisite almost.

The rustling stopped and Karla shone the light into the darkness as she had then, half-expecting to find black rats' eyes staring at her. Instead she found crates of weapons piled high, the re-sawn pine boxes bright in the artificial light. A narrow path trailed down both sides of the pile and some of the crates still had U.S. Mil-Spec numbers stenciled on their sides.

Flashlight in hand, Karla began to feel her way down the stairs. The steps were steep, rounded with wear; the subterranean air touched her skin, tasted coppery, metallic in her mouth. Fear rose like bile in her chest.

Halfway down she stopped and peered up at Sam.

"It's probably just a stray," he said and grinned again.

Karla forced a smile and continued down the stairs, leery still, her skin clammy with memories. Whatever was down here would hide, she told herself. It probably *is* just a stray. Here she was about to take charge of an entire operation, of a man's life, and she was afraid of the dark. *Lächerlich.* If air wasn't so dank and the shadows so long, she would laugh outloud.

A false laugh, Karla realized. Because her fears were real.

She waved the light over the cellar, over the crates and earthen walls, then took another step down and felt the dirt floor, damp, beneath her feet. She waved the light again. Only shadows. Claustrophobic.

The pathway that encircled the crates was less than a yard wide, the pile shoulder-high. Karla could hear the wheeze of her breath as she started down one side and thought of the rats again, remembered the *snick-snick* of their paws on the concrete floor, remembered the way the room went silent when they hopped onto her mattress, the way they pawed at her sleeping bag. The fear paralyzing, not exquisite at all.

Gott!

She wanted to call out to Sam, but remained silent, mute, easing down the path all the while, too proud to let him see her fear.

When she reached the end of the pile, Karla stopped and took a breath, played the light over the dirt wall in front of her, over the ground below. Nothing, nothing at all.

In the far corner two pump-action shotguns were propped against the wall. She hit them with the light; the shotguns were ancient, covered with dust. Cobwebbed.

"What'd you find?"

Karla jumped.

"Hey, it's only me."

Her heart skipped, started. It's Sam.

She took another breath, another moment to gather herself, then turned to face him. Sam stood framed in the doorway; the sky behind him pale, washed-out blue.

"This is some sort of weapons' cache."

Sam scrambled down the steps and she hurried to his side. He took the flashlight. "*Je*-sus," he whistled as he swept the beam over the crates.

Karla edged closer. She wanted to take his arm, to feel his warmth, but settled for having him close, beside her.

The light jounced along the dirt walls then flickered over something in the corner, something she'd missed, and returned to it, picking it out. A prybar.

"Just what we need," Sam said — and slipped from her side.

Karla fought off the urge to follow and remained where she was. She felt the cool cellar air again — damp, musty, fetid — and hugged herself as Sam bent to the bar.

Yowl!!

A cat shot from the shadows and tore past her, brushing against her legs.

"*Scheisse!*"

The cat bound up the stairs and leapt, paws extended, through the doorway. Behind her, Sam laughed quietly.

"Told you it was just stray."

Karla turned to face him and lowered her eyes, embarrassed. "It startled me."

"Scared the shit out of me."

"God," she shivered. Then laughed as well — at herself.

A minute later Sam set to prying open the crates. She retreated to the steps and sat on one of the treads. The sun licked her shoulders as she held the light for him. Warm, lush, comforting.

From each crate Sam drew a weapon, holding it aloft and calling out its name, then set it aside. There were M16s, Uzi submachine guns and M79s, the squat grenade launchers still fresh in their packaging.

"We're looking specifically for a Browning 9mm automatic," she told him. "We're to use it to execute the hostage if necessary."

Sam didn't respond. He just kept opening crates, one at a time, inspecting the contents, taking a sample and moving onto the next. Very orderly. And as she watched it occurred to Karla that Sam handled the weapons as he handled her, with caution and respect.

There were more M16s and Uzis, Redeye missiles and .45s, .22-caliber handguns, and ammunition, cases and cases of it. Karla felt profligate, the abundance almost obscene. Never, not with the RAF in Germany, not even at the camp in Syria where the supply of ordnance seemed limitless, had she seen so much.

The sheer volume, the extravagance, overwhelming. So American, she thought.

Finally Sam produced an opaque plastic bag and handed it to her. The bag felt cool and slick, heavy in her hand.

"That must be it."

Karla nodded, fingers tracing the outline of the weapon through the plastic bag — it was the 9mm automatic, the Browning Hi-Power — and she couldn't help but wonder why Raymond insisted on this particular gun.

She tore the bag away and seeing the condition of the weapon she wondered even more. The handgun had been used, abused. A deep gash ran the length of its wooden grip and a gritty film coated the automatic. She ejected the magazine, racked the slide to clear the chamber and checked the action. The sound — *click-click* — hollow in the confines of the cellar.

She felt Sam's eyes and looked up. The light cast an eerie glow on his face.

"Why the automatic?"

The question sent a chill feathering down Karla's spine. It was as if he were able to read her mind.

"I don't know."

"I'm not killing this guy, Karla."

"We aren't killing anyone."

Sam gave her a look.

"We aren't. Raymond said only if our hideout is discovered."

"Then why that particular gun? Why's it so important?"

Karla felt helpless in the face of his doubts — of her own. She didn't know why Raymond insisted on the automatic, she only knew he had, and that his insistence, the way he kept returning to it as if lecturing a child, troubled her as well, though she wouldn't admit that to Sam.

Sam was still looking at her, waiting for a response.

"Raymond must be setting someone up in case the operation comes apart."

He latched onto her words. "He said that?"

"No, I'm hypothesizing. It's the only explanation that makes sense."

"Who's he setting up?"

"I don't know," she said, emphasizing each word.

Sam's eyes flashed, sparked in the light, suddenly vehement. "I'm not killing this guy. Not without knowing what's going on."

"I said we aren't killing anyone."

But Sam went on as if he hadn't heard. "I'm not killing someone just because Raymond says so. I had enough of that in Nam."

And with that Karla realized this wasn't about the automatic, wasn't about setting someone up, wasn't even about executing the hostage. It was about Vietnam. He always came back to that. Sam seemed incapable of seeing anything beyond the limited framework of the war, and she wanted to feel sorry for him but couldn't. She only felt tired, worn down by doubt — by Sam's doubts, by Raymond's doubts, by her own.

"We were sent to hold Bacchetti, not execute him. And why go to the trouble of kidnapping him? It isn't logical."

Sam didn't say anything. His face half-light, half-shadow, his eyes far away. In some distant jungle, she thought.

"It isn't the killing," he said finally, quietly, softly. "It's having no reason. I *have* to have a reason."

Karla heard the plea in his voice, saw the pain and anguish in his eyes and hastened to his side. She reached up and touched Sam's cheek, his skin smooth and soft, like satin beneath her fingertips.

"We aren't killing anyone," she said again, gently this time and meaning it. "If we have to, we'll have a reason."

Sam's eyes came back, smoldering, burning into her.

"It's the last option, Sam. I promise. The very last."

His gaze wavered — he wanted to believe. She'd spoken with such conviction she believed it herself.

"If they wanted the hostage dead, they wouldn't have sent us. We aren't shooters."

Sam looked away and she felt the tension ease.

"What about the rest of this stuff?"

Her heart thrummed. "Bring what we need. You know better than I."

Sam looked back at her and smiled, a smile of such radiance that it was as if the last few minutes were swept away, as if the pain and doubt ceased to exist.

When he turned back to the weapons, Karla hurried up the stairs, automatic in hand. The day's warmth enveloped her as she emerged from the cellar; the heat felt good now, fresh, reassuring. At the top of the stairs she paused for a few moments to bask in the sunshine, free hand cupped along her brow against the sudden glare. The farmhouse appeared abandoned still, the windows dark against the weathered wood.

Then she saw him again — Bacchetti. He was still looking at her though his eyes were no longer guileless. They were filled with confidence, cocky and arrogant, and something about his eyes, the way they looked through and at her at the same time, stirred memory.

It came to her then. In her mother's favorite photograph her father's eyes possessed the same youthful cockiness, the same arrogance, as if he possessed all the answers and knew it. And in that moment Karla found her rationale, her personal logic. She could execute Bacchetti if she had to, she could put the gun to his head and pull the trigger. But not because she would be killing some proxy for her father. That would be too simple, too clichéd. She would be killing the look in his eyes, the arrogance, the arrogance of his time.

Mao was right, she thought, power *did* come from the barrel of a gun. Though she sensed in its own way that was a cliché as well.

She heard Sam clomp up the stairs behind her. He had two M16s slung over one shoulder, an M79 over the other, and an Uzi in each hand.

"Here, let me help with that," she said.

Sam shrugged off the grenade launcher. The weight dragged at her arm. She had fired an M79 once, in the desert. It jarred her and left her breathless, exhilarated.

"It'll take two more trips," Sam said. "I want to bring up the rest of the weapons we'll need." He sounded relaxed, himself again.

"I have the automatic."

Sam nodded and they started back up the rise. She had already decided that if the operation came apart she would be the one to execute Bacchetti. He was her problem, not Sam's. Her responsibility.

***

The Interstate, like a firebreak, cut through the woods to the south. Last rays of sunlight pierced the thin layer of clouds along the horizon; the land there was cleared and the hilltops appeared flat and without shadow in the fading light.

Karla shifted on the car seat. She and Sam had arrived at 7:10, twenty minutes early, and parked on the shoulder of the overpass that afforded a view of roadway to the south. Sam hopped out immediately and raised the hood. If anyone stopped he would tell them they were having engine trouble. Nothing major, a fouled plug or something. He had it under control. Meanwhile she watched the road.

A vehicle materialized along the horizon, then another as if in pursuit. Karla watched the pair slip down the face of the hill and drop from sight. Moments later they reappeared on the next hilltop, side by side, two light-colored American sedans speeding north on I-91. Then the cars whizzed beneath the overpass and were gone, the gray ribbon of roadway deserted once again.

Raymond told her the kidnappers would come from the south. They would be in a Volkswagen van. *An orange Westphalia camper with Massachusetts plates.*

Karla froze. Did she hear something? Or had she spoken aloud? She tilted her head, listened. But there was only silence, a faint buzzing in her ears, and it made her think of the desert, of the power lines that ran along the dirt track, the way they sang in the stillness — and of her tent flapping gently, invitingly, in the early evening breeze. Already she missed the camp, the dry desert heat.

The hood snapped shut and she looked back to the Interstate. Another vehicle appeared in the distance, a boxy shape shambling along the roadway. The driver's door creaked open and she heard Sam climb in beside her.

"It's them," he said, breathless.

Karla nodded without taking her eyes from the roadway. When the vehicle crested the next hill, she saw that it was the orange Volkswagen camper, exactly as Raymond described.

"It has Massachusetts plates, white with red lettering."

"Yes," she said quietly, "it's them."

The van came straight on, wavering, as if in slow motion. When it was fifty yards from the overpass, the right directional began to flash and the van floated up the exit ramp. At the top it came to a stop, left directional blinking now, then pulled out and parked directly in front of them.

The driver let the engine idle and sat motionless behind the wheel, his features indistinct, the rest of the interior lost in shadow. Karla felt for the Browning 9mm on the seat beside her, found it. The automatic was clean, the barrel and housing oiled, grit-free. She'd cleaned it herself. Doubt had fled.

Sam began to drum on the steering wheel. She reached across and touched his hand. These were just last minute jitters, Karla knew, raging adrenaline, the last moments before the action truly began. She remembered her first time, parked at the curb in front of the Dresdner Bank in Freudenstadt — she had to wait in a car that time too — her stomach churned so violently she thought she would be sick.

He'll be fine, just fine. And it occurred to her that without him she would have been lost, literally. Earlier Sam had suggested the perfect spot for the transfer, a deserted lane not a mile from the overpass. After his military service he had attended Dartmouth College in Hanover, one freeway exit south, so he knew the roads in the area, which obscure lanes were shortcuts, which were dead ends. The day after they arrived he drove her around the campus, narrating all the while, pointing out the College Green, Hopkins Center, Baker Library and where he had lived.

He graduated the previous year and wandered to Europe where Khalil found him in the dead of winter. His expertise with weaponry served as his entrée to the camp, that and his disillusionment.

"What are they waiting for?"

The question startled Karla. Not the question, the fact that she had allowed her mind to wander like that, that under the circumstances it could. She couldn't remember ever having felt so relaxed, so utterly in control.

Sam was hunched over the steering wheel; the van driver hadn't moved, engine still idling.

"They want to make certain we are the right people."

"We're the right people."

Karla smiled. "Patience. We can't fault them for being cautious."

Their caution, in fact, made her feel safe, secure. Her faith in the Red Path confirmed.

At exactly 7:30 the driver flashed his headlights. Sam reached for the key.

"Slowly," she reminded him.

"Right."

The engine turned over and caught; a blast of cool air rushed into the car. Sam backed up and pulled out. As they swung around the kidnapper's van, Karla twisted around on the seat and watched it make a wide U-turn and follow.

They traveled in caravan. After a few minutes Sam turned into the dirt lane, a chute between twin walls of birch; their pale-yellow leaves looked frail, like ashes that would crumble if touched. Underbrush scraped against both sides of the car as they drove down the lane, the van lurching behind them.

The transfer took less than a minute and was anti-climactic. Before the van stopped the cargo door slid open and two Asian men jumped out, neckties flapping. Both of them wore dark business suits as disguises. Hands passed Bacchetti from inside. Twin strips of white adhesive tape covered his mouth and eyes, and his body hung limp, drugged; the toecaps of his shoes traced erratic lines in the dirt as they dragged him to the car.

Karla was already on her knees, facing the backseat. She

pushed open the rear passenger door and without a word the two men dumped the hostage onto the seat and slammed the door. She reached back and propped Bacchetti upright; his head lolled. His hair was thin, yellow with age, and she noticed the grime on the inside of his shirt collar, the stubble salting his jaw and hollow cheeks. His skin waxy, sallow, as if stained by nicotine. Raymond hadn't said anything about the hostage being an old man.

She felt for a pulse at his neck.

"Is he all right?" Sam looked back over his shoulder.

Bacchetti's pulse throbbed, thready. "He's fine."

"He's an old man."

"I know."

Karla bit her lip, her mind a blur, felt the automatic digging into her knee, remembered Raymond's words, his uncompromising tone. *If there's a problem … kill him.* Heard the kidnappers' van, engine screaming, shrieking, as it tore down the lane.

"Let's get out of here."

Sam hesitated.

"Go!" she yelled.

The car lurched forward and Karla grabbed onto her seatback. The old man slumped forward, groaning. She reached back and propped him upright again, wedging him in the corner, then tucked her hair behind her ear and dropped back onto the seat.

Age hadn't occurred to her. The man she imagined, the one who reminded her of her father, was younger — closer to her age. Healthy and robust. Not old and frail.

Er ist ein schwacher alter Mann.

Chapter 4

Empty-handed, headphones draped around his neck, Jim Murphy stood in his office staring at the street seven-stories below. He watched the darkly clad pedestrians move along the sidewalk in haste; taxis, their yellow paintwork bright in the early morning light, floated across town seemingly without sound. Behind him he could hear the bustle in the next room: voices, teletypes chattering, the *dring-dring* of telephones. It was 8:30 a.m. and the squad room was alive already, his office dead still in comparison.

Down on the street an NYPD patrol car appeared, blue lights flashing. Murphy watched the car pull up in front of one of the buildings down the block; two blue-shirted officers got out, grabbed their nightsticks, shut their doors, then waded across the sidewalk and hauled themselves up the stoop in front of the building and went inside. A few minutes later the patrolmen reappeared, a scruffy street person handcuffed between them. They led the man across the sidewalk, pushed his head down and shoved him into the back of the car. As the car pulled away the pedestrians barely took notice.

There was a knock at his office door. Murphy lingered for a moment, gazed at the flat ash-colored sky, then turned and found Charles Plum, one of the newer agents in his command, standing in the doorway. Plum was one of the new breed, in synch with the outside world, and in his creamy-soft silk jacket and open-collared shirt he hardly fit the public's image of an FBI agent. Few of the younger agents did. Or cared to, Murphy thought, fortunately.

The young agent waited to be acknowledged, patient, arms crossed. Behind him other agents shuffled in and out of view.

"Did you want to speak with me?"

Plum came to attention. "Yes, sir. If you have a moment."

"Come on in."

He stepped into the office and closed the door. The act struck Murphy. Normally his door was always left open, but he let it lie. The younger agent looked at him strangely. The headphones, he thought, and pulled them off and set them aside. Earlier, before anyone else arrived, he was listening to Coltrane's *Love Supreme*, letting the music wash over him.

He motioned Plum into a chair and sat himself, clearing a path through the stacks of files littering his desk. "What do you have?"

The young agent looked down at his hands. "I don't want to cause any trouble."

"Let me worry about that," Murphy said quietly.

Plum sat up, cleared his throat. "Yesterday," he said slowly, "I got a call from one of my people. When I took the information to my supervisor he told me to drop it."

"Brinkman's your supervisor?" Murphy kept his voice even, non-committal.

Plum gave him a single curt nod.

"But you think what have is too important to drop."

"Absolutely." Then he looked directly at Murphy, eyes glowing, dark-blue, black almost, like sapphires.

Murphy thought of the closed door, noticed the stillness again. The kid had balls, going over a supervisor's head wasn't easy, and it occurred to him that he really didn't know Plum. They'd spoken briefly twice, once when Plum joined the squad and a second time in passing, but from what he heard and read in the young agent's personnel file he was sharp and ambitious, a mover.

In his four months with the Security squad Plum had managed to assemble a small stable of informants — the radical Left was his specialty — and he had pleased his supervisors in the past. There was only one less than enthusiastic entry in his file, the one that referred to "a proclivity for extralegal investigation," which meant he liked to bend the rules, and Murphy knew all about bending the rules. Sometimes it was the only way to keep an important investigation alive, but other times it made the agent a criminal.

He supposed he should tell Plum that Brinkman, a dull but competent man, knew what he was doing. Then Murphy remembered standing at his office window watching the world flow past. The sense of isolation.

"Tell me about it."

Plum shifted his weight, settled back in the chair. "Night before last I got a call," he said — earlier he'd said yesterday, Murphy recalled, filing the discrepancy away. "My source was very excited. Said the Red Path kidnapped a guy named Bacchetti, Luigi Bacchetti."

The name meant nothing to Murphy and he signaled the young agent to go on.

"I checked it out. Bacchetti lives at 309 East 77th Street, apartment 11B. He's been gone for a while, which isn't unusual apparently. The doorman told me he travels a lot. I used the 'acquaintance inquiry approach.'"

Plum was speaking off-handedly, without caution, eyes easy now. "I called around, visited his office without success. It wasn't much. A couple of rooms and a receptionist. The receptionist confirmed Bacchetti's been out of town, she didn't know where. His apartment was clean and orderly. No signs of a struggle. As far as I can tell they grabbed him somewhere else."

Murphy thought of the time discrepancy, the entry in Plum's file.

"Does Brinkman know you broke into the apartment?"

"No, sir. The black bag work's on me."

Murphy decided to let that go too — for the moment.

"And you're certain Bacchetti was kidnapped?"

"No question."

And he saw it again, the confidence, the younger agent's complete faith in his abilities. Brinkman would think it arrogance.

"What else did the informant have to say?"

Plum shook his head, frowned. "My info is pretty sketchy. The informant says the Red Path is playing it close on this one. Claims they're using outsiders. Says Italians kidnapped him, Japanese handled transport, and a German and an American are holding him now."

He was speaking in a kind of shorthand, Murphy noticed, as if he was trying to avoid compromising his informant — either him or her — in any way.

"Does your guy have any idea where they're holding him?"

"My source doesn't seem to know any more than I've already told you."

And with that Murphy saw the real issue with Brinkman. He wouldn't tolerate one of his subordinates withholding an informant's identity. It went against procedure and Plum had said "my source" as if the informant were his personal property, and Murphy knew *he* shouldn't tolerate that. But in a way he had to respect Plum for wanting to keep his informant anonymous, even if for misguided reasons.

In the old days the Director would have sent Plum's ass straight to Detroit. Would have sent mine there too, Murphy thought, if he'd gotten wind of it. But those days were over — the Director gone, dead. Which was just as well, he thought. Hoover had been the very spirit of the Bureau yet at the same time, especially at the end, an example of its greatest excesses. A caricature. Zeal gone awry. A petty bureaucrat defending his fief.

"The Red Path can't trust their own people," Plum said, excited now, hands animated, flying. "It's a sign of how weak they've become."

"Or how cautious. They suspect we've penetrated their organization. That's why they've brought in outsiders, and we shouldn't forget what the Japanese did at a similar stage."

He never would. In 1971 in a spasm of revolutionary zeal - *zeal gone awry* — the United Red Army tortured those among their ranks suspected of revisionism and left them to die of exposure on the slopes of Mount Haruna.

"Your source could be in danger."

Plum shook his head, hard-blue eyes set. "I don't think so."

God, he was a cold one, Murphy thought. Ruthless. The movers always were. And for a moment he wondered how deep Plum's commitment ran then remembered the young agent was risking his career by trying to protect his informant.

"What about the American holding Bacchetti?"

"My source says he's a Vietnam vet tied to the Palestinians somehow."

"And the German?"

"The same. She's running things."

Murphy sat forward, a chord struck. "She?"

"Yeah. The German's a woman."

Somewhere he had a daughter, a German daughter, a daughter he never knew. But that was thirty years ago.

"What do we know about her?"

Plum pursed his lips, frowned again. "Only her nationality, and that she's in charge."

Murphy eased back in his chair, springs creaking. Thinking. "At least we have the American in place."

"But he isn't …" Plum stopped, incredulous.

Murphy smiled. "No, he isn't one of ours. But at least with an American it's easier to understand his motivation. And if he is a Vietnam vet he'll be easy to trace once we have something on him. See what else your source can find out."

"Right."

Plum started to get up. Murphy sensed there was more, something that made the younger agent decide to come to him.

"Why'd the Red Path grab Bacchetti?"

Plum eased back into the chair and began to recite the facts without benefit of notes as if he had rehearsed it all in advance. When he mentioned that Bacchetti emigrated from Italy in 1935, Murphy asked if the victim was Jewish.

"No, sir. His emigration appears to be coincidental. He did serve in the Army during World War II, however. From 1943-1945. After that he dropped off the grid until '76 when he opened offices here in New York, and in DC and the Bahamas. He's a private security contractor."

Plum paused for effect. He had misjudged Brinkman, Murphy realized. He had good reason for telling Plum to ignore the information. A safe reason. Between them retired Bureau and CIA agents had a lock on the security business. And Bacchetti wasn't ex-Bureau.

"You understand why your supervisor told you to drop it."

Plum nodded.

"Have you contacted the Agency?"

"I figured I'd get the runaround if I contacted them officially."

"True enough," Murphy said — and already he was thinking of Mick Callaghan, his own source. "Let me make a couple of calls. See if this is Company business first."

"Yes, sir."

Plum got up again, then stopped. "It seems ironic. Bacchetti specialized in executive protection."

Murphy chuckled. "Like a barber always needing a haircut."

"Sir?"

It was an old joke, dated. Before Plum's time.

"Never mind. Tell my clerk to fill out my number three card. You do the same. I'll tell Brinkman you're on special assignment for the time being."

"Yes, sir." And for the first time the younger agent smiled.

"Is it Charles, or Chuck?"

"Charles — please."

Then he wheeled around to leave and a stack of files tumbled to the floor. He bent to pick them up.

"Leave it," Murphy said.

Plum left then, the chatter of the squad room filling the office when he opened the door. Then it was quiet again, the door closed deliberately. Just as well, Murphy thought as he picked up the phone and punched in Callaghan's number.

Fellow Iowans, he and Mick Callaghan had soldiered together in Germany after World War II. In the early Fifties Callaghan signed on with the Company while he joined the Bureau and they helped each other out whenever they could ever since, their friendship stronger than the rivalry between the two agencies.

"555-2000."

Murphy allowed himself a silent laugh. Answering with a phone number instead of a name was a holdover from the days when the Company still had some secrets. He asked for Michael Callaghan and the line went silent.

"Callaghan here."

"Hello, Mick."

"Jimmy!" He held the receiver away from his ear.

"How about some lunch?"

"Sure. When?"

Callaghan's voice had turned cautious. An invitation to lunch meant the other wanted a crash meeting. Murphy continued to speak in their private code as did his friend, both of them accepting the taps on their lines and the ones in between.

It took them five minutes to work out the details. They agreed to meet at "the old Irish place," Callaghan's summerhouse on Long Island, in four hours.

When they were finished Murphy hung up, and after a few moments he noticed the quiet again, the silence. A blow-up of the Ten Most Wanted List from January 1975 hung on the wall facing his desk; it was the only memento he cared to possess. He kept the poster, hung it there, because six of the ten were political fugitives, his domain. Two of the six were women, and every day the faces greeted him sullenly. A reminder.

Murphy stood up abruptly and went back to the window, gazed once more at the featureless sky. On the rooftop across the way an old woman, watering can in hand, was attending to her garden, her stooped body hobbling from pot to pot. Watching her, Murphy felt the disquiet again. He mulled over Plum's information — Bacchetti *had* to be ex-CIA. And if Mick told him it was a Company affair he'd back off. Tell Plum to do the same. Anything else would be madness.

Yet even as these thoughts went through his mind, Murphy felt drawn inexorably to the case. As if to a cry in the darkness.

***

Murphy walked into the cavernous garage where the Bureau kept its fleet of vehicles thirty minutes later, his footfalls echoing sharply as he made his way to the back. A series of overhead lamps cast cones of artificial light throughout the building and the cars and vans gleamed.

He fished for his keys as he cut through a row of vehicles. The Ford Granada's engine raced when he started it. He tuned the radio to WQXR, slipped the car into gear and pulled out; the attendant shot him a salute as he glided past. Once he hit the street he turned right, swung around a double-parked delivery van at the corner, then right again and headed downtown, the storefronts and pedestrians passing in a rush of color. Just south of the UN he dropped into the Queens Midtown Tunnel.

Ninety minutes later Murphy exited the Long Island Expressway, the city and suburbs left behind. The landscape had turned low and flat, coastal. Hothouses dotted the vast green fields; in some of the tracts rows of tall conifers formed barricades along the windward edge, the sky above strikingly blue, and he was reminded of the times he and his wife Liz came out here, Liz always insisting they stop at one of the farmstands along the way. On long summer weekends they would visit Mick and his wife at the house in Westhampton and stroll along the shore, arm in arm, the same faultless sky all around them.

Murphy felt the glow of those times, the warmth, and realized it had been nearly two years since they were out here. Time had become too short, obligations too long. And me too maudlin, he thought as he continued along the county road.

Soon the towers of the Beach Lane Bridge came into view. The drawbridge was down and he crossed without delay, radio intoning Glass's *Einstein on the Beach*. A few hundred yards beyond the bridge he made a hard left and headed down Dune Road. The ocean lay beyond a ridge of seagrass-strewn dunes, hidden from view; along the top was a scattering of houses — Murphy thought of them as New Capes with their oddly shaped geometric windows and weathered wood exteriors — all angular in the wind. Callaghan's house was farther along, a few miles down the road, set among the dunes.

When he came to the house, he pulled off the road, engine quieting as the car slipped onto the sandy verge. Fresh tire tracks etched a path to the garage door. Otherwise the house, like all the others along this stretch of beach, appeared deserted, closed up for winter.

Murphy killed the engine and climbed out. On the far side of the dunes the ocean was a murmur, soft white noise. He pressed his door shut, then placed his hands along the small of his back and stretched, eyeing the house all the while. The windows were dark, curtains drawn tight, except at a window on the second floor where they were parted slightly. Until now he believed it possible Callaghan would tell him there was no case, that Plum's informant had it wrong, but seeing the dark house, the parted curtains, the hasty tire tracks in the sand, he knew otherwise. Like the Red Path his friend was playing it close. *Very close.*

A gull swooped low overhead, shrieking, as he started toward the front stairs. Sand crept into his shoes and he felt someone's eyes on his back as he trudged up the shallow rise. At the foot of the stairs he stopped and checked the house across the way, the two on either side. No one. No one but me and Mick, he thought. He felt his friend's eyes as well.

Murphy mounted the stairs and entered the house without

knocking. An off-season stillness greeted him. Halfway across the entry hall he stopped again, listened. Silence. He heard the furnace kick in somewhere deep in the house, and after several moments he could smell the dust baking in the ductwork, feel the heat clinging to his skin.

He crossed to the short flight of stairs that led down to the living room. White sheets were draped over the modern low-slung furniture.

"Mick ... Mick?"

"Jimmy."

He jumped

Callaghan laughed. He was looming in the kitchen doorway, a bear of a man, massive, and with his flushed face and slab of gut hanging at his waist he had the look a drinker. Not a drunk, but someone who took his drinking seriously, a point he proved numerous times over the years.

"Jesus, Mick."

Grinning, delighted, Callaghan strode across the entry hall and clapped him on the back. "Long time no see."

"I was thinking the same thing on the way out," Murphy said, grinning himself, feeling the old warmth again. "We got to stop meeting like this."

Callaghan laughed again, took his arm, hand trembling slightly, and led him down the stairs to the living room. Together they pulled the sheet from one of the sofas and let it fall to the floor. At the far end of the room was a bank of bay windows that commanded a view of the ocean stretching to the distant horizon; gulls soared in the perfectly blue sky, sailing on the wind, and Murphy couldn't help but feel as if he was standing on the deck of a ship, thousands of miles from land, far from home.

"Hey, Jimmy. You want a drink?"

"No thanks," he said, still gazing at the sea. "Maybe later."

He turned and watched his friend lumber across the living room to the portable bar. A mirror was mounted on the wall above the set-up, and it occurred to him that Callaghan was the only person he let call him "Jimmy." Not even his wife Liz called him that.

Callaghan selected a lowball glass from the shelf below the mirror, tossed in a couple of ice cubes and grabbed a pinch bottle of Haig & Haig whiskey. His tastes hadn't changed.

Callaghan held the bottle up in the mirror. "Sure you don't want one of these?"

"Too early for me."

He bobbed his head, unscrewed the bottle cap and began to pour whiskey into the glass. "So what have you gotten yourself into this time, Jimmy?"

"You tell me."

Callaghan didn't say anything at first — he just kept pouring the whiskey. He set the bottle down, raised the glass to his lips and sipped the drink as if testing it, then gazed into the mirror, eyes far away.

"How'd you hear about Bacchetti?" he said finally.

"One of the street agents got wind of it."

"You trust him?"

The question took Murphy by surprise. It hadn't occurred to him not to trust Plum. His mind raced back over the young agent's file. Unlike him and Callaghan, Plum wasn't a farm boy from Iowa. He was a rich man's son and a graduate of Yale Law School. Until recently he served at Headquarters, and before that in Chicago and San Francisco, both assignments unspoken praise.

Then six months ago, inexplicably, Plum requested a transfer to the New York office, to Internal Security and the terrorist squad in particular. The request had troubled him initially, Murphy remembered — it was like a missed note in a virtuoso's performance. Most agents considered New York an office of non-preference and young ambitious agents didn't volunteer for Security. They saw the work, spying on fellow citizens, as demeaning, illegitimate somehow. Mainly he got the drones, the paper shufflers who spent their entire careers latched onto some old Marxist intellectual living on the Upper West Side, whose idea of political protest was subscribing to *The Nation* magazine and spouting slogans at demonstrations.

And what bothered him even more was that Headquarters allowed it. In the end he decided they were grooming Plum, their way of rounding out his file. He imagined Plum saw it that way too.

"He'll probably be my boss some day. Why? What's the problem?"

Still facing the set-up, Callaghan shrugged. "I don't know. The whole thing's strange."

"Strange how?"

His friend turned and met his gaze, seeming to weigh a decision.

"You say the word, Mick, and we back off."

"I'm not saying that." He took another sip of his drink, then drained it and began to mix another.

Murphy heard the furnace kick in again, ice clink against glass.

"How'd you figure Bacchetti for a Company guy?"

"He's in the private security business."

"So are half the Bureau's alumni."

"I'd know him if he was in the Bureau."

Callaghan smiled wryly in the mirror. "I thought I'd know him if he was in the Company."

"So he was," Murphy said.

Callaghan hesitated. "For a time at least."

He came back across the room, glass in hand, surprisingly lithe for a big man. They settled on the couch. Callaghan took a long pull at his drink then lowered the glass, cradling it in both hands.

Murphy waited, patient.

"I checked the files," Callaghan said finally. "You should see what this guy's been into, Jimmy. Everything from the OSS to the DEA. Then when I tried to access his current status with the Company — Bam! I get a no-clearance authorized message."

"Shit."

"Exactly," Callaghan said and took another swallow of his drink. "Any idea who grabbed him?"

"The informant says people working for the Red Path."

Callaghan threw his shaggy head back and laughed, a deep phlegmy laugh. "I knew it. I fucking knew it."

Knew what? Murphy wondered. What was so funny about the Red Path kidnapping Bacchetti? And what did a no-clearance code have to do with it?

Unless, he thought, the whole thing is some convoluted Company plot. The Red Path a Company front, the Company using them to take care of one of their own. Or ...

Murphy closed his eyes, the possibilities swirling in his head. He took a breath, exhaled slowly, and started again: Bacchetti had to have been involved in some of the Company's most covert activities to warrant the no-clearance code. Then another possibility occurred to him. The Red Path could be using Plum's informant to draw the Bureau into the heart of an ultra-secret Company operation. That would explain why Mick asked if he trusted Plum.

"Bacchetti must have been into some really heavy anti-terrorist shit. Looks like it's open season on the Company."

Confounded even more, Murphy shot his friend a look.

"You know the military advisor that was taken out in San Salvador a few weeks ago?"

"Sure, it was in the papers. Congress is making a bunch of noise."

"Nobody's saying, but he was one of ours."

The remark left Murphy speechless for a moment, the case becoming ever more labyrinthine, its very complexity intriguing him.

"So what does the Company want us to do?"

"Beats the hell out of me."

"I'm not getting my ass caught in this, Mick."

"Then let it go."

"I can't act like it didn't happen."

His friend grinned, the skin next to his eyes crinkling.

"This is bullshit, Mick. He's your man."

"I've never known you to be able to resist an interesting case."

Ignoring the jibe, Murphy stood up and walked to the bank of windows. A reef of gray-tinged clouds lay along the horizon, wispy cirrus clouds overhead; whitecaps creased the gunmetal sea and a series of small waves tumbled along the shore. Down the beach a woman in a dark windbreaker and light-colored khakis strolled along the shoreline, her hair whipping in the wind.

He knew Callaghan was right. He should drop it, but he couldn't ignore the kidnapping any more than he could have ignored Gretchen. She was the "interesting case." Callaghan warned him against her too.

He'd met Gretchen in 1948 at the DP camp in Wangen. She was a young refugee from the East, a gentle stray with sunken cheeks and corn-silk hair. Funny, even now he thought of her that way, as a young girl. He hadn't been able to resist Gretchen any more than she had been able to resist him, and from the moment they met they both accepted the attraction they felt as if they had no choice in the matter. Yet for months they avoided physical contact, never letting their eyes meet, their hands twisting away whenever their fingers strayed together.

When it finally happened, their lovemaking was unencumbered and free of guilt, Murphy almost shivering with the memory. He had loved Gretchen and she loved him, but he left her in the end and returned to his wife. He loved Liz too. And that was the part he never quite understood, that it was possible to love two women fully and equally at the same time.

It wasn't until later that he found out about the child. He went back — Liz insisted — but it was too late. They were gone, lost in the currents of post-War Germany. Gretchen and his only child … the daughter he would never know.

Murphy closed his eyes and tried to will the thought away though he knew it was futile. Long ago he accepted the loss as penance for what he had done, for what he hadn't done. He'd walked, left them without a future.

"You okay, Jimmy?"

Murphy sighed, opened his eyes. "Yeah."

The woman was still there, farther down the beach. A wave broke soundlessly at her feet and she trotted back to escape the surging foam. It's past history, lost history. But Murphy knew he was lying to himself. It would never be truly past.

He tried to think about the kidnapping, about the case. There was little he knew. But one thing he did know, an instinct almost, he had to follow. If he didn't, if he let the case go, he would become an old man, another Brinkman. Dull but competent, empty, a cardboard man. And suddenly he felt calm, resolved.

Callaghan came up beside him. "You're going after them, aren't you?"

"I don't see where I have much choice. Tell me what you found."

Without hesitating his friend began: "Luigi Bacchetti was born in Genoa in 1924. He attended schools there until 1935 when he immigrated to the States with his family. The last three years of the war he served in the U.S. Army, Army Intelligence due to his linguistic abilities. Friend Bacchetti speaks French and German as well as English and Italian. Along the way he was recruited by the OSS. No record of the exact date.

"In '47 he made the traveling team when the OSS was absorbed by the Company. Then various assignments in Italy and France. Nothing significant until he surfaced in Indochina. That was in '54, the year the Vietminh kicked French butt at Dien Bien Phu."

Callaghan paused and went back to the bar. Murphy remained where he was and watched the woman amble back in his direction. At one point she bent to inspect something on the beach. A shell? he wondered. She picked it up, examined it, then her arm went back, cocked — no, a rock — and she hurled it out among the waves, the effort throwing her off balance. Then she stood just there, facing the sea.

"In '61," Callaghan continued behind him, "Bacchetti was back in Vietnam and served as moderator between Lodge and the rebel generals during the Diem overthrow. He tried to save Diem and brother Nhu's asses. That was a story, stuff of myths."

Murphy turned from the view. "Tell me about it."

"Not important," Callaghan said, stirring the fresh whiskey with his finger. "Let's just say our man was loyal to his friends. He worked for Bill Colby in the Phoenix program."

And Murphy finally saw the irony, what his CIA friend had found so comical, so bizarre. Phoenix was billed as an effort to neutralize suspected Vietcong officials when in reality it was used to torture and assassinate opponents of the Saigon regime.

"So the Red Path picked the perfect 'victim.'"

"It gets better. Shortly after joining Phoenix, Bacchetti resigned. He claimed the program was ineffective. Too many of the wrong people getting knocked off. 'Unconstructive sanctions,' he called them."

"So Bacchetti's a creep because of Phoenix, but at the same time a Company renegade."

"It was smoke, Jimmy. Pure smoke. I think the whole thing was a ploy to make Bacchetti look like a man of conscience when in fact he was going deeper. Much deeper in my opinion."

Callaghan raised his glass, tasted his fresh drink. "After resigning," he went on, "Bacchetti hooked up with Drug Enforcement and connected with the drug world. There are even hints of a link to the Union Corse from his Saigon days. Possible ties to other criminal organizations. All rumor and innuendo, nothing specific in his DEA file."

Murphy wondered how his friend got his hands on *that* file but didn't ask.

"In '75 Bacchetti resigned from the DEA. A year later he formed Bacchetti & Associates, Ltd. No actual associates from what I can tell."

Smoke, Murphy thought. Mirrors.

"You think the Red Path did it then."

Callaghan beamed. "Oh, they did it, they fucking did it. It's who they did it for that has me confused. My money says we're behind it."

"They'll be onto you, Mick. They'll know you accessed

Bacchetti's file."

"I'll double-talk the fuckers. Tell them I was inquiring into a rumor and when I encountered the no-clearance message I dropped it according to procedure. Of course they'll know I'm fucking lying, but I'll be playing the game their way."

"You sure?"

"I'm sure." Callaghan drained his drink and turned back to the bar. He splashed more whiskey into his glass. He was drinking more heavily than usual and Murphy wondered if it was habit, or the situation. His friend's nonchalance feigned.

"Watch your back on this one, Jimmy."

"You know I always do."

Callaghan snorted.

Murphy glanced out the window. His rock thrower had vanished and in her absence the waves continued to work at the shoreline.

"Thanks, Mick. I have to take off."

Callaghan raised his glass in the mirror, a silent toast.

Then said: "Take extra care, Jimmy."

***

The wind buffeted Murphy when he stepped outside. Grains of sand, like a metallic mist, stung his cheeks. There weren't any other vehicles visible along the road; the woman he saw earlier on the beach was standing on top of a dune a hundred yards away, as if posed there, waiting for him, and he wondered if the Company was already responding to the alarm Callaghan's computer search must have set off.

No — she lives here. In a house overlooking the sea. A year-round resident.

Bits of Bacchetti's career came back to him, the details spinning in his brain. Take your time. It's a puzzle. Fit the pieces together, in different ways. What you need is in the past. Not yours, Bacchetti's. Some betrayal there.

Then he thought of the German woman holding Bacchetti.

Chapter 5

Three weeks earlier winter arrived unannounced, like an uninvited guest, and the days and nights were filled with sleet and rain, and more rain. Endless rain, Karla thought as she watched the old man.

The ceiling light was always left on, the window shade pulled down. The bedroom walls were white and bare. A small electric heater purred at her feet, the warm air wafting against her ankles. On the far side of the room the old man was asleep, one arm dangling, handcuffed to the headboard, a lump beneath the tangle of blankets and sheets.

For more than a month he remained near-silent, refusing to utter a single word about himself. The only time he spoke was when he needed to use the toilet and then he insisted that Sam, not she, accompany him down the hall.

He seemed to have accepted his predicament however — he was their hostage with no chance of escape — and he slept most of the time as if stockpiling his strength, as if he knew there would be a moment of confrontation, a moment that only he seemed to understand.

Karla tilted back in her chair and wedged her shoulders in the corner. Outside, the wind howled in complaint. So far they had learned nothing about the old man. No one acknowledged his disappearance and Raymond revealed nothing further during his weekly phone calls, even when she asked about the Red Path's demands though she couldn't see how knowing what they wanted in exchange for the hostage could do any harm. It might even help their morale, hers and Sam's.

The waiting was toying with her, Karla knew, confusing her, and she remembered Khalil's words. *At times it may seem you are waiting for nothing.* Still she couldn't help but feel trapped, stranded here, as if hibernating in winter. She missed the daily routine of the camp, the exercises, and her body was getting soft. Worse still, the desert was becoming a fading memory.

She closed her eyes and tried to bring the camp to mind, the sun on her head, voices rising from the camp, the warm afternoon breeze. Then the wind outside changed direction and sleet pelted the window beside her, ruining her concentration. It was like having chronic jetlag, she thought, the way she felt, the listlessness, the malaise, her brain getting soft as well.

Karla shook her head and rocked forward, resting her forearms on her thighs. Beside her the wind resumed its assault on the glass; Bacchetti continued to sleep undisturbed. Every night when she brought his food she sat like this, hooded, observing him, and despite his silence she felt she had come to know him in a way. He was a stubborn old man, proud and disciplined, and he seemed more substantial now, less the victim, less frail. At times she even wondered if he was some kind of soldier. He seemed indifferent to his fate. Though his only indifference, Karla sensed, was to them.

The old man stirred, bedsprings creaking, then slipped back into sleep, eyelids fluttering, dreaming, the top of a blanket tucked tightly beneath his grizzled chin. His breathing sawed the air. He has to be important, she promised herself, so important that the opposition can't admit they've lost him. That's the reason for this — for the waiting.

Karla felt the malaise begin to recede. She rolled her balaclava hood up until it cleared her mouth and took a breath of fresh air then eased her chair back against the wall. Even the sleet chattering at the window beside her seemed pleasant somehow.

***

The old man rolled onto his side, groaning. When he came up against the constraints of the handcuffs, his body stiffened. After a few moments he opened his eyes and looked directly at her, fully awake, eyes moving slowly over her hood, like a blind man's fingers tracing the contours of her face.

"Good evening, signor Bacchetti." Karla spoke to him in Italian, trying to keep her accent neutral.

The old man didn't say anything though she knew he understood. She'd heard him babble in Italian in his sleep.

"Come now, Luigi. You will speak to us eventually."

He closed his eyes, which secretly pleased her. This was a game they played; she spoke to him and he pretended not to hear.

"Very well, your dinner is on the floor next to the bed. I hope it's still warm."

His eyes remained closed, silent, unwavering.

Karla stood up, chair legs scraping the floor, and walked to the door but not before nudging the heater around with her foot so that the warm air blew toward the bed. She closed the door behind her, locked it and waited in the dark hallway, listening. After a few moments the bed creaked and she smiled. That was part of the game too. Bacchetti refused to eat until he thought she was gone.

Muffled voices floated down the hall. At the far end lights washed over the living room wall and she pictured Sam hunkered down in front of the TV. Every night he watched the news at five and ten waiting for word — and for reasons. It was all bullshit, he told her, the way no one was saying anything. They were diddling around. And it occurred to her that they each had their own way of trying to figure things out, of dealing with the empty time.

Then, standing in the dark hallway watching the light flicker in the living room, Karla was reminded of another time, an operation before Sam, when everything had been simpler, more black and white. It was two years ago, in Haifa, and that night there hadn't been anything to figure out. The American supply ship carried Lance missiles, Khalil had told her. *Missiles to battle our Palestinian brothers in the Bekaa.*

The water in the harbor was warm that night, and lights washed over the ships and warehouse walls the same way. There were three of them, her and her two Palestinian comrades. They made the swim with masks and air tanks from three miles out, skimming along the surface at first then diving when they were close to the breakwater, and when they resurfaced in the middle of the harbor she felt as she felt now behind the hood in the dark hall. As if she was there without being there.

Quadriceps burning with the memory, Karla sensed her comrades beside her, the warm water lapping gently at her face. The ship lit up like a carousel at night beckoning in the distance. Without a word the three of them split up and dove, Karla kicking, sealing through the water, arms tucked along her sides. When she heard the thrum of a prop she dove deeper, the bubble of her breathing filling her ears.

The ship's hull appeared as a darker place in the murk. Then as she glided closer as an immense black wall. When she was a few yards away she dug at the water, waving her arms in front of her, and came upright, then reached out and touched the hull, the metal rough and flaky with rust. She tipped her head back and saw the light off to her left through the prism of water. *Place the charge in line with the light.*

As if in a dream Karla swam toward it. When she was directly below the light, she unclipped the satchel at her waist, took out the charge and let the bag drift from her hand. She kicked once and rose slowly, free hand crawling up the side of the ship. The charge clunked when she affixed it to the hull.

A sudden shout startled Karla from her reverie. Light from the television danced at the end of the hallway. She had been daydreaming, letting time slip away. *Diddling around.* Still hooded, she put her ear to the door. The bed creaked, a clatter as the platter was set on the floor. Time, she thought, he will speak to us in time.

Karla let her thoughts ease back to Haifa, to the prism of light. After placing the charges she and her comrades regrouped and swam back to the boat, and as they were hauled aboard one of the crewmen detonated the charges. There was a flash of white light along the horizon, then a series of *thumps*, like thunder rumbling in the distance. Red fires in the night sky. And it had been so simple, so straightforward. Not confusing at all.

At dawn a curl of black smoke still hung above the harbor. The press called it a shipboard fire though windows had blown out blocks away. Even after the Palestinians claimed responsibility, the Israelis — and the Americans — denied it was sabotage. Not unlike what they are doing now, Karla thought.

She pulled off the wool balaclava, static crackling, and shook out her hair, then wandered down the hall. She found Sam where she pictured him earlier, squatting in front of the TV. He looked up when she entered the living room. His eyes settled on a spot above her shoulder.

"He's eating," she said.

Without a word Sam turned back to the TV and began to flip through the channels. The volume came in bursts, images flaring on the screen.

"You should turn on the light."

Sam continued flipping through the channels silently. He had set the automatic on top of the television set. Close, at hand. Karla turned and walked back into the hall, then into the kitchen. She turned on the overhead light and went to the table, picked at a scrap of food on one of the stoneware plates.

"Look!"

She ducked her head into the hallway. On the television screen a news commentator sat in front of a bank of monitors, sifting through a sheaf of papers, ignoring the camera. Then a photograph of Bacchetti appeared on the screen.

"It's him," Sam said.

Karla eased back into the living room. It was an old photo and he looked younger, healthier, more robust, as if the flow of time had been reversed. *Endlich.*

The photo vanished and a new scene appeared, a press conference with reporters and rows of chairs. Some of the reporters sat while others stood chatting, gathered in knots. The camera panned to the front of the room and settled on a podium, curtains behind it. There was a seal on the podium: an eagle encircled by stars and the words "Department of Justice, Federal Bureau of Investigation."

The curtains parted and a man in a dark business suit emerged. He ran his hand through his iron-gray hair as he set a sheet of paper on top of the podium. The reporters' voices rose and fell like a wave.

"James Murphy, Special Agent in Charge of the New York Field Office," the newscaster murmured in the background.

"What's his name?" Sam asked.

"Murphy," she replied without taking her eyes from the screen.

Murphy looked uncomfortable and Karla was reminded of the past again, of her mother's favorite photograph. In it her mother and father stood in front of a shabby café, arms entwined. Her father had the same close-mouthed smile, the same fixed gaze. And it occurred to her they were an American type — her father and Murphy. They *looked* like policeman and they both looked like they wanted to be somewhere else.

Behind Murphy stood another man, much younger, hands crossed in front of him. He looked like he wanted to be somewhere else too.

"Today," Murphy began without introduction, "in the course of a routine investigation, we learned of the abduction of a Mr. Luigi Bacchetti."

Karla shot a glance at Sam. He had settled back on his haunches, arms wrapped around his upturned knees.

"The subject," Murphy continued, "is the sole proprietor of Bacchetti & Associates, Limited, a private security firm. Prior to his involvement in the security business, Mr. Bacchetti had a long and distinguished career with the U.S. government."

"What part of the government?" one of the reporters called.

Murphy's gaze flicked to the questioner. "He worked for the Department of Justice."

"Was he in the Bureau?" another reporter asked.

"No, he was not."

"He's a spook," Sam said.

Karla ignored him.

"What part of Justice?" another voice shouted.

"Most recently Mr. Bacchetti worked for the Drug Enforcement Agency."

"He's a spook," Sam said again.

This time Karla shushed him — the old man was a spy.

"Did Bacchetti work undercover?" still another questioner, this one at the back of the room.

"I'm afraid that information is not available at this time."

"How did the Bureau learn about the kidnapping?"

"As I said, it was the result of a routine inquiry."

"What kind of inquiry?"

It was the reporter at the back again. They smelled blood. Karla could sense their hunger.

"I'm afraid I'm not at liberty to say."

"Was an informant involved?" the same questioner.

Murphy was curt with his reply. "No." Then as if realizing it he smiled amiably. "Obviously if an informant was involved we couldn't say."

"Then one was?"

Karla felt her pulse quicken, dismissed it. Only Raymond knew where they were. She stole another glance at Sam; he seemed unperturbed.

"Then one was?" the reporter repeated.

The camera panned to the questioner. He was young, younger than the others, longhaired and bearded — a sympathizer, she thought.

"No," Murphy said, wagging his head. "No informant was involved."

"Did Mr. Bacchetti work with any other government agencies?" The question came from the front of the room this time.

"At this point in the investigation our information is incomplete."

"Have any demands been made?" The reporter in the back again

"Have any?" other voices demanded.

"No," Murphy said. "None."

"Is the Red Path involved?" the young reporter again.

"We have no such indication at this time."

"Isn't the Red Path demanding $5,000,000 and the release of seventeen Palestinian freedom fighters imprisoned in Israel?"

The camera froze on Murphy's face. Bulbs flashed. He closed his eyes for a moment and Karla watched him take a breath, her hopes reaffirmed. *Siebzehn.*

"The fascist state of Israel," the young reporter went on, badgering Murphy, the other reporters transfixed.

Murphy seemed to draw himself up. "If those demands have been made, it's news to me."

"He's lying," Sam said.

"Of course he is," Karla said, "but he can't admit it."

Murphy looked tired, his features drawn. He'd lost control of the press conference and she almost felt sorry for him.

"How are the Palestinians involved?" someone called out.

"At this point in time the only reliable information we have is that Mr. Luigi Bacchetti, sole proprietor of Bacchetti & Associates, Limited, was abducted by persons unknown."

"Unknown or unacknowledged?" the young reporter in the back scoffed, mocking him now.

"Unknown."

The young reporter went on undeterred. "Did Mr. Bacchetti's distinguished career in the federal government include work for the Central Intelligence Agency?"

"You would have to ask the Agency."

"Did he spend time in southeast Asia?"

"I wouldn't know. Mr. Bacchetti was a private security contractor ..."

"In Vietnam?"

Karla saw Sam rock forward, his body rigid, taut.

Murphy shook his head.

"From 1954 to 1969?"

The young reporter was asking all the questions now, not asking questions, providing answers, and Karla finally understood Raymond's reticence. Bacchetti had been in Vietnam.

"Was Mr. Bacchetti involved in the Phoenix pacification program?"

Murphy stared at the young reporter for a moment, the room silent, transfixed once again, then looking directly into the camera said: "The Bureau has no further comment at this time." With that he wheeled around and left, fleeing, his young aide following, the reporters hurling questions at their backs.

Sam reached forward and switched off the television plunging the room into darkness. The wind rattled the loosely fitting windowpanes and Karla could feel the tension in the air as if she were standing in the middle of an electrical storm. When she heard Sam scoop up the automatic, she backed into the hallway.

He was still standing by the TV, silhouetted in the darkness. She could almost feel his brain working, struggling with his demons.

She reached forward blindly and flipped on the overhead light.

Sam blinked, disoriented. His eyes dull and flat, like unpolished stones. Dark, black, mad in every sense of the word.

"Get out of the way."

"No."

"Get out of the way!"

Karla stood her ground. "You can't do this," she said evenly.

"He was there. In-country."

"We were told only if necessary."

"It's necessary." She heard the emptiness in Sam's voice.

Emotionless.

He pulled back the slide, chambered a round.

"I won't let you."

Sam's eyes settled on her, went through her. Frightening, insane.

"Think about the demands," she said. "Seventeen Palestinians."

But it was as if he hadn't heard. "The old man was Phoenix."

"It doesn't matter."

"Yes, it does!" he cried and came at her, barreling across the living room.

Sam stopped when he was inches from her, loomed over her. She could smell his sweat, his absolute rage, feel her own fear. In his eyes was darkness.

"Get out of the way."

"No."

He tried to push her aside.

"Get out of my way!" he cried like an animal in pain.

But she refused to move.

"Please ... I have to," almost pleading with her now.

"We aren't shooters."

"He was Phoenix."

"I don't care. The Palestinians are everything to me." And immediately, saying it, Karla knew she'd made a mistake.

"Fuck the Palestinians!" he shrieked and tossed her aside.

Karla grabbed onto his arm and Sam dragged her flailing, scrabbling, down the hallway. She tried to dig in her heels, clawed at him, fighting him as he towed her toward Bacchetti's door.

"Please," she cried. "Please. This isn't some firefight in Vietnam. You can't kill your problems."

Sam whirled on her with such force that she lost her grip and fell to the floor. He towered over her, breath rasping, seething, and for a moment Karla thought he was going to turn the gun on her. Anything to get at the old man.

"Do you know what Phoenix was? Do you? Do you have any fucking idea?"

Karla shook her head, numb in the face of his anger, his fury.

"Phoenix *was* Vietnam. It was killing opponents of the Saigon regime, regardless of their politics. That's what the whole fucking thing was about. The whole fucking thing. It was politics as usual!"

Sam continued his rant. "They said we were there to fight communism. For democracy. For freedom. Bull-fucking-shit! Those people didn't give a shit about democracy. It was just some bullshit word to them. We were there to keep some cocksucker, our cocksucker, in power."

Karla kept silent, letting him vent his rage, his frustration. In words.

"We died for that. All of us. We killed people — old men, women, children — it didn't fucking matter. We became animals for those motherfuckers. We lost our fucking souls."

Sam stopped abruptly, closed his eyes, trembling. Perspiration drenched his face and hair. Karla reached up and touched his leg gingerly.

His eyes shot open. Flamed out. Lost.

"It's all right." She caressed his thigh. "It's all right."

Sam shivered, twitched.

"It's over. Done." Though Karla knew it would never be over, not for him.

When she tried to ease the automatic from his hand, Sam pulled away. "It's okay, it's okay."

His eyes sparked. "The old man's mine." He was adamant.

"Later," she said quietly, lying to him, doing what she had promised herself she wouldn't do. "We'll do him before we leave. You have my word."

Sam looked at her, his eyes ravaged, burned out. "He doesn't get out of here alive."

"Yes," she said, steeling herself to the lie. "I promise."

She held out her hand and Sam handed over the weapon. He trudged back down the hall, shoulders slumped, head down, and watching him Karla realized that Vietnam had ruined him, stolen whatever innocence he might once have possessed. Khalil warned her.

So had Raymond — several times. She would make it work somehow. She would make him understand.

Chapter 6

Andrew stood on the pedals of his bicycle as he plummeted down the hill below his house, knees flexed, absorbing the shocks that rose in waves from the dirt road. His hair whipped in the wind and he was reminded of times in the mountains when he would hurtle down a gully of scree. Loose, fluid, at the very edge of control.

He ducked over the handlebars, dodged a rock that lay in his path; his eyes teared in the cold as his bicycle continued to gather speed, the trees on either side of the road passing in a blur, limbs uplifted as if in praise, exultant. At the foot of the hill he bumped onto the coast road and headed east — toward Luz. Every day he made this ride, eighteen miles to the beach at Praia da Luz where he would swim in the ocean for an hour, and back. The rides lending a sense of regimen, of discipline to his life, the regularity sustaining him.

Andrew rode steadily, tires whirring on the blacktop. First rays of sunlight flared along the horizon and a faint cool mist lingered along the coast. The exercise warmed him and before long he lost himself in the pace. The miles slipped away.

Last night he heard the news on the BBC wire service. The details of Bacchetti's past didn't surprise him though the kidnapping and the speed with which it was carried out did — he was expecting word of a shooting, the first in a series of three — but after sifting through his recollection of the meeting in Riverside Park he realized that he should have known three kills were too much for Raymond. Even one seemed too many.

Ahead on the left a mule was tethered at the edge of a field. Farther back in the field an old peasant stood stooped over a tangle of brambles and dry weeds, his white shirt chalky in the early morning light. Every day he saw the old man there, working in the field, and every day the old man would rise as he approached and call out to him.

"*Bom dia!*"

Andrew raised a hand in wordless salute and continued on without a break in his pace. Before rounding the next bend he glanced back over his shoulder. The old Portuguese had returned to his work, back bent, *enxada* hacking at the thorny bushes, and it occurred to him that he would miss the old man if he wasn't there. The trumpeted greeting, his own silent reply.

He loved this place, this hard dry land. The Algarve had become his home and he felt settled here, more settled than he cared to admit. He'd become part of the place. No — Andrew thought — the place became part of him. And he cherished that, the feeling, hoarded it.

Yet he knew that he would lose it some day, the sense of connection. They would come for him and he would have to leave. It was inevitable, as inevitable as what he did, and Andrew accepted the inevitability with aplomb. He wasn't a greedy man. He was a gatherer of moments, a collector of simple yet subtle pleasures. A connoisseur.

Soon Espiche came into view. From a distance the town appeared as a clump of white spread over several hills. Then as he rode closer as a concoction of cubist structures assembled at the edge of the road.

He skirted the town on the south side and swung right onto a secondary road that led up the last long hill. His bicycle pitched from side to side as he worked his way up the grade, Andrew standing on the pedals, legs churning. An ache quivered up his thighs, but he kept pumping, breath surging in and out, and he felt powerful, strong, alive. Connected.

When he reached the top of the grade, he dropped back onto the saddle and let the pedals spin freely. A cool onshore breeze washed over his face as he continued along the crest of the hill; he wiped the sweat from his eyes. The houses were more ordered here, well-spaced behind thick whitewashed walls, with proper English gardens, though at this time of year the surrounding landscape appeared stark, bleak. Like the Spanish plateau, he thought.

The town of Praia da Luz lay nestled in the cove below him, red-roofed buildings gathered along crosshatched lanes. At the far end of the town was a swath of white sandy beach; beyond that were headlands, the west face cloaked in shadow. A fogbank clung to the water a short distance from shore, and seeing it Andrew shivered as he started down the backside of the hill.

He let his bicycle go as the pitch steepened, bike jersey flapping, tires whining, screaming in his ears, and for a moment he had the sensation of floating, of weightlessness. Of gliding. As if released, set free.

He braked as he approached Luz's main thoroughfare and coasted through the stop sign, continuing down the hill. The road turned to cobble and he stood on the pedals again, the stones polished slick, and bumped past the butcher shop, past the English pub, past the picture-perfect whitewashed church.

At the foot of the hill was a small promontory, an unpaved area that provided a sweeping view of the broad blue sea. The road cut left and Andrew followed it along the shoreline, pedaling at a leisurely pace now. He could hear seawater trickling down the rocky shelf below the seawall on his right and there was the smell of moisture in the air. Like dew — only thicker.

In the near distance Rocha Negra loomed above the beach, face still dark with shadow. Shuttered caravans — later in the day they would look like booths at a tourist bazaar — were gathered in the roundabout ahead. Andrew swung his leg over saddle and coasted to a stop among the caravans, then wheeled his bicycle to a break in the seawall; he lingered for a few moments, listening to the rhythm of the surf, watching the waves wash and roll along the sandy shore.

From the fogbank came the unearthly shriek of gulls; sand pipers skittered at water's edge. Off to his left a woman lay on her back on the beach, her face turned to the cliffs. A floppy straw hat was set in the sand beside her. She was wearing an ash-gray sweatshirt and a dark bathing suit peeked from beneath the bottom hem, her legs pale-white like the belly of a lizard. Andrew wondered what she was doing here so late in the season. And so early in the morning when normally he had the beach to himself.

A tourist, he decided. Probably English.

He kicked off his shoes, peeled off his socks and ambled down the stairs. The sand felt cool and firm underfoot, still damp from the night air. When he passed close by the woman, she rose onto an elbow and half-smiled at him. She was only a girl, he saw, not more than eighteen or nineteen.

Twenty feet from the tide line he stopped and pulled off his bike jersey, dropped it in the sand. A small wave frothed onto the beach and the shorebirds scattered. He felt the girl's eyes on his back and again wondered what she was doing here.

She's a shop clerk. On late holiday.

Dismissing her, Andrew strode into the surf. The cool water made him shudder. When he was waist-deep he rose onto his toes, arms at half-mast, and floated forward, feeling the cold course through him. He swam hard to warm himself, breast stroking all the way to the fogbank, then popped up and tread water for a while, letting the rise and fall of the surf carry him around. The sun was high above the headlands now and Luz glistened in the cove, stark white against the dun-colored hills. It made him think of an oasis, then of Syria and the camp at Saba' Byar. He felt certain Khalil had sent the kidnap teams from there.

He looked for the girl — she'd lain back down — and set off in a brisk effortless crawl. Each stroke a chant, dull, rhythmic. His mind drifted. At one point he heard the well-modulated tones of the BBC commentator's voice ticking off the details of Bacchetti's career, then of the kidnapping itself. It took place sometime on September 12th or 13th, the announcer said. At most three days after the rendezvous in the park, Andrew thought. Barely enough time for Khalil to have assembled the teams, for them to have driven from the camp to Damascus and fly on to Paris and New York. That would be the most direct route. His friend pulled the teams together fast. Incredibly fast ... unless they were already in place.

The last thought stopped Andrew in mid-stroke. He popped up, felt the jolt of the cool ocean breeze. Could Raymond's plan have already been in motion? The teams set? But why mislead me? What would be the point?

Mystified, Andrew bobbed among the swells. He had swum far beyond the headlands, and the beach and town were hidden from view. At the west end of the headlands an obelisk pricked the sky; someone was strolling there, too far away for him to make out whether it was a man or a woman. The stroller stopped at the edge of the cliffs and gazed out to sea.

It won't be for a few months ... he is an influential man.

Maybe we can use Wit here.

Andrew looked back at the headland. The stroller looked in his direction and he thought of the girl on the beach, the way she'd watched him. He felt a sudden twitch of anxiety. Then the night in Riverside Park came back to him: the shape he'd imagined darting in the night, the way he'd acted — reacted, the fear he'd felt, and he wondered if he, not Raymond, was the one seeing bogeymen everywhere.

No — Bacchetti can't be Khalil's target. If his friend wanted the ex-agent dead he wouldn't waste time kidnapping him. And demands have been made.

Reassured, Andrew rolled onto his back and headed back toward Luz, one arm slipping through the water after the other, the sun warm on his face. Yet even as he swam his thoughts remained fixed on the night in New York. Khalil hadn't trusted the "others" to make the hit — another reason to rule Bacchetti out as the target. Like true believers, the people at the camp were absolutely loyal and followed orders without question. Without qualm.

He had been to the camp once, six years ago, after the first hit. A driver met him in Damascus and took him to Saba' Byar. The heat was incredible, the landscape parched, desiccated, and there were cliffs there as well, red cliffs of haunting beauty.

They followed a dirt track to the camp, the wind howling, funnels of sand swirling like waterspouts in the sky. When they pulled among the tents the place was bustling with activity, people scurrying about as if in the midst of some great task. Andrew pictured their faces in his mind, the Palestinians, the Germans and Italians, the Americans and Japanese, all alike in their fervor and intensity. Their eyes glowed as if fired by some mystical light. The Japanese woman explained it to him, her voice feathery, whispery as she told him about the subjugation of the individual to the collective consciousness. Then she took off her clothes and jumped into his bed without another word.

Andrew shuddered. The woman was a fanatic, devoid of self. Empty. As they all were. Every last one of them.

A wave washed over his face and Andrew sputtered for a moment, then rolled over and slowly breast stroked toward shore. When he reached the breakers, he stood up and plodded through surf; waves, small churners, crashed around his thighs. As he angled toward the beach he brushed the hair from his eyes. The girl had discarded her sweatshirt and sat up on her mat, hugging her legs to her chest, watching him openly now. Along the waterfront the gypsy merchants were beginning to move among their caravans. No sign of the stroller.

Andrew let a wave carry him forward, then jogged out of the surf and dropped onto the sand next to his jersey, his back to the girl. He closed his eyes. She's a clerk, he reminded himself. *Probably English.*

After a while the murmur of the surf lulled him and he imagined himself in the water again, floating on his back, the sun on his face. He heard a gull cry, the gentle lap of whitecaps, the *dip-dip* of a fisherman's oars ...

The soft pad of footsteps broke into his reverie and Andrew whirled around. The girl stopped in her tracks, ten feet away.

"Sorry ..." Definitely English. "I didn't mean to startle you."

He squinted up at her, hand shielding his eyes. She was wearing a black one-piece bathing suit, and had a flat young girl's body. Like the Japanese woman's, he thought. Only hers had been all bone and sinew, chiseled.

"Do you speak English?"

Andrew smiled at the question. "Do you need some help?"

"You're American." She had that surprised way of speaking

some English had, her statement sounding almost like a question.

"Do you need some help?" he asked again.

"Oh, no," the girl said, wagging her head, soft-brown hair brushing the tops of her shoulders. Her skin was milky-white and he thought of the Japanese woman again — *Mariko* — of the velvety texture of her back as she bent to his penis. Resolute. Afterward he felt as if he had been serviced.

"I was wondering how the water is?"

The English girl was peering down at him, her expression open, guileless.

Andrew turned back to the surf, felt her step up beside him, follow his gaze. The fog had burned off and a tanker was anchored miles offshore, its hull deep in the water.

"It's cold," he said finally.

"Very?"

"Tourists mistake this for the Mediterranean all the time."

"I'm that obvious?"

Andrew smiled to himself, her approach transparent, bald. He felt the girl's eyes again, like slivers beneath his skin, and glanced up at her. Her eyes were focused on his lips as if she were waiting to read his reply, but he said nothing.

"I see," the hurt unmistakable in her voice.

The time had come for his graceless departure, Andrew knew, but for reasons beyond him he didn't get up. "I'm sorry. That was rude of me."

The girl's expression brightened and she plopped down beside him. "We've only just arrived, three girls on holiday."

She smelled of suntan lotion, of coconuts.

"Are you on holiday as well?"

"No, I live here."

The girl smiled, shimmied her eyebrows, comic-like. "Must be nice."

Andrew felt her scoot closer. Still he didn't move. It was harmless, a diversion.

He picked up a handful of sand and let it sift through his fingers. "It's late to be on holiday," he said.

"It's less expensive this time of year. We're here a fortnight. Do you live in Luz?"

"I live outside town."

"You have a villa?" She sounded impressed.

"No, a house."

"Where?"

The question jarred Andrew. He stole a glance at the headlands but he saw no one. There wasn't any reason to suspect the girl, that she had been sent. She was merely curious.

Still he was careful with his reply. "It's far from here, down the coast."

"Far from us chattering tourists, eh?" The girl smiled at him, teasing yet flattering him at the same time.

Hit the road. Go!

Andrew hopped to his feet and gathered up his bicycle jersey. "I'm off."

"So soon?"

"I'm afraid so."

The girl peered up at him, her hair swaying lightly in the breeze, and it occurred to him that they'd reversed roles, he and this girl. She was squinting up at him and he was the awkward one.

"Maybe I'll see you later."

"Sure," she said, and turned back the sea.

They both knew he was lying, that tomorrow he would arrive even earlier to avoid her, and for a moment Andrew wished there was some other alternative. But he knew there wasn't. Because in the end he always preferred being alone.

Sand stuck to his feet as he made his way across the beach. When he reached the stairs he jogged up them and scooped up his shoes and socks. He leaned against the seawall to put them on, then walked his bicycle through the parked caravans. A young girl, a child, sat watching him from the back of one of the vans, her feet swinging below the doorway. She wore pink translucent sandals and dirt ringed her ankles.

He thought of the English girl again, then of Mariko. After she had done him she took his hand and slipped it between her thighs and they started again. And not for the first time he wondered if she was a gift, sent to take care of his needs. And if she was a gift what was the girl on the beach?

Andrew looked back past the caravans, past the white poles that supported sunshades in high season. The girl had returned to her mat. And flashing on it, he understood why she was alone. Her friends met someone, holiday lovers, and sent her away.

Shit. But what could he do? If he went back it wouldn't be any different than it had been with the Japanese woman. It would be worse, he knew, far worse. The English girl was a moment, a rare moment of innocence. A moment not to lose.

And knowing that Andrew set his foot on the pedal and pushed off, returning the way he had come, never to see her again.

II

Chapter 7

8:00 a.m. — sky the color of cement.

Snow fell hard and thick, starbursting against the Ford's windshield as Murphy sped down Dune Road. The deserted houses loomed like ghosts among the snow-covered dunes and he pictured the waves crashing onto the beach, spray flying, erupting into the air. The storm-gray sea ripped by the wind.

When the car started to plane, he eased up on the accelerator. He'd been driving too fast, letting his mind glide, thinking of Liz. Murphy felt a twinge of regret — he couldn't remember the last time he spent an entire evening at home. He was never much of a husband: he could be a stubborn, selfish man, quite capable of ignoring his wife, of becoming obsessed as he was now.

For the past three months he'd thought of little but the case, and it got worse after he learned Kiefer's name. Two weeks ago, after months of silence, Plum's informant came up with it out of the blue. Not an alias, not a *nom de guerre*. Her real name. The Assistant Director wanted him to give the name to the press right away, "a token," but he'd held out. He didn't want any more surprises and insisted they wait until they had a chance to look at Kiefer's Interpol file. After reading the file he thought of other reasons.

The car began to plane again and Murphy slowed once more, soft-handling the wheel, letting the Ford drift back to the center of the road, slush scattering, splattering against the car's undercarriage. It made him think of Iowa, of plowing muddy fields, the way the tractor wheel tugged at your arms when you cut back across the deep ruts. Of being a young boy.

Then he thought of Liz again. And of Kiefer, Karla Kiefer, how her past mirrored his own. He felt another twinge. The symmetry seemed uncanny, karmic, as if fated. Murphy forced the thought aside and tightened his grip on the wheel, focusing on the road ahead, on the houses in the mist. On ghosts.

When Callaghan's house materialized, he slowed further and steered onto the shoulder. Lights shone without pretense at the first-floor windows, and as last time, tire tracks etched a path to the garage door. Yves Klein's *Silent Symphony* playing on the radio. Murphy turned it off and sat for a few moments, engine idling, watching the windshield wipers struggle back and forth, the wet snow piling up, his thoughts still in disarray.

He killed the engine and got out. The wind-driven snow pelted him and slush soaked into his shoes as he made his way to the front stairs, and not for the first time Murphy wondered what he was doing here. Then he remembered why he came. He needed someone to talk to, someone other than Liz, someone objective. There had been a second name, an alias, the Herger ID, also out of the blue. It came later and the order troubled him, normally the alias came first not the other way around.

Callaghan yanked open the front door and called down to him. "It's fucking winter out there."

Murphy nodded grimly and marched up the stairs, feeling the sting of the snow again, the icy water trickling down his spine. Callaghan held out a towel as he stepped inside. He took it, mopped his face and brow, then his hair.

"I got to tell you, Jimmy. You look better on TV."

He gave his friend a look, then in spite of everything — the AD, Kiefer's history, his own uncertainty — Murphy smiled. "Just what I needed to hear," he said as he handed back the towel.

Callaghan beamed. "The least I could do."

Murphy peeled off his raincoat and draped it over the standing coat-rack next to the front door, loosened his tie. Together they went down the short flight of stairs to the living room. The sheet had already been removed from one of the sofas and a huge fire smoldered in the stone fireplace. Callaghan went to it, picked up the poker and prodded the logs. Crackling, sparks streaming up the chimney.

Murphy stole a glance at the portable set-up, the capped bottles in soldier-like formation. As last time the drapes were drawn to expose the view. Outside, snow continued to fall in slants, dashing against the glass; the surf pounded the shore. Instinctively he looked down the beach but today no one was there.

"You must be getting it from both directions," Callaghan called from the far side of the room.

Murphy didn't say anything. He just kept gazing at the storm-ravaged sea, unwilling to admit that after three months of nearly nightly barrages from the press he was in a daze, punch drunk, like a boxer who has taken too many blows to the head. And what would he say? That he suspected the Red Path was using Kiefer's past to lure him and setting the hook with the Herger ID. His friend would think him a fool, mad. Rightly so.

"The AD wants me to be more forthcoming with the press," he said, still gazing at the sea.

"Tell the Ay-Dick to fuck off."

Murphy smiled — Plum had suggested the same thing, only more delicately. Then he turned from the view and found his friend still hunched before the fire, poker in hand. He prodded the logs again. The fire snapped, popped; the red-hot coals glowed.

"We have the German woman's name."

Callaghan glanced back over his shoulder.

"It's Kiefer … Karla Kiefer."

Callaghan considered the name for a few moments, lips parted slightly, as if tasting the name, savoring it, then levered himself up with effort and set the poker aside. "Never heard of her."

"She was born in Nuremberg. In 1946." Four years before his own daughter Murphy reminded himself for the hundredth time. "She was part of the Rote Armee Fraktion until six years ago. Shortly after Baader, Ensslin and the others were captured she vanished."

"Was she purged?"

Murphy shook his head. "Not according to Interpol."

He told Callaghan how a Palestinian splinter group had recruited Kiefer — he almost said Karla as if she were a friend — and sent her to a camp in Syria where an international band of terrorists trained. The group owed allegiance to no one, not the Syrians, not the Russians, not even the PLO, and by not repeating the PLO's mistakes in Jordan and staying clear of local political intrigue they had managed to retain a sense of autonomy. They were a force beyond control.

Visibly intrigued, Callaghan waited for him to go on.

"She has a new identity," Murphy said, opening up now, doing what he came here to do. "She's traveling on a Swiss passport in the name of Herger, Ulrike Herger."

Callaghan considered that name, then frowning, shook his head and turned back to the fire. He squatted to a wood chip on the hearth, picked it up and tossed it into the flames. The bark sizzled.

"You remember the supply ship that exploded in Haifa a

couple of years ago."

"Sure," Callaghan said, still facing the fire. "The Palestinians claimed responsibility."

"We have information that a woman traveling on the Herger passport was in Cyprus at the time."

His friend looked back at him, a merry grin on his face. "Jimmy ... you haven't been 'forthcoming' with the press."

"Not completely," he said, almost grinning himself, the funk he'd felt earlier allayed. "According to the INS a woman traveling on the Herger passport arrived on a flight from Paris on August 20th. Three weeks before the Bacchetti kidnapping."

"So you got her."

Murphy wished he could share his friend's enthusiasm. "There's no record of anyone named Herger or Kiefer after that. No hotel reservation, no car rental, nothing."

"The Red Path must be handling logistics."

"Then why leave a trail at all?"

Callaghan seemed to think about that, shrugged. "Don't know. Hey, I'm going to make some coffee. Want some?"

"Sure."

Murphy watched his friend walk across the living room and up the stairs, remembered the way he slammed down the drinks last time he was here. He heard the faucet go on in the kitchen, water drumming against the bottom of the kettle. Then a clatter as the kettle was fumbled onto the stove.

He went to the fire, took up the poker. As Herger, Kiefer had left an obvious trail — marks, Gretel-like, in Damascus, Paris and New York. Why would she chance using an ID from a previous operation? She and her group were more experienced than that.

Murphy felt himself at the edge of insight, of revelation, an idea forming at the back of his mind, just out of reach. He saw it dimly as if glimpsed through a dense wood. Another connection. Something about Bacchetti and Kiefer.

His heart raced, beguiled. Then the idea began to slip away and was gone. Yet Murphy didn't feel any disappointment. It would come, he knew. In time.

"What about the Vietnam vet?" Callaghan called from the kitchen. "You have anything on him?"

"Only one in a couple of million possible suspects."

"You guys at the Bureau always were good at legwork."

"Thanks."

"No problem, Jimmy. Any time."

Murphy smiled. He stirred the coals, the heat made him wince.

"Actually, I was hoping you could help with that."

He heard Callaghan walk back across the kitchen. "How so?" the voice closer.

"You were in Vietnam."

The refrigerator door whispered open, then clicked shut. "If I can. You guys check the flight manifests against veterans' files."

"First thing. All the people on the flight from Paris checked out. Checking those on the Damascus-Paris run was more difficult, but Kiefer was the only one who made the connection. So he must have followed a different route."

"Maybe they're using Kiefer as a decoy."

He'd already thought of that, thought of it during one of his many sleepless nights since the case began. He knew — no, fervently believed — that the woman holding Bacchetti was Kiefer. Just as he knew she was the one who left the trail from Damascus to New York. But what he still couldn't fully understand was why she had.

"Maybe they're setting you up."

Murphy looked up sharply, half-expecting to find his friend

standing in the kitchen doorway.

"If that's the case," the disembodied voice went on, "it means your source is either a plant, or else being fed false information. And if that's the case, he's dead."

Callaghan appeared in the doorway, a steaming mug in each hand. He'd spoken utterly without passion, as if double-crosses and treachery were part of everyday life. But then, Murphy thought, disinformation was his friend's specialty.

The telephone rang and Callaghan ducked back into the kitchen. He spoke quietly into the phone and after several moments reappeared, receiver in hand.

"It's for you."

Murphy gave him a questioning look.

"Some guy."

He went up the stairs and took the receiver. "Hello?"

"I found them, Jim!"

Murphy felt a sudden lightness in his chest, a flutter. "Where?"

"They're holding Bacchetti in Vermont. In a farmhouse there." Plum's words pouring out, tripping over one another.

"Where exactly, Charles?"

"A place called Thetford Center."

"Any word on his condition."

"He's fine. When do we go in?"

Right away, Murphy thought instinctively, without thinking really. Then he remembered his friend's warning.

"Charles, where did you get the information?"

"From my usual source. Why?"

Callaghan was watching him as if trying to decipher the answer from his expression. Murphy put his hand over the mouthpiece. "You know Vermont, Mick. Ever heard of a place called Thetford Center?"

"It's off I-91. About ten miles north of Hanover."

"The nearest airport's West Lebanon, right?"

"It's snowing pretty hard."

But Murphy was already beyond that, mind racing once again. The closest office was Rutland and even if Callaghan was right, even if this was some sort of set up, they wouldn't expect him to go in fast. Then it occurred to him the AD would be pissed if he left him out. He'd want to mount a full-scale operation, dozens of agents, sharpshooters, maybe even some tame reporters. It would be a media circus. Screw the AD. Pure hubris.

"Where are you now, Charles?"

"The East Village."

"Have you contacted anyone else?"

"Not yet."

Murphy looked at his watch, calculating. "Meet me at the Suffolk County Airport four hours from now. At two o'clock."

"I'll be there."

"And Charles ..."

"Yes, sir."

"Where is your informant now?"

"I just left him. Why?"

Murphy left that question unanswered as well and hung up. Callaghan was looking at him, waiting.

"We got them, Mick."

"I gathered as much. But remember what I said."

"We're ahead of them. I can feel it. They won't expect us to go in fast. Why don't you come with us?"

"I can see the headlines now," Callaghan said, grinning as he held up his hands and framed an imaginary headline. "'CIA Assists FBI in Rescue of Disgruntled Agent.' No thanks, Jimmy."

And Murphy felt foolish, like a rookie carried away by the

excitement. Like Plum, he thought.

"I need to make a couple of calls," he said.

"No problem."

Callaghan retrieved one of the coffee mugs and returned to the living room. Murphy dialed his clerk first to find out who handled Security in Rutland. After that he called about the plane. As he expected, the pilot complained and pointed out the danger of flying in such conditions, but he acquiesced finally and agreed to meet him in three hours at the Suffolk County Airport. The storm was letting up, the pilot said, moving north fast.

***

Ten minutes later Murphy left. Callaghan waved from the front door as he pulled out, tires spinning in the slush. The last thing he needed was to end up in a ditch. And then he realized that, for the first time, Plum had referred to his informant as "him."

Chapter 8

Two hundred fifty miles to the north the wind was perfectly calm. Clouds clung to the hilltops and snow fell here as well, drifting over the woods and burying the field in front of the house. Karla had watched Sam drive off an hour ago — he'd gone to Hanover to buy supplies and promised to return within two hours — and after watching him blast down the hill she dragged the rocking chair close to the fire where she now sat rocking quietly, lulled by the motion and hush of the woodstove.

At the back of the house she could hear the old man's footsteps padding back and forth. After the first month they tethered him to the headboard with a length of chain so he could move about and he'd paced ever since.

He was waiting. As they all were. And for what? Karla wondered. For her to lose control of Sam? For the authorities to relent? For Murphy to come to the rescue?

She closed her eyes and waited for the moment of doubt to pass. It was the weather, she knew, that made her feel this way — that and the not knowing. It seemed months since she last saw the sun and felt its heat. Each gray day the same, as if time were frozen, non-existent. Still her commitment was beyond reproach, beyond question. She had found her purpose; freeing the Palestinians made it all seem worthwhile.

Beside her, a piece of bark ignited in the stove. Karla snuggled deeper into her coat, focusing on the sound. *Crinkling* — like a piece of tissue paper being crumpled. Then she heard another sound, farther away, a rumble almost.

She scooped the Uzi from the floor and cocked her head. It was a car coming from the west, from farther back in the hills, not the east, someone else headed to town. The car kept coming, traveling slowly, deliberately, the thrum of the engine growing as it approached, and she pictured the driver hunched forward, squinting over the steering wheel as he tried to pick out the road ahead, driving blind.

Without slowing the car passed below the house and continued on. Karla eased back in the chair and rested the Uzi on top of her thighs, listening to the sound recede. Then the sound died as if cut off and she was on her feet running to the front window. She could barely make out the faded image of the road at the foot of the hill so she moved to the window at the far end of the room where she had a better view of the road entering the woods. Nothing. And for a moment she wondered if she'd imagined the sound, if her mind and mood were playing tricks on her.

No — she'd heard the car. And when Sam drove away the sound faded slowly, gradually, not stopped abruptly like a faucet being shut off.

She scanned the area again, looking for movement this time. Her breath fogged the glass and she wiped it away, her fingers stiff, achy in the cold. Finally, seeing no one she decided the storm muffled the sound and returned to her chair and warmth of the stove.

Karla set the Uzi back on the floor and began to rock gently once more. Quiet. At the back of the house the old man resumed his pacing. *Er hörte es auch.* She got up again and went back to the window. Still no one, nothing. Only the silence of the woods and the drifting snow. And the old man's pacing.

***

Five minutes later the telephone rang. Karla turned from the window and watched it ring. Perhaps Sam was delayed? Or could it be Raymond? Though he'd called only yesterday.

The phone continued to ring, insistent, and she began to count outloud. "*Sechs, seiben, acht …*" She thought of the car that passed by — someone else going into Hanover for supplies. "*Zwölf, dreizehn …*"

You can answer, pick up the handset and listen. If it's Raymond or Sam they will speak without prompting. If it's someone else they will think they have connected to a dead line, a natural result of the storm.

Karla glanced out the window again, then turned and went to the phone. She tucked her hair behind her ear as she lifted the receiver.

"Karla …" It was Raymond.

"Yes."

"Where were you?" He sounded excited, panicky almost.

"You normally call on Mondays. Why? What is it?"

"Murphy knows where you are."

The words jolted Karla, taking her breath away. She looked back at the window. *Scheisse.*

"There was a car," she said, sharing his panic now.

"When?"

"Not ten minutes ago."

Raymond's reply was surprisingly calm. "It can't be him. He's just left New York."

"He could have sent someone."

"No, the car was coincidence. He wants to handle this himself."

How could he be so certain? she wondered. How could he know? Then it came to her. Raymond, like Murphy, had an informant. It was how he knew they were on the way.

At the back of the house the old man stopped again.

"How long do we have?"

"Three hours. Four at most."

Karla glanced at her watch. Until half past four. Her hopes shimmered.

"There's time then."

"Remember to use the Browning 9mm."

But Raymond had misunderstood.

"We can save the operation."

"No."

"There's still time!" Karla heard her voice rise in the silent house, pictured Bacchetti standing with his ear to the bedroom door.

"It's possible," she said, keeping her voice down.

"No, it isn't possible." Raymond was adamant.

"But what about the Palestinians?"

"We'll try for them again later."

"We can do this," she insisted, her voice barely a whisper. "We can get him out of here."

"I know you can, but we don't have anywhere for you to go."

Again Raymond's words stunned her. How was that possible? How could he have neglected to organize a second hideout? And a third.

"I thought you said the authorities were ready to negotiate."

"They reneged. It's over."

Yet her every instinct told her not to panic, to keep the operation alive as long as possible. They could kill Bacchetti any time, even as Murphy and his men crashed through the front door.

"Don't sacrifice yourself, Karla." It was as if he could read her mind. "They aren't worth it."

But they were — to her. The Palestinians were her hope, her dream. And why else were they here?

"Listen," Raymond continued, reasoning with her. "The operation is blown. I wish it wasn't but it is and there isn't anything we can do about it. Bacchetti deserves to die." Then his voice changed as if he was searching for the right pitch: "Hey, if you don't want to do it, let your friend. From what I've heard he'll love it."

His name is Sam she wanted to scream. And she promised herself she wouldn't use Sam. Nor would she let Raymond. Not against himself.

"*I'll* execute the hostage," she said, "when necessary."

"You'll execute him now."

The line was quiet then and she could sense Raymond's will, his power. "I wanted the Palestinians too," he went on, reasoning with her again. "We have to be realistic. At least we can show them we are serious. Khalil said I could depend on you."

Karla didn't say anything. She had never refused an order before; she was always dependable and loyal, a good soldier, and she knew to refuse was pointless, futility. Madness regardless of how she felt. And she accepted that now.

She picked up the automatic, phone still pressed to her ear, and hefted its weight in her hand. *A good soldier.*

"We'll take care of everything."

"Good. Use the handgun we discussed. Then get the hell out of there. Ditch the car when you get to Montreal. You have the contact's number." The Montreal contact's name and phone number had been among the packet of information delivered to the apartment in New York. "He'll have ID for both of you."

Karla nodded, numb, all of it going fast. She looked down at the gun in her hand.

"You can do it, Karla."

"I've told you I will." Her voice testy.

"All right." Raymond's tone had changed again, fairly purring now. "You've done well. I'll make certain Khalil knows."

He hung up and Karla slowly set the handset back in its cradle, eyes fixed on the wall before her. For a few seconds she considered calling the number in New York, the emergency number Khalil made her memorize before they went their separate ways in Damascus.

Yet even as she contemplated it, she knew it was wasted energy. There wasn't time — it was over. As with the RAF they had been reduced to gestures. And she accepted that too.

Karla ejected the magazine, checked that it was fully loaded and slammed it home, then chambered a round, thumbed on the safety and returned to the front window. She had little faith in what Raymond said about the car.

It had stopped snowing and the contour of the road and the woods beyond were clearly visible. The snow-laden maple and birch swayed lightly and it occurred to her that finally, after all these months, she was going home, to the *hamad*. To warmth.

But she didn't feel any warmth. She only felt empty, failed. She thought of her Palestinian comrades abandoned in their cells, pictured their gaunt faces behind the bars. Then as if experiencing a vision she saw her mother's face and remembered how she looked at the end: frail, a wisp, yellow-gray hair scattered across the sheet. Still waiting for her lover to return. Loyal to death. Loyalty was her vice.

No — Karla thought — loyalty wasn't her mother's vice. Nor was it hers. Loyalty to the wrong person was.

Fuck Raymond.

And in that moment, standing in a farmhouse in America, Karla began to accept that she was going to die. Maybe even today. But she wasn't afraid. If anything she felt unburdened, as if commitment had set her free.

She wheeled around and headed for Bacchetti's room. The light in the hallway was shadowy, dim, the air stale as if it had gathered there for months. The old man's room quiet except for the purr of the electric heater. It was ironic, she thought, that last day at the camp Khalil should have warned her against herself. Not that it would have done any good. Her decision was made long before that, long before Khalil recruited her. Even before she left university to join the Rote Armee. It was just now that she realized it.

She grabbed the old man's clothes from the hook next to the door, draped them over her free arm, then unlocked the door and pushed it open. Bacchetti stood cowering in the corner, naked, hands splayed modestly in front of him. When she tossed him the key his hand shot out instinctively and he snagged it in mid-air. He looked at the key for a moment, then his head came up and his watery gaze skimmed over her, pausing on her uncovered face, and settled on the handgun.

Karla dumped the clothes on the bed. "Get dressed."

"Why?"

She thumbed off the safety in reply.

Without another word the old man sidestepped to the bed, hands crossed to conceal his nakedness once more. He turned his back to her and unlocked the handcuffs. When he bent forward to step into his briefs, bony knobs poked out along his spine. His skin was blotchy, Karla noticed, the color of beeswax, and hung in folds from his haunches.

Bacchetti dressed quickly, each article of clothing seeming to restore a measure of his dignity. When he was finished he turned to face her. He seemed taller, more erect.

"The handcuffs," she said.

He retrieved the handcuffs from the bed and fastened them around his wrists.

"The key."

Bacchetti shuffle-tossed the key to her.

"Now turn off the heater. Please."

Again he did as he was told.

She waved the gun toward the door. "Out."

And with that the old man balked.

"Now!"

His eyes rose to meet hers.

"Don't worry, I'm not here to execute you. But if you don't do exactly as I say, I *will* kill you. I promise."

He nodded and inched past her, eyes on the handgun all the while. Karla followed him down the hallway to the living room. She unlocked the cuff from one wrist and fastened it to the rocking chair, then returned to the front window. Not for a moment had she forgotten the car, and when she was in Bacchetti's room she heard another sound, like a car door slamming. Though it could have been anything, she knew, the wintry wind gusting among the trees, snow falling to the ground, her imagination.

She stole a glance at her watch — 2:10. Outside, it was snowing again, thicker now; huge wet flakes floated to the ground, burying the tire tracks. Only ridges remained where Sam drove down the hill.

"Where are we going?"

The words startled Karla, unnerving her for a moment. She'd nearly forgotten Bacchetti was in the room with her, and she didn't know where they were going. She only knew that they were.

"It isn't important."

"*Per me lo é.*"

"*Un posto.*" He seemed more accommodating when she spoke to him in Italian, and Sam would know a place, a safe place … if *he'll take us there.*

Her mind flashed back to the night of Murphy's first press conference, Sam looming over her, shrieking, the pain and hatred in his eyes. *He doesn't get out of here alive.* She was able to pacify him that night.

"*Che posto?* the old man asked.

"*Un posto lontano da qui.*"

"*Che lontano?*"

"*Basta cosi Luigi, ti ho giá detto di non fare domande.*"

"*Ero solo un pó curioso.*"

Karla shook her head — he was more than curious — and turned her attention back to the scene out front. Snow continued to fall and the road had nearly merged into the frozen landscape once again. She shivered and went to her duffel bag, which lay next to Sam's near the front door. They always kept them there, packed, ready for flight.

She squatted down, set the automatic on the floor, unzipped her bag and began to dig through it, her clothes — an extra sweater and jeans, tops, panties and socks — cold, damp almost beneath her hand. Sam bought her a hat a few months back, a hand-knit cloche; it was shortly after the weather changed and he was shy, she remembered, when he handed it to her, as if embarrassed by the sentiment. *Too keep you warm.* That was the side of him she would appeal to, his thoughtful side. She would convince him somehow.

Karla continued rummaging through her bag. Finally she located the hat, the wool fabric scratchy against her skin, and pulled it out. She gathered her hair into a high ponytail, twisted it and piled the result on top of her head, and pulled the hat on. As she was tucking the last wayward strands beneath the brim, she heard a sound outside and stopped.

Behind her, the rocking chair creaked. "*Sta zitto!*"

After a moment she recognized the sound — another car, traveling fast. She snatched the automatic from the floor and ran back to the window, saw the Datsun shoot from the woods.

"*Chi è?*"

"We're leaving," she said, scanning the woods and hillside opposite the house.

The car skidded as it swerved into the field, fishtailing in the drifted snow, wheels spinning, digging for traction, finding solid ground finally. White waves of snow curled from the fenders as the car plowed slowly up the hill. As he crested the rise Sam gunned the engine and slid the car sideways so that it was pointing toward the road when it came to a halt. He got out, grabbed the grocery bags and plodded toward the house, postholing in the calf-deep snow.

Karla wondered what she would say to him, the words she would use to convince him She knew she couldn't lie to him, not again. She had to tell him the truth. Otherwise it would be for nothing. Delusion.

Out front, Sam was shaking the snow from his hair. When she opened the door he looked up, stomped his feet on the porch floorboards.

"There's a car parked along the road," he said.

"Where?"

"Back a bit. Toward town," he said, his voice fading as he

turned and pointed to where the road slipped into the woods. "Whoever it is broke down."

Karla stood on her toes straining to see over his shoulder. "Are you sure?"

Sam turned back to her. "It seems okay. There's a note on the dashboard and his tracks lead toward the next farm."

Which explained the sound, she thought, the way it cut off so abruptly.

"You spooked?" Sam was looking at the gun in her hand.

"We had a call," she said, keeping her voice even, matter-of-fact. "Murphy knows about this place."

Sam pulled open the screen door and pushed past her. He stopped when he saw Bacchetti handcuffed to the chair. "What's he doing out here?"

"We're leaving."

Sam looked at her. "With him?"

Karla felt the old man watching her. "Yes."

Sam seemed to consider that for a moment, then said, "Where are we going?"

When she didn't reply, he set the grocery bags on top of the television console and held out his hand.

"We can do this," she said. An echo.

"They told us to take care of him if there were any problems. You said so yourself."

He wasn't arguing, Karla noticed, just stating the facts very reasonably.

"I'll do it," he said.

"The Red Path is panicking," she said, trying to keep any hint of desperation from her voice. "They won't be here for a couple of hours. You must know a place where we can go?"

Sam studied her face for several moments, her eyes, trying to fathom her and her motives. "Do you know what they'll do to us?"

"I have to at least try," she said, keeping nothing from him now.

Sam gazed at her a moment longer, then shook his head and smiled. "The shit I put up with."

Karla felt a surge of relief, of gratitude. He was setting his past aside. For her.

"Next time," he called over her shoulder, "you're mine, old man." Then he reached down for their bags.

Karla slid the automatic into her coat pocket and hurried to Bacchetti's side. She unlocked the cuff attached to the chair, pulled him to his feet and refastened his hands behind his back. "If you don't do exactly as you are told," she said again. "I will kill you." The old man nodded.

Sam was standing at the front door, their duffel bags clutched in one hand, a pair of Uzis in the other. "Let's get the fuck out of here," he said, then butted the screen door open with the bags and went out.

Karla prodded the old man forward. Even with her wool hat and winter coat she felt the stab of cold when she stepped outside. She ran her eyes over the woods on either side of the house, over the hillside. Everywhere was quiet. Harmless. Nothing moved.

Sam was out front leading the way, following his tracks back to the car, leaping from one posthole to the next. Bacchetti slogged through the snow a few yards behind him, lurching from side to side; Karla reached forward to steady him. His arm felt frail, stick-like. Their footsteps crunched in the snow.

A shot rang out and Sam fell, duffels and Uzis dropping like stones.

"Down!" Karla screamed, too late. Bacchetti dove to the

ground beside her.

Sam lay on his back, blood darkening the front of his fatigue jacket. Gutshot. Another sharp crack. Karla scrabbled forward on all fours, grabbed Sam's collar, and mindless of the danger rose and dragged him to shelter behind the car.

More shots, like dry twigs snapping. She pulled Sam close, touched his cheek, his skin pale, shocky. His hands covered the wound; dark-red blood seeped between his interlocked fingers.

"Shit …"

Sam's breath caught and his eyes misted, then he managed an ironic smile. "I guess this is it."

"No. We can get you out of here. We can take you somewhere."

"Where?"

"I don't know."

She looked away, blinked at the snow.

"Listen …" His breath caught again. Sam wheezed. "You can't take me and don't let them." His hand came up then and she could see how badly he was wounded, that without proper care he would die soon.

"Cut your losses," he said. "Finish it!"

She shook her head. She couldn't do what he was asking, not after what they'd been through together, not after what they shared, the moments coming back to her, the first time they made love, the times since, the way he'd touched her, filled her emptiness. And the moments became minutes, and the minutes hours, and the hours days, until they turned back on each other and all she had left was this moment and she couldn't let it go. She couldn't let *him* go.

"Please, Karla …"

Sam stopped again, his chest heaved. Bright-red blood foamed from his mouth. "I know it isn't easy."

"I can't," she cried. "I just can't."

"Please," he said softly, gently. "Do it for me."

She nodded then, sniffed at the cold, understanding for the first time what true commitment was and meant. She reached down and brushed the snowflakes from Sam's forehead, touched his cheek; bits of ice clung to his sandy curls. There wasn't any reason to hurry now.

"It's okay, it's okay," his voice singsong, a lullaby. Absolution.

"Remember," he said, "I'm with you. All the way."

Karla bit at her lip, choked back the tears. She raised the automatic and pressed the tip of the barrel to his chest. Sam smiled serenely. He was with her now. *All the way.*

The gun bucked when she fired, echoing. Sam shuddered once then died. His last breath a gush.

Karla remained where she was for several moments, kneeling like a supplicant at his side, watching the snowflakes drift down and settle on his wide-open eyes then melt away.

"I can't believe you did that."

She turned and saw the horror, the disbelief on Bacchetti's face. He had retreated to the far end of the car and was crouching next to the back panel.

"Kneel."

He shook his head.

"Kneel!" she screamed.

"You can't do this."

But she could. She had to now.

She raised the automatic and Bacchetti fell forward onto his knees; she crawled to his side.

"This doesn't make any sense. You don't have a chance."

"*Stá zitto!*"

He was silent then; the shooting had stopped. Ferret-like, Karla peeked above the back of the car, scanned the woods on the hillside facing the house. Then she thought of the car again, the car door slamming, and knew it hadn't been imagination.

"You tried to save me."

Bacchetti was looking at her, his eyes yellow and rheumy, trying to engage hers. She prodded him face forward so she wouldn't have to look at his eyes, put the gun to his temple.

"You're not one of them. You're different."

But I am — Karla thought — I am one of them.

"You can live!"

She braced her arm, pictured Sam shaking his head and smiling. *The shit I put up with.* Then the moment in the hallway. *We became animals for those motherfuckers. We lost our fucking souls.* Feeling his anguish, his rage, his past, letting it wash over her. Embracing it, absorbing it.

"*Dio mio!*"

The sound of the shot cut off the old man's cry and Karla watched his head slam against the rear panel of the car, bone, blood, brains spraying the paintwork.

She dropped the gun and felt for a pulse automatically, then crawled back to Sam and patted his pockets. All reaction now, all training. When she found his money and ID she took them out, shoved them into her coat pocket with her own and ran for the house, keeping her head down, chin almost touching her knees, expecting the pepper of more shots. But there weren't any more shots, not even when she plucked one of the Uzis from the snow.

She took the porch steps two at a time and tore open the screen, crashed through the front door. Once inside she paused for a few moments to catch her breath, chest heaving, then peeked out the window expecting to find men swarming up the hillside below the house. But only the dead lay in the field, Sam on his back, hands folded on his stomach in repose.

Karla swayed with grief, then caught herself and fled down the hall, allowing herself only his name as she ran into Bacchetti's room.

Sam — as she opened the window.

Sam — as she dropped to the ground.

Sam, Sam, Sam.

***

Uzi slung over her shoulder, Karla kept the house between herself and the hillside as she fled across the field, the snow knee-deep, slowing her down, still expecting the slam of a bullet at any moment. When she reached the cover of the woods she kept moving, running faster now, weaving through the trees, the snow-laced undergrowth crunching beneath her feet.

She looked for tracks in the shadowy light, found none. Manic almost, Karla ran faster, faster. Saplings tore at her legs, whipped at her face. Then she tripped over a buried rock, feet racing to keep up, and slammed shoulder-first into a tree. The bone buckled and a sharp pain like an electric shock ran down her arm; pinpoints of white light flashed before her eyes but she kept running, running as fast as she could.

Without conscious thought, lost in the act of flight, Karla worked her way north until she came to the top of an embankment that overlooked the road a mile from the house. She paused and hunched forward, hands braced on her knees, heart pounding, her breath steaming in the cold.

Please ... it's okay.

No — not now. You have to go on. To survive.

Karla straightened up and rotated her injured shoulder. White-hot pain. She slid her fingers along her collarbone, probing the area gently. There was soft swelling where the bone attached to the scapula. But it wasn't broken, she knew. There wasn't enough pain.

Clasping her arm tightly to her side, she set off again, moving along the edge of the embankment toward town. The road below was deserted, a white trail cutting through the dark thicket of trees; icicles clung to the tangle of branches on the far side. Beyond that the river was silent, frozen. The light dim, perpetual gray. She stopped again, listened for the crash of pursuers. Quiet.

She replayed the ambush in her mind. The shots came in series. One at a time, she remembered. Maybe there was only one of them, someone local Murphy sent to cover the house until he and his men arrived.

Karla pressed the backlight button on her wristwatch — 3:23. Better to wait here rather than thrash aimlessly through the woods. It would be dark before they could follow her tracks and someone was bound to come along before that, some local in a rusted-out car or truck. Darkness was on her side.

She looked for flaws in her logic. She could flag down the vehicle, tell the driver she'd gotten lost, caught out in the storm. While walking through the woods, she'd say. "I love walking in the woods."

Karla heard the hollowness in her voice, then the wind rising among the trees, snow plopping to the ground around her. The sweat on her skin turned cold and she shivered. Then she noticed the red splotches on her coat and hands. Her lips trembled, but Karla made herself ignore the memory.

She unslung the Uzi and set it against a tree, reached down, grabbed a handful of snow and began to scrub at the stains on her coat and hands. The cold made her fingers ache but she ignored that too.

When she was finished she reclaimed the Uzi and leaned against the tree. The snow started again and snowflakes floated down and settled on her shoulders and bare head. Somewhere along the way she'd lost her hat, the one ...

Karla closed her eyes. She wouldn't even allow herself his name.

***

Sometime later Karla watched a night-darkened pickup truck chug up the road toward her. The pitch of the engine changed when the driver shifted down a gear. She lowered the Uzi by its strap to the ground and eased off her coat, careful with her injured left shoulder, but before she could drop to the road she heard the rush of vehicles approaching from the east.

She eased back a step, then another. When the caravan appeared, she froze. The battered pickup continued chugging up the road; the caravan slowed as it approached, a Vermont State police cruiser in the lead, blue lights flashing. She caught a glimpse of Murphy and another man — the one who stood behind him during the first press conference — in the second car as it passed below. The man appeared to be talking to him.

The last car in the line swung out to block the truck's path, the lead cruiser cutting off any chance of escape. Karla used the diversion to retrieve the Uzi and duck behind a tree. She shook off the snow and set the fire-selector to semi-automatic, flexed her fingers — they felt stiff, arthritic, like blocks of wood. The caravan wasn't thirty yards away and for an instant she considered engaging them, stepping from behind the tree and spraying the vehicles with bullets, but she knew that would be pointless, a gesture, an act of despair, and she had given up on gestures and acts of despair. She had to focus on the present, not the past. On here, now.

137

She could hear the engines idling smoothly down on the road. A car door opened and snapped shut. She pressed her back into the tree, held her breath. The squeak of footsteps on the snow-packed road, mumbled conversation. A radio squelched, then another door swung open and closed. More footsteps.

She closed her eyes, concentrating …

The footsteps stopped.

"Good evening, sir."

"What's the problem?" The man in the pickup truck sounded tentative, uncertain.

"Can we see your driver's license and registration, please?"

"Why?"

"Please, sir. Driver's license and registration."

Quiet. The thick-sweet scent of exhaust in the air.

"What are you doing out here, Mr. Scott."

"I live here." The driver sounded peeved now.

"Where you headed, Mr. Scott?"

"Into town."

"Where are you coming from?" a second voice, less cordial.

"My house."

"Where's that?"

"Back a ways."

"Where exactly?" the second voice again, impatient.

Another long pause. The man's contrariness pleased Karla. His unwillingness to cooperate, to go along.

"I have a farm," he said finally, "near South Strafford."

"Thank you, Mr. Scott. One moment please."

Karla heard footsteps move away. A radio screeched, more mumbled conversation.

Then closer: "Seen anything unusual?" The second man had remained by the truck; he sounded more congenial now.

She pictured the driver tight-lipped, obstinate, and slung the Uzi over her good shoulder and trudged back into the woods making for the thickest part. The sound of the engines faded as she moved away, blue lights like strobes flashing among the trees. After a while she turned back to the north, following an arc that would bring her back to the road. In places the snow had drifted so deep she sank to mid-thigh but she slogged on, numb, indifferent almost, as if she had been at it all day. Beyond cold, beyond feeling.

Eventually the woods thinned and she spotted the road, a white gap among the skeletal trees. When she heard the stutter of the truck's engine she dropped the Uzi and, chancing it, rushed headlong for the road. The headlight beams caught her as she broke from the woods; she raised her right arm and waved. The truck, rusted-out panels and all, rattled past, then slowed and came to a halt a short distance away.

The passenger door swung open and Karla ran for it.

"Hey, thanks," she said as she set her hand on the door handle, thinking American, saying the words at the front of her mouth. "Thanks for stopping."

"What the hell are you doing out here?"

The driver was a big man, massive behind the wheel, in denim overalls, with long hair and a dark bushy beard. She could smell the wet scent of hay in the bed of the truck.

"I was out walking."

The driver regarded her with suspicion. "In this weather?"

Karla avoided his gaze. "I got lost. I love walking in the woods."

Not a word in response.

Yet she sensed he would help her if she stopped lying to him. "I must get to Hanover."

The man continued to gaze at her, as if measuring her, assessing her, who she was, what she was. Then, almost imperceptibly, he nodded. "Hop in. I'm going into Norwich. It's just up the hill from there."

"Thank you," she breathed, feeling her hopes revive.

"No thanks required."

She stepped onto the running board and swung up and onto the seat. The pain jarred her as she landed.

"You okay?" The man was looking at her again.

Karla pulled the door shut, stared at the road ahead.

"I'm fine," she said. Perfectly fine.

The driver shrugged, then wagged his head and reached forward and put the truck into gear. The tires chattered on the icy road as they pulled away.

Chapter 9

The caravan rolled to a halt and they sat in silence for a few moments, Murphy and Plum in the back of the number-two car, the lead cruiser stopped directly ahead, blue lights off now. Off to the left, beyond a stand of stick-like paper birch, a clearing could be seen rising gently from road. The snow let up and a dark wall of woods materialized on the far side.

"The house is at the top of the rise," Plum said.

Murphy nodded slowly without taking his eyes from the clearing. He rolled his window down a crack. The late afternoon was quiet, eerie almost, and he could feel the tension, the expectation in the air. Like a contagion. All of it reminding him of a day long ago. As now it had been snowing the day he had returned to the DP camp in Wangen, and there had been the same sense of expectation, the same heightened awareness. As if every moment, every detail, were etched indelibly in his mind.

He had been nervous, anxious, like a proselyte waiting by a river, but they were gone when he arrived. Lost in the post-War chaos.

Plum shifted on the seat beside him. "If you like we can work our way up through the trees for a better look."

"No, we'll wait. It'll be dark soon and they'll be watching."

And for a moment as if he were one of them, Murphy pictured the view from the house: the gentle white slope, then the flat of the road and the steep hillside opposite where the maple and birch were winter-bare.

He hunched forward, ducked his head. He moved his eyes

over the hillside slowly — he hadn't forgotten Callaghan's warning. The snow was unmarked, untouched, and mounds had formed where it had settled on the rocks and brush. The trees swayed benignly in the light breeze, the storm seemingly spent.

Reassured, Murphy turned his attention back to the clearing where snow was falling once again.

"What do you see?"

It was Plum again — and he sounded skittish all of a sudden as if the silence had spooked him.

"Nothing," he replied, easing back on the seat. "I was just thinking how isolated they must feel."

"Not exactly the place I'd want to spend the winter." Then his young colleague smiled and he smiled in return.

"What did the informant say about the layout?"

"Only that they're here."

"The Staties might know something," one of the agents up front said. The agent, an older man, had twisted around on the seat and faced them, his arm resting on the seatback. He was a vision of the resident agent, thickset with close-cropped, steel-gray hair, and Murphy had to think for a moment to remember his name. Smithers, that was it, Randy Smithers. Smithers was the one he spoke to earlier on the phone, and he led the contingent over from Rutland himself; they were waiting at the Lebanon Municipal Airport when the plane touched down. Smithers also arranged to have the State Police meet them when they crossed the Vermont state line.

"Let's see what they know."

Smithers nodded smartly, then swung back around and unhooked the radio mic. The radio squawked as he spoke into it. Beside him the driver remained silent, face forward, both hands on the wheel. Plum remained silent as well.

After a few moments the front passenger door of the lead cruiser swung open and a state trooper stepped out. He was wearing a drab-green uniform coat with pants to match, and had gold sergeant's chevrons on his sleeves. A flat-brimmed DI hat was set squarely on his head.

As he came toward them the trooper's step was steady and sure on the ice road. When Smithers rolled down his window he veered toward it, his face flushed, raw from the cold.

He leaned forward and rested his hands on top of the car. "The house's at the top of the clearing ahead," he said, eyes skimming over them as he spoke.

"How far is it from the road?"

"About two hundred yards."

"What's behind it?" Murphy asked.

The trooper's eyes settled on him. "More open field. There's fields on all sides. This used to be the old Tyson place." He paused and Murphy motioned for him to go on. "A school teacher from New York owns the place. She used to come up here summers, but no one's seen her in years. Folks were surprised when these people showed up."

"Have you been out here already?" Plum said, sounding spooked again.

The trooper gazed at him for a moment, then cut his eyes back to Murphy. "One of my men lives out this way. People talk." Then he grinned, giving Murphy a look at a mouthful of nicotine-stained teeth. Still he liked the man instinctively, his bluntness and lack of frills, the way he had made it clear that Plum's question was completely out of line.

"When was that, Sergeant?"

"Early September. A week or so after the holiday."

Murphy felt a rush. They'd arrived — Kiefer at least — in late

143

August, two weeks before Labor Day and Bacchetti had been grabbed the week after that.

The state trooper was still looking at him.

"Any idea how many of them are up there?"

"Seems there's just two of them," the trooper said. "A man and a woman. The male is in his mid-to-late twenties, six feet, sandy hair, scruffy looking."

"And the woman?" Murphy kept his voice even, matter-of-fact.

"She's tall, trim, long blonde hair. No one's gotten a good look at her face. She keeps to the house mostly. The man goes into town once or twice week."

"Makes sense," Plum said.

"It does," Murphy agreed. "With her accent Kiefer would limit her interactions with the local people."

"You think they're the ones grabbed this Bacchetti guy?" the trooper asked.

"We think so, Sergeant."

"Do you want to do a drive by?" This time it was Smithers who cut in.

Murphy glanced over the driver's shoulder. The light in the clearing was dim, dusky; night was falling fast and he felt the impatience all around him.

"Let's do it."

The trooper took a step back. "We'll lead the way," he said, then turned on his heel and started back toward his vehicle.

"Wait," Murphy called.

The trooper stopped, turned back to him.

"Your cruiser might spook them."

He gave Murphy a look. "Sir, we have reason to be out here. The storm and all."

"We'll do it all the same," Murphy said, knowing the other man was right. They did have reason to be out here. But then so did he.

"Thanks for the info, Sergeant."

The trooper touched the brim of his hat and continued toward his car. Murphy reached forward and tapped the driver on the shoulder and they pulled out, engine nearly silent on the snow-covered road. Up front Smithers was murmuring into the radio, Plum leaning forward behind him, hands on the back of the seat.

"Charles, I want you to keep your eye on the hillside facing the house."

"Got it," he said, and turned to the side window.

The trooper shot them a salute as they crept past, exhaust pluming soundlessly from the cruiser's tailpipe. Beyond the trees an icy stillness hung over the clearing.

"Not too slowly," Murphy cautioned.

The driver nodded and the car picked up speed. When they broke from the woods the landscape opened up; fresh tire tracks led up the hill to the house. Lights, like hot embers, glowed on the first floor. A car was parked out front.

"What kind of car is that?"

"A Datsun," the driver said, speaking for the first time. "A 210, I think."

"It has New York plates," Plum said.

"Definitely New York," Smithers agreed quietly, glassing the car. "She flew into JFK, right?"

"That she did," Murphy said. The puzzle pieces falling into place: the timing, her trail ending, the Red Path logistics.

They were nearly even with the house. Cold air streamed through Smithers' cracked window. Murphy looked for silhouettes. For shadows. But there were only blocks of light at the first-floor windows; the second floor dark, silent.

Still something about the scene nagged at him, something about the fresh tire tracks, something about the light, the light at the front …

"Go!" he yelled.

The driver hesitated.

"Someone's been here. Go! Go now!"

"Go! Go! Go!" Plum yelled too.

The car leapt forward and skidded as it swerved into the field, back end yawing, sending Murphy flying, crashing into Plum. He grabbed onto the seatback in front of him, clawed himself upright.

Up front was chaos: the driver fighting the wheel, trying to stay in the tracks; Smithers yelling into the radio mic: "We're going in! We're going in!"

The State Police car screamed up the hill behind them, siren wailing. They're dead, Murphy thought. They're all dead.

He was out before the car had come to a halt, weapon drawn, running through the calf-deep snow. The bodies lay behind the car as if sheltering there: the Vietnam vet was sprawled on his back, a dusting of snow. Bacchetti wasn't far away, head shattered. Murphy spun around looking for the third body. But there wasn't a third body.

All around him men were running, shouting wildly as they fanned out in front of the house. Murphy forced himself to slow down and searched the area again, more deliberately this time. A smear of gore on the car's rear panel, the Browning Hi-Power next to the body. A bloody trough led from the Vietnam vet halfway to the house, then tracks like craters in the snow.

Gun still in hand, Murphy ran for the front door, Plum following. His footsteps clattered as he raced up the steps and across the porch. He pulled up at the edge of the screen door, heart pounding, thoughts scattered ... *even if she were your daughter you'd have no choice.*

At the edge of his vision he saw Smithers and a small knot of men start down the side of the house; Plum had drawn up alongside the screen door opposite him. The balance of the men took up positions behind the vehicles, riot and handguns aimed at the house.

Most likely she was in there, Murphy knew, wounded and frightened.

Or — she could be lying in wait. *Waiting to put one between my eyes.*

He shook off the thought. Plum nodded at the door. With his free hand Murphy reached across and started to ease the screen door open. When the hinges whined, he stopped. Plum rolled his eyes and grinned. Murphy counted off with his head — one, two, three — and yanked the door open and the young agent rushed inside. He followed close behind, gun leveled, covering the room. But she wasn't there.

They'd stopped in the middle of the living room. Murphy looked for blood on the floor, in the hallway beyond. A shabby sofa leaned against the wall facing the front door; beside it were a small table and rotary telephone. Two bags of groceries on top of the television console. At the far end of the room were a rocking chair and woodstove; hot coals glowed behind the intake vents.

Gun held upright and close to his cheek, Murphy slipped past Plum and into the unlit hallway. On the left was a kitchen; on the right a staircase led up and into darkness of the second floor. Farther down the hall was an open door, a light burned in the room beyond. He motioned Plum up the stairs and started down the hall, keeping to the left, free hand trailing along the wall.

He ducked his head into the kitchen. Boxes of ammunition were heaped on the table, the remnants of a meal. More boxes littering the countertops, an M16 propped in the corner. He continued down the hall, pulse hammering in his head, mouth dry, sour from the adrenaline rush. He heard the murmur of voices, felt a cool draft and saw the open window in the bedroom, the curtains swaying lightly.

He crept up to the doorway and stopped, sucked silently at the fresh air. "This way … over here," the voices moving away.

It could be a ruse, Murphy knew, a ploy to draw him into the room. He craned his neck for a better look. The walls in the room were white and bare, rumpled blankets were strewn across the bed, a chain trailed from the headboard out of sight. In the corner was a single straight-backed chair. They'd kept Bacchetti here.

The ceiling overhead creaked. Plum, he thought and looked back down the hall. At the far end one of the agents from Rutland was standing in the doorway, shotgun held at the ready across his chest. He hadn't even heard the man enter the house. He told himself to relax, to lighten up.

He turned back to the room, felt the Smith & Wesson sweaty in his hand. He took a breath, gathered his wits and burst into the room, body low, gun swinging, searching the corners. But there were only shadows. Ghosts.

Murphy straightened up slowly and crossed to the window, nudged one of the curtains aside with the barrel of his revolver. The snow was packed down where Karla had dropped to the ground, and again he looked for blood. But the snow beneath the window was white, glistening even in the night.

In the distance the trackers' light flickered among the trees as they followed her trail into the woods. Too late, he thought. She was gone. And once again Murphy was reminded of the day he returned to the DP camp. He felt the same disappointment as he had that day when he learned Gretchen and the child were gone. And the same contradiction, he realized now, loss tempered by relief.

He pictured Karla running, fleeing across the field, head back, her hair streaming behind her. It must have been hell, struggling through the knee-deep snow, expecting the slam of a bullet at any moment. Then he remembered the scene out front and saw things that, in his haste, hadn't registered earlier, their belongings scattered in the snow, the discarded Uzi, her comrade's wounds. He'd been gutshot. A wound he never would have survived. Yet even knowing this Karla dragged him to shelter behind the car.

There was a second wound, a neater wound, in the center of his chest. She'd done that. Then she'd ...

Murphy's mind recoiled at the next thought, at the next sight, Bacchetti's mouth rounded in a silent scream. But he made himself look at it — the lopsided face, features twisted and askew, the blank stare. The ex-agent's head was canted strangely as if the force of the shot had broken his neck, his wrists handcuffed low behind his back.

A series of flashes. Bacchetti's head snapping, blood, bone, brain matter spraying ...

She shot him like a dog. Without a moment's hesitation. Like some kind of animal.

But she had no choice.

The thought stopped Murphy and for a moment he wondered if he was allowing his personal involvement to skew his perspective. But it *was* a matter of perspective, he reasoned, Kiefer's perspective. Her comrade dead, believing herself dead as well, she had no choice. In her mind executing the hostage was duty, obligation.

And a righteous act, an act of total commitment. It was the reason he half-expected to find her here, waiting for him. Taking him out would have been her last act of defiance. *And a righteous act.*

The concept — so literal, so dogmatic — made Murphy shudder as he watched the trackers' lights move deeper into the woods.

He heard footsteps creeping up the hallway behind him.

"All clear," Plum called.

He nodded, still watching the lights. Every so often they would fade and disappear, only to reappear moments later. Like Kiefer, he thought.

"Charles, I want a team to search the hillside facing the house."

The young agent stepped into the room behind him. "You think there was a shooter?"

"You saw the wounds," he said, eyes still on the lights. Then they were gone.

"Who do you think it was?"

Murphy sighed, letting the curtain slip back into place. "I wish I knew, Charles. I wish I knew."

When he turned from the window, his young colleague avoided his gaze. "You think my informant had second thoughts."

"Could he have?"

Plum looked at him then, eyes dark, penetrating, fierce almost. Then his gaze softened and he shrugged. "I don't know. Anything's possible. Maybe their leaving was coincidence."

Murphy almost smiled. "That still doesn't explain the shooter."

No, Plum seemed to agree, it didn't.

"Let's have another look outside."

Plum stepped aside to let him pass. The agent from Rutland

had disappeared. Murphy retraced his steps down the hallway to the living room. He paused at the front door, hand splayed on the screen. Outside, it was full night. Snowflakes reflected in the headlight beams as they floated to the ground. Men were milling around the bodies.

Murphy pushed the screen door open and stepped onto the porch. "I want those men away from the bodies," he said to Plum. "Then get the forensics team into the house. Let's see if anyone else's been here."

Plum went down the steps without a word and ordered the men back, then huddled with Smithers and the State Police sergeant. After several moments Smithers called out to his driver and the trooper signaled two of his men. Then Plum summoned the forensics team, exchanged a few words and pointed toward the house.

Watching all this transpire Murphy felt a sense of detachment, as if by relinquishing control for a single moment he had become separate, an observer, disconnected somehow. He shook off the feeling and walked down the stairs. As he approached the bodies the stink of death — of feces, voided bowels — struck him. He turned his head away and breathed through his mouth, saw the cars bucking down the rise. At the foot of the hill the State Police cruiser peeled off and sped away, light-bar flashing, returning the way they came.

Smithers' searchlight began to work the opposite hillside, sweeping back and forth like a brush of light. "You'll have to do on foot," Murphy said, thinking outloud.

The light stopped as if Smithers had heard him. A minute later two dark figures emerged from the trees and began to move crab-like across the lighted area, and seeing them searching, looking for signs of the shooter, Murphy realized this was what he had caught a glimpse of earlier at Callaghan's, the other connection, his almost insight. The Red Path intended to execute Bacchetti all along. The rest — the Red Path's demands, Plum's source, his bouts with the press — were pretext. Manipulation.

He wondered if Karla knew. Nothing in her file led him to believe that she had. She wasn't an assassin — her actions were preordained, he thought, not premeditated. They were set up. But by whom?

Murphy felt someone come up beside him. When he looked to see who it was, he was surprised to find the State Police sergeant standing there, gazing at the lighted area.

"You think someone was up there?"

"Someone was," he said, not sure how much to tell the other man. "I heard the guy in the truck was uncooperative."

"These people are different," the trooper said. "Always difficult."

"I should have asked you to hold him. Questioned him myself."

"No reason to. He had valid ID."

Murphy turned back to the bodies. The Vietnam vet stared up at him in admonition. The trooper squatted beside the body, plucked at the bloodstained fatigue jacket. A bulge of intestine, distended and silvery, caught the light.

"How long do you think it's been?"

"Not much snow on the bodies," the trooper said, pulling the jacket back farther, holding the zipper pull between his thumb and forefinger as if it were fragile, delicate. "Looks like you're right. This was done with a high-powered rifle."

Murphy stepped closer to the body and dropped down beside the trooper. Just then Plum rushed up, out of breath. "The forensics team is checking the house."

"This one," the trooper went on, ignoring Plum and pointing to the chest wound, "was probably the automatic over there."

"She saw he wasn't going to make it," Murphy said, "so she finished him off."

The trooper squinted at him, hard. "She didn't finish the other guy off. He's handcuffed."

"True. But in her mind we killed her partner."

"Her lover most likely," Plum said.

"That still doesn't justify it."

"No," Murphy said, "it doesn't. But it explains her actions." And again he was struck by an inner vision, Karla fleeing, crashing through the woods without direction or plan, out of control. And it occurred to him that after three-plus months of investigation he had gotten absolutely nowhere. Except now he had two dead bodies and a terrorist on the run. In a way he failed them all, though he knew thinking that way did no good. Figure it out.

Slowly Murphy began to assemble what he knew, the details of Bacchetti's career, the connection to his past, the fortuitous timing of the source's information, their attempt to escape, the presence of the shooter, Karla's disorderly flight. Then, in a moment of startling clarity, it all came together, the logic simple, revelatory. They were tipped off to get Bacchetti into the shooter's sights. But he missed.

No — he didn't miss. The shooter hit her partner intentionally to force Karla's hand so it would look like a Red Path operation gone awry. Disinformation. Fucking Callaghan. I should have known.

Murphy set his hands on his thighs and pushed himself up, knees aching in the cold, and suddenly he felt old, disgusted, betrayed even by his friend.

The state trooper had gone off somewhere.

"I'm still wondering if my informant had second thoughts," Plum said.

"Think it through, Charles. Obviously they knew we were coming, and we were 'given' the location."

"That means my informant is a plant."

"Not necessarily. He could have been duped too."

"Either way it must have been the Agency," Plum said. "A disciplinary action."

The swiftness with which his young colleague put it together surprised Murphy. Impressed him too. "Not a word to anyone."

"Whatever you say. So what do we do now?"

"What we always do. Investigate. Bag the weapons, take special care with the automatic."

"Right."

As Plum walked away Murphy saw the silhouettes of the forensics teams moving in the living room. Then he saw one last thing, one horrifying thing: Karla was dead. Not yet, but soon. And she didn't know it.

***

Ten minutes later Smithers and his men produced the shooter's rifle, a Winchester Model 70. The last thing Murphy expected was for the Company to leave the weapon. He wondered if it was meant to lead him somewhere.

The rifle's more misdirection. Follow Kiefer. She's the trail. And it occurred to him that the case had changed, morphed somehow. Become something else. A quest … a crusade though he knew that wasn't the right word.

Redemption.

And he was secretly pleased.

Chapter 10

Twilight had settled over the woods, the forest dark, monochromatic. Night was falling fast and Karla watched the headlight beams pick out the road ahead. The road ran dead straight, like a chute hewn in some primeval mountain ridge. At the edge of the road, icicles caught the light making the trees shimmer and sparkle, the truck rattling along, transmission whining whenever the driver shifted gear.

His movements were smooth and fluid, powerful, and in a way he reminded Karla of the reedy old men who had welcomed her and her mother to Heidelberg when they first arrived as refugees. Together with those men, she and her mother tilled their tiny plot of land on the outskirts of the city, her mother and the men speaking familiarly of the farms they had left behind when the Russians came.

Like those men, the man beside her had the look of a farmer. His skin was weathered, his eyes set in a nest of crow's feet and his beard shot with gray. The resemblance ended there however, because this man wasn't old — at most he was ten years older than she — and he wasn't gaunt and thinned by years of war and adversity. He filled his side of the cab and his hair and beard were so bushy and overgrown that it was difficult to tell where one began and the other ended. People like him were scattered among the remote hills of Vermont, hippies whom time had left behind. *Unreconstructed freaks.*

Karla felt her heart seize. She took a breath — Sam had called them that.

"What is it?"

The driver was looking at her, his gaze clearly sympathetic.

"Nothing. Nothing at all."

His eyes flicked back to the road. The glow from the dashboard lit his face and he seemed to accept her reticence as if he understood she needed time to herself, time to think and plan.

Karla sat back and rested her head against the side of the cab, the passenger window cold, vibrating against her temple. The storm had broken and faint starlight showed where there were gaps in the clouds overhead.

First, Hanover — she thought — then the train to Montreal.

∗∗∗

Twenty-five minutes later the truck rolled into the town of Norwich without incident. They passed the Norwich Inn, then Dan and Whit's general store, a row of cars and pickup trucks parked side by side out front.

"Anywhere along here is fine," she said.

"I'll take you into Hanover," the driver replied without taking his eyes from the road.

"You don't have to do that."

"It's nothing."

But Karla knew it wasn't nothing.

"Thank you."

"It's no big deal," he said to her, eyes still on the road. "I need something at the Co-op anyway."

"Still …"

The driver smiled, a gleaming crescent in his dark beard, reached forward and shifted up a gear.

They drove in silence under the Interstate and started across the bridge spanning the Connecticut. The truck shuddered beneath them as they passed over a series of washboard ruts in the icy road, then they were on a steep hill, the night-dark woods closing in once again. When they reached the top the town of Hanover lay before them. They crossed Main Street, the shop fronts and street alive with holiday lights, and chugged past the Hanover Inn. Facing the inn was the College Green, and seeing it Karla remembered the first time she came here. A lush plot of grass covered the Green then and students, some of them in shorts and barefoot, tossed footballs and Frisbees in the warm afternoon air. But now there was only cold and the white of the snow — and Sam's staring eyes.

Karla willed the vision away, banishing it from her mind as the truck pulled up in front of Hopkins Center, front tire nudging the curb. With its vaulted roofline and broad glass façade the arts center looked out of place among the red brick and white clapboard buildings of the town. A pale-blue placard with white lettering ran the length of the upper floor:

ASHKENAZY 12/11 8:00 PM Tonight!

"You sure you're going to be okay?"

The driver had turned and faced her.

"Yeah," she said, thinking American again, lying to him and knowing she was. *Now is when you find out who you truly are.*

She reached for the door handle. "Hey, thanks. Thanks for the ride."

The driver shrugged. "No problem."

She knew she owed him more than that. But what could she say? What could she do? It would be wrong to involve him any more than she already had.

Karla shouldered the passenger door open and a jolt of pain shot down her left arm. She bit her lip, stifling the cry, and clambered out. Another jolt as she stepped to the ground.

"Take care," the driver called.

She nodded mutely and swung the door shut with her good arm. Then, knowing better, she mouthed a silent: *Danke*.

The driver grinned and wagged his shaggy head, then peering back over his shoulder backed out.

Karla watched him drive away. At the corner of the Green the pickup turned left onto College Street, then made another left in front of the library, its tower bathed in a mist of pale-white light, then left again, and not for the first time she wondered if she would ever understand the innate hubris of Americans, tempered by acts of extraordinary generosity.

Her eyes misted, but she wouldn't let herself cry. Because it would do no good. And because she knew she had to be strong — as he had in the end.

Clutching her arm to her side, Karla swung around and headed back toward Main Street. Students swarmed past her, heads down, their voices low, muffled against the cold. The thawed and refrozen snow on the sidewalk crunched beneath her boots. Off to her right a horn tooted. She looked up and saw the battered truck had completed its circuit of the Green. The driver waved amiably, a salute of comradeship, then turned right and headed back down the hill, right rear directional blinking red in the night.

Just then the chimes in the library tower sounded. Karla glanced at her watch — half past five — nearly three hours since she fled the farmhouse. She pictured Murphy and his men gathered around the bodies, spotlights lancing the night. Then as if time were out of sequence she saw their chaotic arrival, light-bars flashing, men racing toward the house, others pursuing her through the woods, torch beams darting among the trees.

Following her trail would be simple enough, she knew. Her tracks apparent, distinct in the snow. They'd find her coat near the edge of the embankment, the discarded Uzi farther along, near the road, figure someone picked her up and eventually track her here.

But by then I'll be gone, on the train to Montreal. The contact will be waiting.

And so will Murphy.

The thought stopped Karla in her tracks, paralyzing her for a moment. She felt a throb of fear, of recognition: she couldn't trust Montreal. The emergency number, she thought. No one knew about the phone number in New York — not Murphy, not anyone in the Red Path, not even Raymond. Only Khalil who would expect her to rely on her instincts and training ...

"Meinen Tagen in der Wüste."

Karla froze again, glanced at the faces nearby. The stream of muffled students continued past, unconcerned, heads still down, indifferent to her, to her presence even. New destination in mind she started off again and turned left onto Main Street. She inspected her clothes, tugged at the hem of her sweater, combed her fingers through her hair. Partway down the block she entered a women's clothing store nonchalantly — Campion's read the sign out front — and let a saleswoman talk her into an understated wool suit, a silky blouse and slip, hose and a belted London Fog raincoat. As if an afterthought the woman selected an expensive pair of boots and pocketbook to match. When the woman commented on her accent Karla told her she was from Switzerland, a medical student at Mary Hitchcock; she was going home for the holiday, the lies coming easily now, the saleswoman smiling, nodding, taking it all in.

The purchases came to just under $950 and Karla paid cash. As she counted out the bills she thought of Sam, remembered digging through his pockets, taking his money and ID, but she remained cool and calm. She was operating on instinct now, pure instinct.

In the pharmacy next door she bought a pair of scissors, a long-handled comb, lip-gloss and an inexpensive mirror. The mirror had a cheap metal frame with a hanging bracket. Her last purchase was the local newspaper.

Shopping bags in hand, Karla hustled along the alleyway that ran between the two buildings and made for the rear entrance of the arts center. The wind rose, gusting, and sliced through her wool sweater. Her skin felt stiff, like parchment; her shoulder began to ache but she ignored the pain, compartmentalizing it, concentrating on her footing instead, on the bags bouncing against her thigh. Without slowing she entered Hopkins Center. As she expected, the rear entry area was deserted. A staircase led to the upper floor. At the top, out of her line of sight, someone was practicing an etude. Karla paused for a moment to listen, the sound of the flute light, feathery, then she crossed to the women's toilet and pushed through the door.

She kicked open each stall as she made her way to the back to confirm she was alone and locked herself in the last one. She felt the sudden confinement, disregarded it and set the bags on the floor, then unfolded the newspaper and spread it on the floor in front of the toilet. The newspaper rustled beneath her feet as she dug the mirror from one of the bags and hung it from the hook on the back of the stall door. Then she removed her boots and massaged her feet, her toes cold, numb, lifeless. As I am, she thought.

More rustling as she eased off her sweater gingerly, folded it and placed it in the bag. Her skin was pale, Karla noticed, wan in the mirror, though there was swelling along the fleshy part of her injured shoulder, red going to blue. When she touched the area,

160

the pain took her breath away and for a moment she thought she'd be sick.

She huffed twice, hard, and focused on her image in the mirror. The strain of the past few months showed around her mouth and eyes, along her brow; bits of ice and flecks of gray clung to her hair and as if from a great distance she watched her fingers drag through her hair, catching and snagging in the snarls.

He begged me. I had no choice.

Karla closed her eyes, tried to summon up the shimmering heat of the camp, late afternoons on the ridgetop, the muted sun in the pale sky — but all she could see, all she could feel, was the cold as she waited at the edge of the road, as she scrubbed the blood from her hands.

Unable to keep Sam at bay any longer she remembered their first night at the farmhouse, his hands roaming over her, then felt the gun in her hand, pressed to his chest, the blowback …

"I'm sorry," she whispered. "I'm so sorry. We both knew death was a possibility, a likelihood even. Only I survived. And now I must go on. You'd want that."

Karla opened her eyes. They looked flat, dead in the mirror, spent. She tilted her head back and shook out her hair, her neck stiff, crackly. Then she bent down carefully and drew the scissors from the bag, the metal blades flashing in the fluorescent light. Pain flared in her shoulder as she reached up and grabbed a handful of hair, but this time Karla didn't try to ignore the pain. She welcomed it, embracing it and the searing heat. The desert heat.

Metal sheared against metal as she sliced through her hair, handful after handful, and it was as if she couldn't see the clumps falling away.

✷✷✷

The next day at half past twelve Karla found herself moving with the crowd up Fifth Avenue, an anonymous businesswoman in a charcoal-gray suit. She felt the noisomeness of the place all around her, heard the cars beeping, honking. People jostled her as they hurried past, their intensity so complete, so absolute, that it was as if each of them moved in a world of their own.

Overhead, the narrow strip of sky sparkled and her cheeks glowed in the frosty air, though the sun held little warmth. When she had called the emergency number a man with an American accent answered and she gave her name. Khalil came on the line right away. He would meet her in one hour, he told her. There was a pond at the southeast corner of Central Park. Did she know it? She said she would find it, then hung up and purchased a street map at one of the kiosks in Penn Station.

At the corner of 57th Street and Fifth Avenue foot traffic stalled. Karla waited patiently among the crowd, the air thick with exhaust. A whistle trilled and the crowd surged forward carrying her with it, and as she passed Bergdorf Goodman's department store she caught a glimpse of her reflection in one of the display windows.

For a moment she didn't recognize herself: the sober business suit, the dark boots, the ragged hair. Her eyes began to tear. It hadn't been until the very last moment kneeling at Sam's side that she realized how much she cared for him and what that meant. And the hardest part, she'd come to realize, was learning to go on without him, alone.

As she continued up Fifth the crowd peeled away and the scene opened up. The sky cloudless, pristine-blue. Central Park lay across the broad avenue ahead. On her left was the Plaza Hotel, the doorman resplendent in his gold-braided livery. The Paris Cinema — *The Lost Honor of Katharina Blum* declared the marquee.

Karla waited at the corner for the light to change, then hurried across Central Park South. A band of derelicts partially blocked the park's southeast entrance, their hair filthy and matted, their faces an unnatural rosy hue; the men shouted at one another and waved their fists ineffectually in the air. The one shouting the loudest and most vehemently had a deep-green bruise beneath one eye and a crusty scab on the bridge of his nose. The others pounced on the man, punching and shoving him as she detoured around them. She made no attempt to intervene.

The sound of the drunks and traffic faded as she wound down into the park, the frozen stillness of the pond visible through the trees. Halfway down she came upon two young Arabs standing in the ankle-deep snow at the edge of the pavement, their eyes watchful and intent, and she couldn't help but think they looked half-dressed without their kaffiyehs.

The guards acknowledged her with a nod as she walked past. She spotted Khalil near the bottom of the slope, at a fork in the path. He was pacing with his head down, hands thrust deep in his pockets, breath pluming around his head. She called out to him and he raised a hand in greeting.

The Palestinian's eyes moved over her as she approached, paused for a few moments on her hair. "You look tired," he said. "You've cut your hair."

"Yes," she said, reaching up absently and touching her hair where she had chopped it off just below her ears. It felt soft and thick, like the bristles of a paintbrush. As if it belonged to someone else.

When Khalil reached out to take her arm, she winced and pulled away.

"Are you injured?" His voice was full of concern.

"I'm fine," she said. In truth she felt numb, disoriented; she couldn't even feel the cold. "I tripped while running through the woods."

Khalil's arm went up and one of his bodyguards hurried toward them.

"It's nothing," she said. "A bruise." Though she wondered if it sounded more like a whine.

The guard stopped a few yards away and Khalil looked at her. Assessing her, Karla knew. She drew herself up.

"I'm tired. The train was delayed and I haven't slept." She didn't tell him that she'd tried, but her dreams were filled with nightmarish images, Sam's intestines bulging and silvery like snakes.

The Palestinian studied her face a few moments longer then indicated the path that rimmed the pond. The guard retreated and rejoined his comrade as they started along the path. The path was a mix of black ice and clumps of refrozen snow. In the distance, traffic hummed.

"I tried to save the operation."

"I know."

She shot Khalil a glance — that he knew surprised her — but his attention seemed elsewhere, on his bodyguards who were trailing along the slope above them. Something drew their interest, a lump among the trees. One of guards prodded it with his foot. The lump muttered in complaint. A sleeping drunk wrapped in rags.

"I wanted it to go on," she said, her voice like the traffic sounding far way. "It seemed pointless otherwise."

Khalil nodded.

"Raymond said we had three hours, but someone was already there."

Khalil stopped abruptly. "Who?" His eyes bore into her.

"There was a car …"

"What car?"

Karla tried to think, to concentrate, but her brain felt soft, cottony, as if she had too much to drink the previous evening.

"It passed earlier and was parked down the road …" *It's seems okay.* "We thought we had time."

"The FBI must have alerted the local authorities."

"But it wasn't a police car."

"You were in a place where the police would be volunteers."

That has to be it, Karla thought, my initial impression correct, the note left on the car's dashboard a ruse.

They started off again, walking side by side.

"How did they find us?"

Silence as if something shameful had passed between them and it occurred to her that she already knew. Raymond told someone in the Red Path the location of their hideout, and rather than appalling her, the knowledge pleased Karla. Raymond had fucked up in every way. It wasn't her fault.

Then she saw Sam again, the blood seeping between his fingers, bubbling from his mouth, and knew that it was.

"He was wounded," she said quietly, speaking to herself as much as Khalil.

"You don't have to explain, Karla."

But she did — she owed Sam that.

"I wanted to take him somewhere, but he saw it was hopeless …" *Finish it.* "I had to execute Bacchetti."

"You were supposed to."

"But not that way." Her voice rising, sharp and strident. Then softly, guiltily, "I wasn't thinking about the operation."

"You did what you had to."

"But what about the prisoners? What about them?"

They stopped again, Khalil facing her.

"We'll get them next time. At least we showed them we are serious." An echo.

The words stunned Karla — Raymond used those very words — and she felt as if her mind was ready to implode. Did Sam die for that? To show they were serious? And what good was the old man dead? The Palestinians still imprisoned.

"It's over," Khalil said. "It's time to regroup. You need a rest." His arm went up again and the young guard came on the run, coattails fanning out behind him.

Khalil spoke to him in Arabic — his name was Majid. He was to escort her to the airport and travel with her on the flight to Paris. From there they would take the train south, then west across the Spanish plateau to Portugal.

"Why can't I return to the camp?"

Khalil turned back to her. The guard stepped away.

"There are problems, I'm afraid."

"What problems?"

"Just problems. Nothing to worry about." Then he smiled, a wintry smile, and Karla realized she was being banished, sent into exile.

"You said I did what I had to."

"It's only temporary. I'll be honest with you. Raymond wants you out of the picture. He blames you for Grossman's death."

"*He* blames me. Don't you think ..."

Karla stopped, felt the tears again. She promised herself she wouldn't do this; she wouldn't fall apart, not in front of Khalil. And last night on the train she had found a place for Sam, a private place, a safe place in her mind ... a secure place.

The young bodyguard rejoined Khalil. He spoke in Arabic

again. Majid was to take care of her, he was saying, to protect her with his life if necessary. A car would be waiting for them at the Portuguese frontier. He handed Majid a key. He was to drop her in Praia da Luz. A man would meet her on the beach. He would make the approach.

Karla didn't argue anymore — the whole thing had the ring of inevitability — and this time when Khalil reached out to take her arm she let him.

"The place I'm sending you to belongs to a friend," he said, stroking her arm "He is very good, a sympathizer, but quirky. You can rest there. Majid has a passport for you."

The young Arab handed it to her. It was a U.S. passport, green-jacketed and well worn, with a bent cover. Karla thumbed through it, stopping on the photo page. The woman in the photograph had long blonde hair partially obscuring an unremarkable face.

"We didn't have much time," Khalil said. "The resemblance isn't very good. We're depending on it being an American passport. Leave everything to Majid, he's very good as well. You must go now."

The young guard tugged at her arm more gently than Karla expected and she let him guide her back along the edge of the pond. They would buy her new clothes, Majid told her, something a peripatetic American would wear. He spoke flawless English.

Karla looked back over her shoulder as they rejoined the paved walkway. Khalil had vanished. A magician.

Chapter 11

Legs trembling, Andrew walked slowly across the porch behind his house. Sweat seeped into his eyes. He stopped at the back wall, breath rasping, and put his hands on his hips. He took a slow deep breath and exhaled sharply. Below him a gust of wind lifted the leaves scattered on the ground and sent them tumbling down the hillside. They came to a rest for a moment then rose again, swirling and dancing around the trunks of the trees.

He'd ridden hard all the way back from Luz. The same wind, stiff and blowing onshore, battered him along the hilltops slowing him to a near standstill in places, his thighs burning with the memory.

Andrew took another breath. It was December, he reminded himself. Winter. And here, wind *was* winter.

Behind him, as if in counterpoint, the wind chimes stirred in a wayward breeze. A caprice, he thought, a whim. He closed his eyes and focused on the sound — the chimes moaned, soft, ethereal, delicate — and after a while his breathing eased. The burn in his thighs softened to a glow and he saw the dead leaves again, swirling in his mind. Then the men in the field, dead as well.

It isn't your concern. And Andrew refocused on the sound of the chimes, gentle, like a children's round. Round and round and round …

Another sound intruded, discordant, the sound of an automobile speeding down the coast road. The car slowed abruptly and turned into his drive; tires crept up the dirt lane but

Andrew was already running for the house. He bolted through the back door, bound over the sofa blocking his path, socks slip-sliding on the tile floor as he hurried toward the kitchen. In the cupboard above the stove he kept a .22-caliber High Standard pistol, always prepared for this moment.

He tore open the cabinet door, hand diving, scrabbling inside, settling finally on the familiar pistol grip. As he drew the weapon from the cupboard, the silenced barrel caught on a bag of flour and sent it tumbling to the stove — *pfooft* — but Andrew ignored it. He chambered a round, then yanked open the drawer next to the stove, grabbed two extra loaded magazines and shoved them into his jersey pocket.

Out front the car had pulled up, engine rumbling smoothly. He knew they would check out the house first, get a feel for the place, and Andrew had a vision of his house, the blue-framed windows and front door. He saw his bicycle leaning against the wall next to the door, his beat-up car parked in the carport beneath a layer of fine red dust.

His finger moved instinctively to the trigger. "Not yet," he whispered. Not yet.

Andrew rose onto his toes and moved swiftly to the window at the far end of the kitchen, careful to stay far enough back so he wouldn't be silhouetted through the curtain. There would be four of them, he imagined, two up front and two more in the back. They'd split up once they got out, one pair would take the front of the house while the other circled around back, and again he was struck by a vision — of two men this time, crouched low, weapons drawn, creeping along the side of the house. Facelesss.

He'd take them first, pop them as they stepped onto the back porch, quickly and in rapid succession, then flee down the hillside and wait for the others. Among the trees and dead leaves. He reached back and felt for the extra magazines, touching them as if they were talisman. Thirty rounds in all, more than enough for what he needed to do.

Outside, the engine died. Andrew took a breath and exhaled slowly, quieting his mind. He heard a car door slam and waited for others, for echoes. But there was only silence and the soft dance of the chimes.

Slowly, with his free hand, he gentled the curtain aside and saw Khalil scurrying toward the front door. His finger went to the trigger again — it could even be your friend — then he belayed it. Khalil was alone except his driver who had remained in the car, both hands clearly visible on top of the steering wheel.

Andrew pushed the curtain all the way back, showing himself. At the foot of the hill was another car, a dark Mercedes sedan parked just off the blacktop, four men standing beside it, and seeing it, seeing them, he felt a chill shiver down his spine. He hadn't heard the second car.

There was a pounding at the front door. Gun still hand, Andrew retraced his steps across the kitchen. Before entering the living room he ducked his head through the doorway and glanced out back. No one. Only the chimes swaying soundlessly in the breeze.

The pounding continued, insistent. He crossed to the front door, unlocked it and eased the door open partway. Khalil looked up, surprised.

"Ah, you are here."

At the foot of the drive the men were still standing beside the car, leaning against it. Harmless.

"What are you doing here?"

"Such a welcome."

Khalil was smiling broadly though his eyes were riveted on the gun and Andrew felt his face go hot with shame. He set the handgun on the table next to the front door.

"I wasn't expecting anyone. You've never come here before."

"For good reason," his friend said. Then he laughed, a full deep-throated laugh, and Andrew couldn't help but join him. It had been undisciplined. More hyped-up imagination, he thought, flashing on the night in New York. Craziness.

"Come in, come in," he said, swinging the door wide and stepping aside.

Khalil swept past him and circled the living room as if on inspection. He stopped in front of one of the wall hangings, an ancient hand-carved African mask, the mask dark against the whitewashed wall. Primitive.

His hand went to the mask, fingers tracing the contours of the mouth and eyes lightly as if it was an object of reverence. Modern art hundreds of years old.

"It's from Ghana," Andrew told him.

The Palestinian nodded appreciatively, hand still on the mask.

This was prelude, Andrew knew. The opening act though his friend's interest was genuine.

"How much time do you have? I was about to eat."

Khalil turned from the mask. "Only an hour, I'm afraid."

"Time enough then."

Without waiting for a reply Andrew returned to the kitchen. He noticed the bag of flour on the stove, its side split open, the fine white powder dusting the burners. He felt foolish once again and this time he didn't have four days of nonstop travel to blame.

Chastened, Andrew swept the bag into the trash and brushed his hands. He heard Khalil amble out back, the chimes clattering as if struck by a gust of wind.

"The place suits you," his friend called. "It's modest and

simple, ascetic almost, yet quite lovely."

"I don't need anything more," Andrew called back.

For a man of spartan sensibilities, of simple tastes, anything more was superfluous, decoration, just so many things. It was the feel of the place that appealed to him. In Portuguese they would say it was *sympática*. Pleasantly agreeable though it was more than that. This was his retreat, his home, the place where he felt he belonged.

He'd inherited the house twelve years earlier, shortly after his parents died. They lingered for months after the automobile accident then passed away within days of one another as if some vital organ were shared. Seven years later, after graduating from Stanford, he moved to the house and lived simply. Modestly, as his friend put it.

Khalil on the other hand accepted a position with Credit Suisse after Stanford. The fortunes of the al-Fasani family had come a long way since their flight to the refugee camp in Lebanon. His father was a peasant, Andrew had heard Khalil declare more than once with pride. In truth his father was a highly respected artisan and a Palestinian leader committed to the liberation of his homeland. If he had been a peasant, Khalil would be a street fighter in Beirut, not a banker in New York.

The al-Fasani family remained in the refugee camp out of ethnic pride, not necessity.

Khalil attended private schools in Lebanon and Saudi Arabia, then went on to university in Cairo, then England and the United States, and in time his outlook became more global than his father's.

All of this Andrew had learned when they studied together at Stanford. It was a time of rebellion, of dissatisfaction, of mutual discontent, and it was then that they discovered the mountains as an outlet, finding release running the fields of scree.

After university they went their separate ways. Then six years ago, shortly after Andrew's move to the Algarve, Khalil came to him with the proposal for the first hit. He wanted to take out the American Secretary of State. Coming to him hadn't been illogical — they had a shared past, and at Stanford Andrew had a reputation as a skilled marksman. Yet to this day he marveled at his friend's sense of timing. It was as if Khalil knew the precise moment when his ideas matured, when he accepted "destructive passion could be creative passion." When he became a man of pure instinct, of pure will. The act itself.

Thinking it, Andrew felt a surge of righteousness, then noticed the fine white flour residue on his hands and smiled. Madness. He went to the refrigerator and opened the door. Before his ride he had prepared a pitcher of orange juice and a platter of fruit and cheese. He took them out, added a few rolls and two glasses to the platter and carried it all out back.

Khalil had drawn one of the wicker chairs up to the table and was gazing out over the hills to the north, the top of his dark head peeking above the back of the chair. Andrew set the platter and pitcher on the table and pulled up a chair opposite. He felt the cool breeze on the back of his neck as he sat down.

"I should have called."

Andrew smiled, shame gone now. "Next time you will."

The Palestinian laughed, then glanced over his shoulder, at something behind him, but Andrew resisted the urge to look. It would be paranoia, he knew.

He reached forward, picked up the pitcher and poured juice into the glasses and handed one to Khalil, raised his own and took a sip. The juice tasted sharp, yet sweet.

Khalil looked at him, studying his face. "You were tired in

173

New York."

"And angry." Andrew could talk about it now, see it objectively, the way he had acted, reacted.

Once he returned home he'd decided he was done for a while, finished, at least for the time being. When his rifle arrived in late September, he cleaned and oiled it, recalibrated the scope, then cleaned and oiled it again and stashed it in the cubbyhole behind the steamer trunk in his basement. He alone would know when to take it out.

"I'm not interested in any jobs."

"I'm not here about one."

A moment of silence passed between them, a moment so fleeting that it would have been undetectable to the casual observer, but Andrew noticed it, felt it like a shift in wind direction while standing on a mountain ridge, and in that moment he knew that he hadn't been completely wrong earlier. His friend, or his people, would come for him one day. And it wouldn't be in daylight. They would come at night, in darkness.

None of this appalled Andrew, however. He always accepted the nature of their alliance — so did Khalil. Their acceptance was a bond of sorts, a bond of mutual consent. And of mutual destruction.

"Why are you here, Khalil?"

"A friend can't just visit."

"You don't just visit."

The Palestinian smiled, a smile that was confident and acquiescent at the same time. "You heard about Bacchetti?"

Andrew nodded. They were there, prelude completed.

He leaned forward and picked up the pitcher again and refilled their glasses, juice sloshing against the pitcher's clay walls.

"Sounds like a fiasco."

Khalil fluttered his hand in dismissal. "It didn't work out the way we planned."

"Your people were holding him?"

"Yes, Karla, the one who escaped, and her American comrade."

"Surprising. But then it *was* Raymond's plan."

His friend didn't respond.

"The Palestinians won't be released now."

"They weren't supposed to be."

The remark confused Andrew. Then he flashed on the night in the park again. *Maybe we can use Wit here … It won't be for a few months.*

"You intended to kill Bacchetti all along," he said, seeing the logic, skewed as it was. "He was the 'influential man.'"

Again Khalil didn't respond.

Andrew stood up and walked to the edge of the porch, rested his hands on the half-wall. The wind had died and he felt the sun on his face; a pair of lapwings flapped erratically above the tree-studded hills.

"Why were they taking Bacchetti with them?"

"They were trying to save the operation."

"They didn't know."

"Raymond wanted the kidnapping to appear genuine."

Andrew felt a wave of contempt not unlike the one he felt the night in the New York. Even then he had intuited Raymond's duplicity, his capacity for betrayal.

"Who was the shooter?"

"Raymond's man."

Andrew pictured the scene at the farmhouse. Khalil's people hustling Bacchetti through the snow toward their vehicle, Raymond's shooter lying in wait, cold seeping through his clothes.

He flexed his fingers instinctively. "How did the FBI find them?" Yet even as he asked, he knew. The answer obvious. The whole thing contrived, corrupt.

He swung around. His friend's eyes flitted away. "What does Raymond do, exchange notes with the FBI?"

Khalil made no attempt to argue. Instead he selected a piece of cheese from the platter, the *queijo da serra* white against his dark skin, and popped it into his mouth, tendons rolling along his cheekbones as his jaws worked the cheese, mashing it.

"Raymond gave them plenty of time," he said finally. "All they had to do was execute Bacchetti, instead they tried to save the operation."

"What did you expect? As far as they were concerned, the kidnapping was the operation."

"They had their orders."

"Bullshit! You knew they wouldn't do it. That's why you needed the shooter."

"He was only insurance. I thought they would do it when the time came. Grossman had every reason to and I had absolute faith in Karla. Her loyalty is beyond question."

"Which is why she tried to save the operation."

"I misjudged her. A mistake, I admit. Her commitment to the prisoners was even greater than I imagined. But they weren't the point of the operation."

"No, killing Bacchetti was."

"Yes and no."

Then Khalil stopped as if he had gone too far.

"What aren't you saying, Khalil?"

The Palestinian looked away, shifted his weight in the chair. "The whole point of the operation," he said finally, "was to prove the Red Path was serious. If an attempt to rescue the hostage was made, they would execute him. That was their threat and they carried it out. When Raymond's man saw them leaving with Bacchetti, he took the shot but missed and wounded Grossman. He couldn't travel so Karla finished him off. Then she executed Bacchetti as ordered."

It wasn't an execution, Andrew thought. It was revenge. The killing misguided, charged with emotion, personal.

"Raymond's plan was brilliant," Khalil continued. "Even the weapon Karla used was planned for. At first the press will believe the Red Path carried out their threat. Then after they tire of that, and with the proper guidance, they will trace the weapon to the FBI. In the end they'll think it was the FBI doing the CIA's dirty work. We win both ways."

Disgusted, offended, Andrew went into the house and grabbed his sweatshirt from sofa and draped it over his shoulders. He heard Khalil come into the room behind him.

"I know none of this is your style."

"That isn't the point. For you it has become about power, politics."

"I would have instructed you personally … and you wouldn't have missed."

Andrew turned to face Khalil. Their eyes met as if each was measuring the other, examining the remains of their tattered friendship.

"Why are you here, Khalil?"

The Palestinian was silent for a moment. "I need a favor."

"No."

He went on undeterred. "The woman has become a problem. She disobeyed orders and Raymond wants her taken care of."

Andrew felt sullied, insulted by what Khalil proposed. "No

fucking way. I'm not killing someone just because she displeases Raymond."

"You misunderstand, my friend. I don't want Karla killed. I want to hide her here."

"Here?"

"It's the last place Raymond will look. He met you only the one time. He doesn't know anything about you. He doesn't even know your real name. Fuck Raymond. Karla's the best."

"You just said she didn't follow orders."

Khalil grinned. "Like you."

And Andrew knew his friend had him. He would shelter the woman, protect her, even if for no other reason than to spite Raymond, and it occurred to him that he still couldn't remember where he had seen Raymond's photograph, the man's arrogance. Then he remembered a line from Lenin. "There are no morals in politics … only expedience."

Still he didn't give up without a fight. "She'll bring the GNR, Interpol, the FBI. God knows who."

"We were very careful. She hasn't been followed. One of my personal bodyguards is escorting her. You can meet her in Praia da Luz."

Andrew wavered.

"It will only be for a couple of weeks."

"Why don't you send her back to the camp?"

"Raymond will know. Plus the mullahs are gaining influence there. She'll be gone within days."

"You're using me."

His friend grinned again. "I don't deny it."

Andrew sighed. "All right. Two weeks only. When does she arrive?"

Khalil glanced at his wristwatch. "In one hour."

Andrew shook his head, smiled.

Khalil laughed. "I've told you before, we know each other too well."

Yes, Andrew thought, too well. But then on another level his friend didn't know him at all.

Chapter 12

Exhausted after the long trip Karla sat on the beach thinking of Sam and seeing his eyes in the aquamarine surf. She didn't cry yet she still felt the pain, imagined the salty taste of tears on her lips. I will mourn him later, she promised herself. In a different place, in a different way.

A flock of gulls swooped low over the swells, cawing, and there was the smell of ocean in the air. At one end of the beach a rocky shelf tapered into the sea while at the other end a cliff rose to form a headland, its west face cast in shadow in the midday light. Behind her lay the village of Praia da Luz.

An hour earlier Majid had dropped her along the town's main thoroughfare and she walked down the hill to the beach alone, past the shimmering villas, dazzling white in the sunlight, past the tourist gift shops and shuttered gypsy caravans. When she came to the seawall, she paused for a few moments to gaze at the broad white strand, then trod down the steps and found a place in the sand.

Ten minutes later her young Arab escort motored along the road that rimmed the shoreline. He parked along the seawall and trotted up the steps to one of the restaurants along the waterfront. A few minutes later he reappeared on the restaurant's terrace and took a table that commanded a view of the sea.

Karla glanced back over her shoulder — he was still there, sitting at the table, seemingly indifferent to her or anyone else for that matter. In his dark glasses and white dress shirt, a pale-blue sweater draped over his shoulders, the young Palestinian looked like a pampered Saudi prince. Exactly the opposite of what he was. He was a warrior, Majid told her. A *feyadeen*. And a devout Muslim. Karla remembered the way he averted his gaze when she changed clothes in the back of the car on the way to JFK.

They had boarded the flight without a hitch and it was raining when they landed at Charles De Gaulle, the skies as gray and leaden as her soul. As Khalil promised, the immigration officials didn't give the passport more than a cursory glance. From Paris they took the train south to the Spanish frontier and disembarked with the rest of the passengers and walked to the border and waiting RENFE train in Irún. At the border station the French authorities detained Majid for several minutes though his papers were in order — he was traveling on a Moroccan passport, a guest worker on holiday. He'd acted humbly as the blue-uniformed officers questioned him, subservient, absolutely in role.

All this Karla had watched from a distance. They traveled separately until Vila Real. A young Arab and an American woman traveling together would attract too much attention, Majid told her. But he would be close, at hand. He would watch over her.

From Irún they traveled west to San Sebastian and continued south across the broad Spanish plateau, the rain following them. The landscape was rocky and barren, desolate; the towns lost along the horizon. Only the cathedrals distinguished the towns from the dun-colored plain, and even they appeared faded, dusty-brown. Then sometime during the second night, after changing trains again in Madrid, the towns had turned stark-white as if bleached by the sun.

Near the larger towns were freshly cultivated fields, new green sprouting among the peat-colored fields, and it made Karla think of her mother, of tilling their tiny plot of land on the outskirts of

Heidelberg. But that life seemed long ago, far away, as if it were a mirage, a faded dream, fiction.

A light ocean breeze swept onshore, insinuating itself into her thoughts. She rubbed her arms, chilled, the cotton sweater she wore soft against her skin, and glanced back at the headland. A slash of trail marked the west face; at the top was a monument of sorts, an obelisk piercing the faultless sky. The location was less than ideal, she knew, the sea and cliffs cutting off any chance for her to escape. But she was certain no one had followed. Even in her fragile state she watched for a tail.

Reassured, Karla eased back around and gazed at the empty horizon, felt the sun warm on her head, and for a few moments she let herself imagine she was back at the camp, sitting cross-legged on the ridgetop, the dry breeze whispering across the desert floor, Sam calling up to her …

In a different place, in a different way.

***

Twenty minutes later a man appeared soundlessly on the rocky shelf. He squatted to examine something on the exposed rock, then stood back up and peered at the sea, hands deep in his trouser pockets, pale-brown hair blowing in the breeze; in profile he was tall and thin, slender as a reed. Karla wanted to call out to him so certain was she that he was Khalil's sympathizer, but Majid had told her to wait, to let the man make the approach.

She stole another glance at the restaurant — the young Palestinian was paying his bill, the white-shirted waiter hovering nearby. When she looked back to the man, he gazed directly at her for a moment then turned his attention back to the sea, seemingly as indifferent to her presence as Majid.

A wave broke below him and the man jumped back. He was acting, Karla realized, as Majid was acting, as even she was acting, as if for some hidden camera, some unseen observer, though they were alone.

Another wave broke and the man made his move. Still he took his time meandering across the tide-polished shelf, eyes moving without seeming to, taking everything in. When he came to the edge of the shelf, he hopped down to the sand and wandered across the beach in her general direction.

When he was a few yards away, the man paused as if to exchange a momentary pleasantry. "*In fünf Minuten,*" he said quietly, "*folgen Sie mir.*"

Karla nodded with her eyes and the man smiled though she knew the smile wasn't for her. Then he set off again down the beach. That he spoke to her in German surprised her. Majid told her the sympathizer was American but his accent wasn't American. At least not like the GIs in Heidelberg when they spoke their clumsy *Deutsch*. His accent was gentle, Bavarian almost, and as she watched him continue down the beach Karla couldn't help but think of Sam — he was never far from her mind. They had the same walk, loose-hipped and relaxed, hands settled deep in their pockets. An American walk.

The man strolled to the base of the cliff face and followed it to where the headland jutted into the sea. Another wave crashed thrusting itself against the rock face, erupting, confetti-like. The man watched it retreat. Then as if he'd had enough he turned and marched across the beach and up the steps into town. Meanwhile Majid had disappeared.

Karla grabbed her pack and got slowly to her feet. After one last long look at the sea she turned and followed the American. A local fisherman, his face and hands the color of tobacco, had spread his net over the seawall. A black sportcap was slung low over his eyes. He didn't look up when she trotted up the steps, a net-shuttle clenched between his teeth, his fingers working the net nimbly. As if on cue Majid appeared in the restaurant entrance.

Keyed up, Karla stopped and slipped off her shoes, shook out the sand. The shops along the street she passed earlier were closed, shut down for siesta, and it occurred to her they planned it this way, Khalil and his friend, for the sleepy time of day. Still, she took her time studying the shop windows and for a moment she imagined Murphy and his men there, behind the glass, watching their every move, though she doubted anyone would think to look for her in this remote corner of the world.

She felt the fisherman's gaze and started up the hill, following the American at a safe distance, her pack thumping against her back. Back in the town she could hear music, a woman singing a melancholy lament. Then it was quiet and she sensed Majid behind her. Watching over her.

The American climbed into a beat-up car parked halfway up the hill, cobblestones shimmering in the sunlight. As she approached, Karla noticed the driver's side window was down. The man called out to her softly as she came alongside.

"Excuse me," he was speaking in English now, "can I offer you a lift?" His tone was friendly and unassuming. Perfect, harmless.

Karla looked back down the lane. Majid was peering into one of the shop windows as if something there had caught his interest.

Then playing along, she turned back to the American. "Which way are you going?"

"Down the coast." His face was all angles, the bones sharp beneath the wind-burned skin. An ascetic's face, a monk's face.

"East — or west?"

"West, toward Sagres. I can drop you wherever you like."

Karla feigned indecision for a moment, then without another

word walked around the front of the car. Majid was crossing the cobbled lane below her and she realized she hadn't had a chance to thank him. She thanked him now. Silently. Without him she would have been lost.

Sam came back to her, unbidden, his last benevolent gaze, his tolerant smile … *the shit I put up with*, and Karla felt the sadness once more, bittersweet, shattered blue, but she put him from her mind. Because right now, she knew, sadness and thoughts of the past — even the future — were a hindrance.

The car rumbled to life beside her. After checking the shop windows one last time she climbed in.

"Welcome."

Karla bobbed her head and hugged her pack to her breast as the car pulled from the curb and she felt as if she was leaving the world behind, a refugee once again.

The car rattled around them as they went up the hill.

"That was very clean," she said.

"It never hurts to be careful."

"You were more than careful."

The man smiled, seemingly pleased by the observation, otherwise his expression gave nothing away. As they neared the top of the hill, he double-clutched deftly and shifted down a gear, then craned his head forward to check for oncoming traffic and turned left onto the town's main thoroughfare. He was even more focused than Majid.

They passed a small cluster of shops on the right, a grocer's, a pharmacist's, a bank and newsstand. On the dashboard lay a confusion of maps, paperback books without their jackets and folded up sections of newspaper, all covered with a fine layer of clay-colored dust as if the car was driven regularly along dirt roads.

Quirky, Karla remembered Khalil saying.

At the next intersection they turned right and started up a long grade, engine laboring. As they approached the edge of town they drove past a strip of squalor, dilapidated buildings, half-dressed children playing along a dirt track. Then they were out in the country driving through orchards and open fields.

Karla eased back on the seat and watched the landscape wash past, letting it transport her as she had on the train, a mute observer of the passing scene. Soon they came to an enclave of villas sheltering behind a whitewashed wall, the terracotta roof tiles burnt-red in the sunlight.

"Who lives there?"

"Brits," the man said evenly, indifferently almost. He seemed intent on the driving.

"What should I call you?"

"What did Khalil say?"

"He said you were a sympathizer … a friend."

The man smiled again without taking his eyes from the road, a private smile.

"You can call me Andrew."

"Kiefer," she said. "Karla Kiefer."

"I know. You're from Saba' Byar."

"You've been there?"

"Once … a long time ago."

Karla could see the camp meant nothing to him.

"Is that where you met Khalil?"

Andrew gave her a look then turned his attention back to the road.

"I'm sorry. It isn't my business."

"There's no harm in being curious. How did the FBI find you?"

186

The suddenness and directness of the question startled Karla. Then she remembered the way he looked at her on the beach, his eyes taking her in, assessing her without being obvious, his unhurried approach, his absolute confidence and control. Clearly he was more than a sympathizer, more than Khalil's friend.

"There is an informant in the Red Path."

Andrew dipped his head without comment. He drove conscientiously, without flourish. They were going downhill, the car humming along, heat radiating through the floorboards. At the edge of the road, blocks of native schist were piled high to form a wall.

"Khalil said your partner was wounded. That you had to finish him off. That must have been difficult."

"Not that difficult," Karla said, lying, then remembering. "Not until afterward."

"That's what I meant."

She looked at Andrew again, and again his expression gave nothing away.

The car slowed as they approached a T-intersection. On the far side was a village, a cluster of one-story buildings ascending a rise. To the right the road trailed into the shade of some eucalyptus trees and around a bend. A milestone — N125 — and Karla realized it was a continuation of the road she and Majid followed after they had ferried across the Rio Guadiana and picked up the car on a side street in Vila Real.

"Espiche," Andrew said, then turned left onto the main road and headed west, true to his word.

They drove in silence, the car seeming to coast effortlessly over the hills. Every so often, at breaks in the landscape, they caught glimpses of the cobalt sea; the sky above faded, washed-out blue.

Before long they came to a series of orchards, row upon row of trees marching to the ocher-colored hills in the distance. In some of the orchards the tree trunks looked raw, flayed, stripped bare.

"Cork oaks," Andrew said, breaking the silence.

Karla nodded. "And those?"

She was pointing at another orchard where the trees were smaller and more compact, where swollen buds appeared.

"Almonds," Andrew said, straight-arming the car through a curve. "But most of this is cork oak. You've never been here?"

"No."

She was silent then, head turned to the passenger window, elbow resting on her pack. Her hand went to her hair, tugged at the blunted ends, and Andrew wondered about her emotional state. Then he thought of the woman at the camp — *Mariko* — her line about the subjugation of the individual to the collective and wondered if Karla was the same way. *A fanatic, devoid of self.*

He had watched her in the wing mirror as she strode up the hill, all broad shoulders and long legs. The impression was one of power and strength, yet she freely acknowledged that finishing off Grossman was difficult, and she had the presence of mind to realize they had been set up in some way.

The engine began to ping and Andrew shifted down a gear and returned to his thoughts. Khalil said she was the best. *Like you.* But he knew his friend would say anything to get what he wanted, and for that reason Andrew decided to be careful with her. In every sense of the word.

He glanced at Karla out of the corner of his eye. She was still facing the passenger window. Her hand went to her hair again — a reflex. The woman is your guest, nothing more. Which was bullshit. His reasons for taking her in were far more complicated than that. His dislike of Raymond had been instantaneous, instinctive — the man was without scruples, a politician — and despite his initial misgivings he was beginning to find her plight sympathetic. And *that* Andrew knew was dangerous. For all of them.

"What else did Khalil tell you?"

She spoke slowly, seeming to measure each word: "He said I could trust you. That you were good, but quirky."

Andrew almost smiled. Quirky.

"Majid told me you were American," she continued, her voice quiet. "I was surprised when you spoke to me in German."

"Majid was the young Arab with you?"

He had recognized the young Arab from the night in the park, from the shadows, and recalled thinking Khalil was foolish having him escort her. They had stuck out, an Arab with a blonde-haired woman, stuck out as the three of them had as they wandered up the deserted lane. He wanted to wait until later, until the shops reopened and the streets were alive again, but Khalil insisted the time was fixed; he didn't want to leave Karla exposed. And that was how she looked sitting on the beach, her exposure almost palpable.

For nearly an hour he had watched from the headland. He watched the Mercedes drive into the town, watched Karla climb out and walk down Rua da Praia, watched the car circle through town and approach the beach from the west. Then watched the young bodyguard get out, recognizing him then, and trip up the steps to La Praia.

Still he waited. At 1:45 the fisherman appeared and spread his net over the seawall. He'd watched him too, watched until he was certain the man had nothing to do with the woman. Then he traversed the headland, half-running, half-sidestepping down the dirt path that led to the backside of the vacant villas at the east end of town, and joined the route Majid had taken. The rest followed naturally, uneventfully, cleanly as Karla put it.

Almost too cleanly. Andrew glanced at the rearview mirror. The road behind them was deserted, the oak groves closing in, seeming to erase their path. Illusion.

"I don't know why you are doing this," Karla said. "But thank you."

"Don't thank me. It wasn't my idea."

She didn't say anything in reply, her head still turned away, and Andrew wondered if she was crying.

"I'm not accustomed to having guests," he said, stumbling, awkward. "I've always lived alone."

She turned to face him then, her eyes shiny. "I understand. I'll try to stay out of your way."

They crested the last hill in silence. Andrew swung into his drive, suspension squeaking in protest as the car climbed the dirt lane. He parked out front, close to the front step. His bicycle still tilted against the whitewashed wall.

He pushed his door open and climbed out. Heard Karla get out the other side. She was facing the sea, back to him, pack in hand; he let her linger. The sun hung low above the horizon. Wisps of cirrostratus in the southern sky. There was a winter chill in the air.

"How far is it to the sea?" she asked, her *esses* sounding like *zees*.

Andrew considered replying in German but settled for giving her the distance in kilometers instead. "About ten kilometers if you cut through the orchards."

She nodded as if that sounded about right, then flung the pack over her shoulder and winced.

"What's wrong?"

"Nothing!"

He went around the car. "Here, let me help with that."

Karla pulled away sharply, clutching the pack strap to her chest. "I can handle it."

Andrew let the silence linger, thought of the English girl he encountered a couple of months back. He'd insulted her too.

"I was rude earlier," he said. "You weren't the one who asked to stay."

Karla looked at him, tight-lipped, eyes cold as crystal, and Andrew remembered how their clarity struck him when he stopped to speak with her on the beach.

"We all have our quirks."

A glimmer of a smile flitted across her face. "Mine is stubbornness."

And contrariness, Andrew thought and as if to prove just that Karla cinched the pack strap tight.

"Come," he said, extending his arm toward the house. "I'll show you your room."

"*Danke*," she replied, her voice barely a whisper.

Andrew was careful not to touch her as she walked past. He checked the road below — no one had followed, not even Majid — and fell in behind her.

As she mounted the front step he noticed her hair was uneven in the back where it had been chopped off. Bare white skin showed along the line of her neck.

"Tomorrow we'll have to get you a proper haircut."

Karla stopped, looked back over her shoulder. "Does it look that badly?" A lilt to her voice.

"You were butchered," he said, realizing too late what he was saying.

She smiled again, sadly this time, her eyes so pale they appeared almost without color, translucent, lightest gray, and

Andrew knew what she was seeing: *the men in the field.*

He shuddered. It was as if a spirit, a ghost, had passed close by.

Chapter 13

Murphy woke with a start, disoriented, the dark of night all around him. He lay on his back and could hear a faint tapping sound like a dog's paws on a hardwood floor. Off to his right files lay scattered on a desktop in a halo of light and all at once he realized where he was. He had been working on the files earlier — half-heartedly, Murphy recalled — but gave it up to pace. After a while he gave up on that too.

He swung his legs off the cot and sat up, rested his palms on his thighs. He felt tired, worn-down. Like an old man, he thought, a relic. For nearly a week he had been pushing himself hard and the nap offered little respite.

Murphy hauled himself up, swayed slightly and made his way to his office window. Raindrops beaded on the glass. Down on the street a car cruised slowly past, headlight beams washing over the buildings like a beacon in the night. Two days after the shootings they abandoned the search for Karla in Vermont and returned to New York. They had found the spot where she stumbled, the scuffle of footprints — her panic real, not imagined — then discovered the bloodstained coat at the top of an embankment not thirty yards from where they pulled the truck over and even now Murphy wondered if she had been there, listening.

He shuddered at the thought, then thrust out his arms and stretched, rotating his spine, and settled before the window once more. Outside, rain continued to fall; another car slipped silently past. Within a few hours they found the truck abandoned on a side street in Norwich and decided the man they stopped was most likely the shooter. For a while they even suspected he intercepted Karla, and Murphy called in extras teams and sent them out to search the woods for the body, but they found nothing. Except the discarded Uzi and the weapons' cache.

The next morning one of Smithers' men came up with the woman in the clothing store in Hanover. The woman recognized Karla's photo right away. She'd been a sight, the woman told them, memorable, which had surprised Murphy until he remembered the chaotic scene at the farmhouse, her panicked flight.

Later that morning they located the cab driver who took her to White River Junction. Unlike the saleswoman he didn't recognize Karla's photograph. Her hair was different, the cabby claimed. "It was chopped short, a home-cut if I ever seen one. Dropped her at the Tip Top." That afternoon they found the bag of hair and wet clothing in a trash bin at the White River train station. Somewhere between the clothing store and cab ride the panic ended.

Murphy replayed her movements in his mind as he continued to gaze at the street below, the seeming randomness yet underlying order — for a German, taking a train was normal, natural, a logical means of escape — and he knew that the Red Path operation was still running, as was Karla. Executing Bacchetti was only the beginning, the weapons proved that.

Murphy tried not to think about the weapons, about his disastrous meeting with the AD earlier that day, the memory painful, raw. That morning he had received the initial ballistics reports. The results from the Browning Hi-Power matched those of a handgun the Bureau confiscated a few months back. When they checked the evidence room, the gun was gone.

He'd suspected as much after reading the ballistics reports. Just as he suspected — no, believed — the Red Path had someone inside the Bureau, someone close to the investigation, someone watching his every move. They couldn't have managed it any other way. They played him, played him as they had played Karla, were playing both of them even now. Using her as bait.

All this Murphy knew without a doubt, felt deep inside, viscerally, and the irony didn't escape him. It was Germany all over again.

Behind him the tapping sound resumed. Earlier he had set Hendricks — Dick, not Richard — the task of tracking the Winchester rifle though he assumed it would ultimately lead to the Company, another suspicion. Meanwhile he sent Plum out to meet with his informant; they could factor whatever he had to say.

There was a murmur of voices in the squad room. Plum, Murphy thought. He turned and walked across his office to the door. Plum was standing at Hendricks' workstation. The two young agents were speaking quietly, the shoulders of Plum's overcoat dark with rain.

Murphy switched on the overhead light and Plum looked up. She was gone — he could see it on Plum's face — and to his surprise Murphy felt relieved, dispassionate almost.

"You were right, Jim. Kiefer took the train here. The source says she flew to Paris."

Hendricks was watching him as if to gauge his reaction. Could it be him? Murphy wondered. Could Hendricks be the "someone inside?" Hendricks was new, newer than Plum, and when he asked Hendricks to stay late to work the rifle he jumped at the chance. But then, he thought, it could be anyone.

"When?"

"The night after the shooting."

Hendricks had turned back to his terminal; he tapped a key and the screen flashed to life.

Murphy motioned Plum into his office and closed the door. "Where is she now?"

Plum shook his head. "He claims he doesn't know. I'm beginning to wonder if anything he says is legit?"

"They're playing us. They want us to know about Paris."

"So what do we do?" He had never seen his young colleague so perplexed, so completely at a loss.

"We act like we don't know they want us to know. Request the passenger lists for flights from New York to Paris that night, and don't be quiet about it. Check Germans, Swiss, Austrians … and Americans," he added, thinking aloud.

Plum's expression brightened. "Of course. No one would look closely at the passport of an American leaving the country."

Murphy smiled, pleased that his young colleague made the leap with him. "There'll be a trail. A not-too-obvious trail. A funny passport or something …" He had a flash, a moment of sight, a flicker at the back of his brain as he had that day at Callaghan's. When he tried to focus on it the insight slipped away.

"I'll request the manifests from Logan and Dulles too," Plum said.

Then he saw it again, clearly this time. The passport will be easy, they want us to follow … but she'll be gone. As she was in Vermont. As Gretchen and the child had been when he returned to the camp in Wangen.

Murphy felt light-headed, dizzy, moments of darkness threatening his equilibrium. He reached out and steadied himself against the desk.

"You okay?" the voice far off.

Plum looked at him with concern.

"I'm fine. I just got dizzy for a second." So much for dispassion, he thought.

"You should get some rest. You haven't been out of here in days. I'll put in a request for the manifests."

"I think I will. A good night's sleep will help and I haven't seen my wife in days. Only phone calls."

Plum smiled. "Good." And headed for the door.

After taking a few steps he stopped and turned. "Shouldn't we alert Interpol at this point? They can help out at the Paris end. Don't you have a friend there?"

"I know a few people." He did have a friend, one in particular from his days as Bureau liaison in Saint-Cloud, Georges Depardieu, but he was reluctant to use a friend again, or anyone from his past. So far the Red Path had been using his past against him.

"Let's hold off for the time being. See what we can learn from the passenger manifests."

"Whatever you say. Get some rest, Jim."

He left then, the door clicking shut quietly behind him.

There wasn't any reason to hurry, Murphy knew. The Red Path would wait — he could control the pace. And it occurred to him that was the only advantage available to him.

∗∗∗

An hour and a half later Murphy found himself parked in the driveway in front of his house in Stamford. Exhausted, he slumped back on the seat, listening to the rain tattoo the roof of the car. He lost track of how many times he had nodded off at the wheel, the drive like a mad dream. The angry blare of horns echoed in his head, the smear of headlights on the rain-wetted windshield blinding him, the bridge abutments like ghosts leaping into his path.

Murphy shunted the vision aside, shouldered his door open and climbed out. The rain was letting up, and an unexpectedly warm breeze brushed across his face. Lush, tropical. Another dream, he thought. The streetlights glowed in the evening mist, corona-like, and lit the crusty snow-berms along both side of the street. At the end of the block a dog moaned, as if abandoned.

He turned and headed for the house, weaving through the puddles that lay in his path. The porch light flared and the front door swung open. Liz stood in the doorway in her white terrycloth robe.

"You shouldn't have waited up," he said quietly.

"I didn't. I woke when you pulled in."

She'd cut her hair, Murphy noticed, cropped it in line with her jaw, the dark salted with gray. It made her face look rounder, fuller, her skin radiating good health even at this ungodly hour, and it made him think of Gretchen, his gentle stray, their idle moments together, private moments.

Murphy swallowed hard, accepting the guilt he felt as penance. Ever since the case began he couldn't look at his wife without thinking of Gretchen and the child. Our surrogate child, Liz called her without a hint of derision. Not once had she directed her anger at the child. Of course she had been angry, her faith in him bruised, but eventually she forgave him and took him into her arms as she did now. A prodigal.

They lingered for a few moments, their bodies close. Then Murphy reached across and closed the front door, and returned to his wife's embrace. He could smell the sleep in her hair. Fresh, clean.

"You look done in."

"I feel it. I'm getting too old for this."

Liz pulled back, studied his face, his eyes. "It's more than that." He never had been able to get anything past her.

"Kiefer's gone."

His wife put her head back on his shoulder, held him tight. He had told her everything since the day Plum walked into his office, his suspicions, how Karla's past resonated with his.

"The AD wants me to disappear the weapons," he said, still not believing it, the smallness of the man. "The ballistics tests, the lab work, everything."

Liz tipped her head back again, gazed at him. "That's obstruction of justice."

"I know."

"You can't do that!"

He loved her for that. For her fire, her spirit.

"Not a chance."

After confirming the Browning Hi-Power was missing from the evidence room he went directly to the Assistant Director's office and was waiting at the AD's door when he arrived promptly at 9:30 a.m. The AD waved him into his office and pointed him into a chair.

Benjamin J Liker was a vain, colorless man. His office, unlike Murphy's, was immaculate. An American flag hung draped from the flagpole behind his desk. On the wall behind it hung a series of black-framed photographs, one of the AD with the Director, another with Kelly, still another with Nixon, each of them with a rigid smile in place.

His desk gleamed as always, cleared the previous evening by the AD himself and polished by his personal staff. Liker was one of those men who believed that no day should end with a single item left unattended, the ultimate organization man. Some in the

New York office joked that "the BJ" wanted to be ready when the call for his triumphant return to Headquarters came. Murphy believed otherwise. He distrusted orderliness instinctively, the sign of an inflexible mind.

The AD was livid when he told him about the automatic, face scarlet, a tic like a cliché twitching at the corner of his mouth. "Do you have any idea what the repercussions will be like? The effect it will have on us."

When he said "us," Murphy knew Liker meant "me." The AD was small, petty even, but he wasn't without adequate survival instincts.

"When was the weapon last inventoried?"

"August. But you know how the clerks wing it sometimes."

"It's their fault then."

Murphy wanted to laugh, then cry. Liker already had found someone to blame.

"It doesn't matter whose fault it is. The press will say we shot Bacchetti. It's what they want to believe, and they'll sell more newspapers that way."

The AD glared at him, then stood up and began to pace. Murphy could almost see the man thinking, looking for a way to cover his ass.

He stopped, looked at Murphy, smug. "We have plausible deniability." Plausible deniability meant that everyone would believe the Bureau did it but couldn't prove it.

"At best we'll look like idiots," Murphy said. "At worst like we're doing the Company's dirty work. The Red Path wants us to look like criminals, like the real terrorists."

"Don't spout that revolutionary crap to me. They're a bunch of thugs. And did it ever occur to you that the Company might be using the Red Path against us?"

"It did. But why would the Company leave the rifle? It's obvious the Red Path wants to attack their credibility too."

Liker waved off his words. "I want the weapons disappeared."

The order stunned Murphy.

"Do you hear me?" The AD was livid again, chins quivering with rage. "I want all the evidence to disappear. Especially the ballistics reports."

He had nodded, nodded that he heard not that he agreed. And immediately after leaving the AD's office he collected the weapons, the lab analyses and ballistics reports and stowed them in the trunk of his car.

Liz was smiling at him, knowing him well enough. "What are you going to tell Liker if he asks what you did with it all?"

"I'll tell him he doesn't want to know."

His wife's smile broadened.

"It could ruin my career, Liz. Everything we worked for."

"And the other choice …"

She kissed him then, lovingly, unconditionally, her body melting into his. And Murphy knew what he would do. In the morning he would hide the weapons and documents in the shed behind their house, then contact Georges as Plum suggested. He wouldn't tell anyone.

Except Liz.

III

Chapter 14

Ever the silent observer, Andrew was stationed at the kitchen window, Swarovski 8x42 binoculars dangling from his neck. He watched Karla come to a halt at the top of the far ridge, left arm cocked, hand poised on her hip like a dancer at rest. She stood facing the sea and was wearing tan khaki shorts and a cropped sleeveless blouse; a floppy-brimmed straw hat was set squarely on her head and he pictured her squinting in the glare, sweat trickling down her brow, breathing deeply yet evenly after the steep climb.

Her discipline pleased him. Every day she took these walks, long solitary marches to the sea, and every day he stood at the window like this, watching until she dropped from sight, watching for reasons that until yesterday seemed to have become gratuitous, excessive even for him.

As he continued his vigil Andrew remembered the way her eyes gravitated to the coastline the day she arrived. Later that day she told him she needed to walk. The long winter in America had left her body soft, she said, but he knew that what she truly needed was time to herself, time to reconcile her actions, time alone. Unlike him she wasn't able to objectify the killing and she was still struggling with guilt.

She wasn't without courage however, Andrew thought. She took care of her lover — he was certain Grossman had been that — when she had to and against all reasonable odds she managed to escape, and once she arrived at the house she didn't retreat to her room, didn't let the pain consume her. Instead she made these daily treks. *Long solitary marches to the sea.*

Across the way a gust of wind caught Karla's hat. Her hand went up, arm arcing gracefully, and held it in place, her hair riffling lightly in the breeze. Andrew took up his binoculars and brought them to bear. Months in the sun had left her skin nut-brown and he could see the highlights in her hair, flecks of gold, the downy fuzz on her sun-baked arms, the dampness along the tunnel of her spine …

Andrew lowered the glasses abruptly — he felt like a voyeur. Don't, he told himself. Only peril lies there, complication, complication for both of us.

Karla set off again. When she dropped behind the ridge, he let his gaze ease down the hillside. Near the bottom was a rundown cottage with grubby whitewashed walls. The front door hung forlornly from its hinges and all the windows were broken, dark, shattered long ago. Rubble lay everywhere: shards of glass, a legless chair, slash from the trees. Not far from the cottage was what had once been a substantial garden. Waxy spears of native agave grew wild there now, the rest of the hillside given over to cork oak.

The previous day he had spotted the man near the cottage. He followed Karla all the way to the beach then held back as she picked her way down the jumble of rocks to the slender spit of sand. He seemed content following, shadowing her from a distance, never hurrying. It was as if the stranger knew her route.

Andrew raised the binoculars again and trained them on the building's shadowy interior. When a flash of white rushed across the lenses he followed it, anticipating it from window to window. It was the same man as yesterday, the same crisp white shirt.

The stranger exited the cottage and Andrew tracked him with the glasses as he worked his way up the hillside. At the top he stopped and took shelter behind one of the trees, the gray-felt leaves fluttering around his head. Andrew fine-tuned the focus and the man's features sharpened. Dark lank hair hung to his collar and his skin was pale, pockmarked, like some subterranean creature that rarely ventured into the sun.

Then, as if sensing his interest, the stranger turned to face the house. His gaze was unfocused, far way, and for a moment Andrew felt as if he was staring into a blind man's eyes.

He shuddered. Bad karma.

Or — he wondered — was it an omen? A sign?

He unslung the binoculars and set them on the counter. It was over, he knew, ended. This place as his retreat, as Karla's sanctuary. Someone had found them and he had been considering a journey ever since reading about the series of lectures Jorge Velasquez, the Mexican energy minister, intended to give at the Hoover Institution. Velasquez presented the perfect target — liberals loved him for his internationalist views, conservatives for his country's internal politics — and he would be in Palo Alto in three weeks.

And now, Andrew thought, so will I. The man following Karla was merely hastening his departure.

That he wasn't disturbed by the prospect of leaving surprised Andrew somewhat. From the beginning he accepted that he would lose this place — it was inevitable, as inevitable as what he did — yet he had always wondered if his acceptance was a pose, denial. But now that the day had arrived he knew his doubts had been unwarranted, his connection to the place, to its history, broken, severed forever ...

He saw the men entering his house, swarming from room to

room, doors and windows flung open, furniture overturned, artwork ripped from the walls, book and record collections scattered, brutalized. It was violation. An outrage.

Yet he felt no anger, only a preternatural calm. A strange concurrence. Like a dovetail in time. Make the arrangements, an inner voice whispered. Call Albert.

Andrew waited until the stranger dropped from view then made his way across the kitchen to the living room. He glanced out back instinctively. The porch was deserted, the back door closed; remnants of their afternoon meal lay on the table undisturbed, their white cloth napkins crumpled in tiny heaps. Then he walked briskly to the telephone.

Andrew checked his hand as he reached for the handset. Better to be safe, he thought, to make the call from somewhere else, paranoid even. A shard of memory, the shadow darting in the night, racing up the walkway. Irrational. He scooped the car keys from the table and went out the front door. Outside, the air smelled of blossoms, of spring full-blown. Swathes of wild geraniums flared along the side of the carport. Without so much as a glance at the far hillside Andrew hopped into his car and fired up the engine.

Fifteen minutes later he pulled into the gravel parking area in front of the restaurant a few miles from Luz. The afternoon meal had ended and the lot was deserted. He left the keys in the ignition and made his way to the front door. Inside was dimly lit, already dusk. He could hear the metallic clang of pots in the kitchen, water rushing into a sink; the tables were cleared, the wait staff gone for siesta. Off to his right the proprietor sat at one of the tables, hunched over the afternoon's receipts. When he raised his head, Andrew pointed to the payphone on the back wall. The man nodded and returned to his accounts.

For a while Andrew stood by the phone, listening, patient, watching the cleft of light at the front door. That no one followed pleased him; it indicated a lack of urgency on their part and left him with time to finesse their departure. It also meant the man following Karla would leave her alone for the time being.

The kitchen door crashed open and the dishwasher appeared in a flood of light, a pile of plates balanced in his arms. The dishwasher's hair was wet, slick with steam. The man was so intent on his work that he didn't notice Andrew standing in the shadows as he waded through the sea of tables. He dumped the dishes on a sideboard, righted the stack and returned to the kitchen, the door twitching behind him. All the while the industrious owner remained bent over his accounts.

It's as if I'm not here, Andrew thought. As if I exist on a different plane, in separate dimension, a different world.

He lifted the handset from the hook quietly and dialed the number. It was a Geneva exchange. When the long-distance operator came on the line, he recited his calling card number and she placed the call.

The phone buzzed over and over at the other end; Andrew let it ring. Finally a woman answered and he asked for Albert.

After several moments the Swiss shipper came on the line. They spoke in French, Andrew careful to keep his voice low, a murmur beneath the din coming from the kitchen.

"I need some items moved," he said.

"When?"

"Right away."

"A moment please."

The phone clunked at the other end. Andrew could hear static, scratchy voices on the line, garbled conversations he wasn't able to make out. Dying echoes.

The shipper came back on the line. "There is a flight to London this afternoon. I can make a connection and arrive in Faro late this evening. I'll arrange a car."

"Perfect." He and Karla could close down the house as if they were bedding down for the night and leave before dawn.

"How soon will you require delivery?"

"Three — four weeks," Andrew said. "I'll give you the details this evening."

"Simple enough then." The shipper spoke as if the deed were already done.

Andrew remembered an earlier shipment, also to America. The rush was at the other end that time and the planning more frenzied, the shipper more ebullient. In the end Albert hid the weapon in a quadriplegic's gurney and the rifle traveled to New York first class.

"There's one other thing …" Andrew paused, glanced at the kitchen door, at the proprietor, at the sliver of light along the side of the front door. "I need a passport."

"Nationality?" Again Albert seemed unfazed.

"U.S.," he said, then quickly added: "It isn't for me."

The shipper hesitated for a moment. "Male or female?"

Andrew turned his back to the dining room. "It's for a woman."

"When will you need it?"

"Tonight."

"That's unfortunate. I can't guarantee a perfect match."

"Not a problem. We can make the necessary adjustments here."

"Very well. I'll try for something close. I'll need the details."

Andrew pictured Karla on the ridgetop, more objectively this time, her powerful walker's body silhouetted against the cloud-riddled sky.

"Slender," he said, "about 170 centimeters. Blonde hair, gray eyes."

"Age?"

"Late twenties, early thirties."

"That shouldn't be a problem."

Receiver tucked between shoulder and ear, Andrew turned back to the dining room. The owner had stood up and was shoving the afternoon's receipts into a bank bag.

"The passport," the shipper continued, "you mustn't trust it for more than a few days."

"You know me, Albert."

"Of course. Until this evening then."

"This evening," Andrew said.

But, a thousand miles away, the line was already dead.

Andrew hung the handset up slowly. Suddenly the urge to flee rose in his throat. Go.

You can drive away. Leave her.

Until now he hadn't considered leaving Karla, abandoning her. He gave his word to Khalil.

Screw it. Let them have her.

The keys are in the car. Disappear.

Andrew smiled. It was rat thinking, he knew. Stories in his head. Ego.

The proprietor still stood by the table, zipped bank bag secured under one arm. He was looking directly at him.

Maybe we're both just being paranoid.

***

When he got back to his house Andrew went straight to the kitchen and opened the cellar door. He left the light off and a damp wintry chill greeted him as he felt his way down the stairs;

he could just make out the bulky shape of the steamer trunk against the far wall. Behind it in a cubbyhole he had carved out years ago were his SSG rifle and, since Karla's arrival, the .22-caliber High Standard pistol.

He intended to have Albert take everything stored there — both weapons, the boxes of 7.62 and .22-caliber cartridges, the cleaning kit and extra magazines — because he knew they would come into house after he and Karla left, and again he saw the men swarming through his house, trashing it. For a moment he felt a twinge of regret, of grief almost, and he acknowledged it, then set it aside. It was meant to be, fate.

Struggling with the weight Andrew dragged the trunk from the cellar wall. The bottom grated loudly on the concrete floor and he glanced back over his shoulder. At the top of the stairs was a nimbus of light, the house quiet, still, and again he was struck by a sense of separation, of living in parallel world.

Andrew shook off the feeling and ducked into the hole, grabbed the rifle case and set it on top of the trunk, flat side down. When he popped the locks, the lid sprung open and he reached blindly inside, hand brushing over the stiff-foam lining. He pried the rifle from its nest, the synthetic stock cool in his hand. After inserting the cold-steel bolt he brought the rifle to his shoulder and swung on the light at the head of the stairs, remembering how it felt, the purity, the absolute lack of ambiguity. Everything black and white.

A soft scraping sound upstairs.

Andrew froze.

The front door rasped shut. He reached back, calm, and plucked a loaded magazine from the case and slipped it quietly into the rifle.

Footsteps — a single set — padded across the floor overhead

and stopped at the back door. He took a breath, rifle still on the doorway. He would take him when he stepped into the light.

The footsteps reversed direction, more deliberate now.

Andrew breathed slowly, easily, imagined the sharp report of the rifle shot echoing in the basement. Soundless in the distance.

"Hello?"

He eased up, took his finger off the trigger, heard Karla start toward the kitchen and began to break down the rifle, hurrying. He fitted the magazine back in its slot, then the steel bolt.

"Are you down there?"

He froze again, rifle still in hand, and saw Karla standing at the top of the stairs, framed by the light.

"Andrew?" She sounded nervous.

"I'll be right up," he called.

She lingered for a few moments then moved off as if he had willed her away. He eased the rifle back in the foam cutout, closed the case and set it back in the hole, then went to the stairs, leaving the trunk where it lay.

He found Karla standing at the far end of the kitchen, peering out the window. His binoculars lay on the counter beside her, untouched. She whirled around when he pressed the door shut.

"Someone's following me." Her words urgent, clipped.

"I know. I noticed him yesterday."

Her eyes flicked to the binoculars. "You should have said something."

Andrew ignored her and went into the living room. He walked toward the back door, stopped just short of it and scanned the hills to the north, looking for reflection, for light off a lens.

He heard Karla walk into the room behind him.

"Is someone else out there?"

"I don't think so," he said, still scanning the hillsides.

The ocean breeze had died, the leaves at rest. Nothing moved. Karla came across the room, stepped up beside him, followed his gaze. To the east, in one of the ravines, a sedge of pall-black cranes rose, wings rippling.

"He seems to be alone at this point," Andrew said. "Did you recognize him?"

"No. Should I have?"

"I thought maybe Khalil sent him. That he was from the camp."

Karla was silent for several moments. "I have never seen him before. I must go now."

Andrew turned from the view and watched her snatch her weathered sunhat from the sofa and hasten toward the stairs. Her room, like his, lay on the second floor.

"Where will you go?"

"I don't know," she said, tossing the words over her shoulder. "Away from here."

"What about Khalil? The camp?"

She stopped, foot on the bottom stair. She refused to look at him as if she knew she was being irrational, reactive, that her ID was blown most likely, that there wasn't anywhere for her to go. Yet Andrew sensed the firmness of her resolve — *I can handle it* — and he realized after nearly three months sharing the same house, the same meals, he still didn't know this woman. They'd been too busy keeping out of each other's way.

He thought of the times they moved side by side through the crush of shoppers at the Lagos market, the crowd forcing them close together, their bodies just touching, both of them pulling away as if from a hot flame. The drawn-out silences that followed.

Andrew turned back to the door, saw their empty plates, their crumpled napkins, the wind chimes swaying silently. It's better this way, he told himself. For both of us. To remain strangers, alone.

"You should at least wait until we can arrange new papers for you."

No reply.

Karla came back across the room, stepped up beside him again. He could feel the heat emanating from her body. "It's more dangerous for you now."

"I don't think they'll bother us for a while," Andrew said, mouth suddenly dry.

"Who is he?"

"Interpol most likely, or the local GNR. Maybe the FBI. Raymond would have …"

The memory struck him, like a flare of white light, blinding him for a moment. Then the photo of Raymond emerged, the shadows stripped away. His arrogance more emphatic, accentuated in gray-scale.

"What is it?"

Andrew raised a hand, quieting her as he focused on the photograph. He'd seen it in *Time* a year or so ago — a small photo, he remembered, a snapshot almost buried deep in the pages of the magazine, one among many. TWO HUNDRED YOUNG PEOPLE BUILDING AMERICA'S FUTURE.

Then he saw the name beneath the photograph, the organization below that, and felt a chill of recognition. The name was Plum, Charles Plum. FBI.

"Son of a bitch."

"What?"

Plum didn't need to go far. A simple intra-Bureau phone call would have done it. He would have claimed he had an informant, a confidential informant. All of it made sense, how he set Karla and Grossman — and the FBI — up, how he arranged it, known when to have the shooter in place, the weapons even. Plum was working both sides. And in that moment Andrew knew, not as revelation but as confirmation. The sides were the same.

A rational calm descended upon him, perfect objectivity. The same calm he felt when he had the rifle at his shoulder, familiar, like a place returned to after a long absence. And it occurred to him that he almost had it figured the day Khalil visited, without realizing it. *What does Raymond do, exchange notes with the FBI?*

Khalil hadn't objected. He'd become pensive, rationalized the set up. And the night in Riverside Park his friend warned him off. Twice ... *it's better you don't know.*

Again the urge to flee rose in Andrew's throat.

Walk away.

You don't owe her anything. She's a lost cause.

Illusions. More stories in his head. Delusion.

There was no getting out, no walking away. Because in the end, Andrew knew, for a man of commitment, of obligation, what truly counted was the way in which he comported himself, the way in which he made his stand, in which he faced his friend ... and enemy. And the irony wasn't lost on him.

Karla was tugging at his arm. "What is it?" Her eyes troubled, guileless.

Of all of them — he thought — Khalil, Plum, Mariko and the others at the camp she was the only one with an honest agenda, with a single pure-thought in her head. But how can I tell her that? How can I tell her that Plum betrayed them? That her lover died for nothing. That the Palestinian prisoners were pawns, pieces in a far-fetched drama. It would shatter what remained of her world.

Yet at the same time Andrew knew he had to tell her, that not telling her would be another form of betrayal.

Without realizing he had turned back to the view. The sun hung low in the west and cast a fiery glow across the sky. Uncertainty had fled.

"Have you ever met Raymond?"

"We spoke only on the telephone."

"I did, once." Even to him his voice sounded strangely distant, far away, disembodied almost. "You were right. There is an informant in the Red Path. His name is Plum, Charles Plum. Only when I met him Khalil introduced him as 'Raymond.' Raymond's FBI."

He felt Karla draw away. "Raymond? FBI?"

"Sit down," he said gently.

Karla resisted.

"Please."

She went to the sofa then and sat down, knees pressed tightly together, her hands interwoven in her lap.

Andrew reached up and yanked the drape across the back door. "The whole point of the operation," he said, using Khalil's exact words, "was to attack the credibility of the FBI and the CIA. Raymond ... Plum was positioned to orchestrate that. There was no deal for prisoners, no negotiations. They intended to execute Bacchetti from the beginning. Even the gun you used was planned."

Karla looked up at him, her eyes dim, disbelieving. "Who are you? How do you know all this?"

"I just do. They sent the shooter to make certain."

Her hand went to her eyes and she lowered her head. Andrew could see her mind working, putting it together.

"They used you, Karla."

"Of course they used me," she cried, hand still covering her eyes. "I let them use me. As I used Sam." Her voice cracked. "I killed him. You'll never know what it was like. I can still see their eyes …"

Her words trailed off and Andrew went to her side. He sat on the arm of the sofa beside her; she was crying softly and he could sense the sadness in her, the unrelenting guilt. He touched her shoulder and she pulled away sharply. He wanted to tell her that he did understand, that he *had* looked into their eyes. As far as he knew she knew nothing of the weapons in the basement, of his life. To her he must seem a wastrel.

His own first kill came back to him. It had been July, the rainy season in Querétaro, and the air in the storeroom where he waited had been heavy, drenched with humidity, barely enough space for him and his rifle. He remembered the sweat soaking through his clothes; the clutch of security men swarming around the hotel in their dark glasses, communication buds plugged in their ears; the rose-colored granite of the Jardin Zenea.

For hours, hours that seemed without shape or dimension, he waited in the cramped room, enduring the heat, watching the ticket vendor slouched in the shade of the park bandstand, the locals strolling past in their vertiginous *paseo*, part of the ebb and flow. Not a hint of a breeze.

When the Secretary of State's motorcade finally arrived, he took up his rifle and settled himself. Earlier he was nervous but now he felt calm, loose, detached almost, a sense of weightlessness in his chest.

He saw the light flare in the hotel room across the way and put his eye to the scope. The Secretary lumbered into view, his face close, seeming only yards away, exactly as Khalil said. He could see the man's eyes, the dark shadow of beard, the flecks of silver at his temple when he turned and offered his head.

Andrew took a breath, let it halfway out, and squeezed off a shot. Then another, the second shattering the glass, and he felt nothing. No joy, no remorse. No jubilation. Only an absolute equanimity.

Killing like that required a certain amount of detachment, a certain remoteness, a willingness to be alone, a solitary. Nothing of what Karla was feeling.

"He's gone," he said. "You can't change that."

Karla sniffed, head still down, took a deep shuddery breath. "I know."

"Sometimes death can be merciful."

She looked up at him, her eyes red-rimmed, cheeks streaked with tears. He saw a spark there. Of understanding perhaps — though he knew it could just as easily be hatred.

"We can get out of here."

"No one else is dying because of …"

"No one is dying," he said, cutting her off sharply. "Not here." Not yet.

Karla continued looking at him, her gaze indecipherable.

"We'll split up after we get out. You can go wherever you want. I'll go on alone."

Anything else would be madness, Andrew knew. Folly.

Tempting fate.

***

The room was like a Benedictine's cell, the whitewashed walls stark, without decoration. A tiny box-shaped window was set high in the wall facing Karla's bed. Earlier, before lying down, she had opened the window, swinging it inward. A crescent of moon was etched on the glass and the briny smell of ocean filled the room. Karla pictured the breakers at the base of the cliffs, rising and falling, the *whump* as they crashed onto the rocks, the salty spray on her face.

She reached out with her foot and felt for her pack at the end of the bed, confirming once again that it was there. They were leaving before dawn. Before first light, Andrew had told her. He told her many things that day though nothing of himself. The operation was a sham, a lie; Raymond sent the shooter — insurance, Andrew called him — only he missed. The operation was never about the Palestinian prisoners, or the old man.

A wedge of anger rose in her chest but Karla held it off. Anger was destructive, feckless; it indicated a lack of control. But it also could be a sign of strength, she knew, of recovery. Her thoughts turned to her mother, to another lie. Her own hopes were no less illusory than her mother's. And for the first time she felt a special kinship with her mother and began to understand why her mother let the promise of her lover's return shape her life. The illusion that the dream was shared.

Karla looked up at the open window, at the starpoints in the night sky. She and Sam had shared a dream, a misguided dream …

I'm with you. All the way.

Her eyes misted. That wasn't a lie. That was real, pure. Untainted.

Never again, she promised herself. No one would die for her ever again.

***

Downstairs, music etched the silence. The recording was modern, sharp and dissonant, atonal, jagged as shattered glass. She envisioned Andrew sitting in the living room, in a straight-backed chair, listening, fingers steepled in front of his face, placid. A spider perched on glass.

He was a mirror image of Sam, she realized. Everything

reversed. Where Sam resisted he flowed, where Sam was passionate Andrew was composed. And he *was* right — sometimes death could be merciful. And now she must learn to live with the knowledge that Sam died for nothing.

She thought of their last moments together, brushing the snow from Sam's hair, the way he smiled. *It's okay, it's okay.* It hadn't been until then that she realized how wrong she was, about him and everything else.

A tear trickled down Karla's cheek, then another as she wept. Unheard, a cry rendered mute by the crashing waves of sound.

***

Sometime later the music ended abruptly. Hands pillowed beneath her head, dry-eyed, Karla listened to the silence. At the window a moth beat its wings ineffectually against the screen. Then she heard the wheeze of an automobile's suspension as it came up the drive. Andrew told her there would be a visitor. She was to stay out of sight.

The headlights washed over the ceiling as the car pulled in front of the house. The driver killed the engine and doused the lights. Darkness. Karla swung her legs off of the bed, sat up and slid her feet into her sandals. Then, thinking better of it, kicked them off and crept into the hallway, the terracotta-flooring cool beneath her feet.

A light burned brightly at the foot of the stairs. She edged toward it, stopping well back from the staircase, shoulder touching the rough plaster wall. She heard Andrew talking quietly, then the visitor's voice.

"*Tous?*"

"*Oui, ils ont découvert la maison.*" They found the house — Karla translating in her head.

"*Quand?*" She heard the urgency in the visitor's voice.

"*Hier.*"

"*Êtes-vous certain?*" Even alarmed the other man sounded cultured, his accent melodic.

"*Qui.*"

"*Sont-ils là-bas maintenant?*"

"*Très probablement,*" Andrew replied.

"*Qui sont-ils?*" She had asked that too, but Andrew didn't know who sent the man.

"*Ce n'est pas important.*"

Then silence — and Karla pictured the two men facing each other, Andrew's steady gaze.

"*Très bien,*" the other man said, his voice subdued now, as if Andrew's confidence was contagious.

"*Vous aurez de la livraison en trois semaines?*"

Karla struggled with her limited French — something about a delivery.

"*Oui,*" Andrew said.

She crept closer to the top of the stairs, remaining out of sight.

"*Là où vous aurez besoin de la livraison?*" Yes, delivery.

"San Francisco," Andrew told the visitor. "*Je vous contacterai une fois que je suis en place.*"

"*Très bien. J'aurai mon homme là en trois semaines.*" In three weeks.

"*Il pourrait avoir à attendre.*"

Waiting for what? Karla wondered.

"*Ce n'est pas un problème. Aurez-vous besoin de tout?*"

"*Non,*" Andrew replied. "*Je n'ai besoin que le fusil.*"

Karla cocked her head, uncertain of her French once more. *Le fusil ... le pistolet. Ein Gewehr?*

The men stepped into the entryway, into the light, and as if to confirm his words Andrew was holding a metal rifle case.

Karla felt dizzy, short of breath.

The light went off, plunging the house into darkness. The front door clicked shut.

"You heard?"

She flinched, saw Andrew standing at the foot of the stairs, a silhouette in the moonlight.

"You think it was me."

She didn't know what to think, to say.

The light flashed on, blinding her for a moment.

"You were there."

"No."

"But you knew."

"Yes." He seemed indifferent almost. As if he were beyond everything. Emotionless, untouchable.

"I don't miss, Karla."

And somehow she knew that he didn't, that he wasn't lying to her.

"They came to you, but you refused."

"Yes."

"You're a shooter."

"You expect an apology?"

Karla didn't know what she expected anymore. At the camp there had been a rumor about a shooter. Mariko had told her about him — her fabled lover. He hadn't shared their cause, she'd said. And his motives were ultimately selfish.

Andrew still stood at the foot of the stairs, eyeing her. "I won't lie to you. It could have been me. But I didn't kill your partner."

And it all came flooding back to her, kneeling at Sam's side, the severity of his wound, the blowback, the old man's cry.

"You fucked up, no question. You tried to save the operation and your partner died as a result, but he chose death the moment he joined your group. And I suspect he died believing in what you were doing. And Bacchetti? Everyone wanted him dead."

"But what good was there in killing the old man?"

"What good was there in not killing him?"

Karla felt lost, confused.

"Listen, the guilt you feel isn't real. It's what you think you should feel. People die. It's that simple."

"It doesn't feel simple," she cried.

"Have you ever watched anyone die?"

She looked down at Andrew, even more confused. Of course she had, Sam, Bacchetti, her mother.

"I mean *really* die. They suffer. They linger on and on until all you want is for it to be over for them." An edge of sadness in his voice. "Life is more than just taking a breath. Death isn't that big a deal."

Then he changed direction. "The first time I expected to feel guilty. After a while I felt guilty because I didn't feel guilty." Andrew paused and smiled, a private smile. "I was trying to feel how I thought I was supposed to feel. Not how I actually felt. Now I just do it. For my own reasons.

"But none of that is important," he ended abruptly, and came up the stairs.

He reached into his sweatshirt pocket and pulled out a green-jacketed U.S. passport and handed it to her.

"The resemblance is extraordinary," he said and started down the hall toward his room. "Almost too extraordinary."

Karla thumbed back the cover: the woman in the photograph could have been a younger version of herself.

"I leave in two hours," Andrew said. "The choice is yours." Then he stepped into his room and closed the door.

Go with him, her every instinct told her. Trust him.

He isn't a lie.

Chapter 15

Murphy stepped onto screened-in porch behind his house, breath frosting in the pre-dawn chill. Liz had risen early and gone to the gym and he was alone. From within the house came the timeless riffs of Miles and his horn feeling their way through the darkness.

Coffee mug in hand, Murphy turned his attention to the dark outline of the shed at the back of the yard where he secured the weapons and ballistics reports months earlier. Only Liz and Plum knew he didn't destroy them.

The telephone rang and he went inside to answer. He lowered the volume on the stereo set to a murmur as he picked up the handset.

"Can you talk?"

He recognized Georges' voice, the French accent, immediately. They agreed his French colleague would contact him only when he had something — and only at home. The AD and Hendricks were watching his every move; Plum seemed his only ally.

"Yes. Where are you?"

"A place called Praia da Luz," Georges replied.

Murphy cast about for the place in his mind. *Luz* meant light — *la lumière* in French.

"It's a small resort on the southern coast of Portugal," Georges said, seeming to read his mind. "It's approximately one hundred fifty kilometers from the Spanish frontier."

The coast west of Spain was unfamiliar to him. "Where do I fly into?"

"There isn't any point. Kiefer's gone."

Strangely Murphy felt unmoved, untouched, as if he had just learned of a distant relative's death. He hadn't expected Georges to find Karla, only her trail.

"She was staying with an American expatriate in a house not far from here," the Frenchman went on. "Three weeks ago they disappeared. The trail is dead."

Still Murphy felt compelled to go. "What's the nearest airport?"

There was silence at the other end of the line, as if Georges didn't approve, as if his going was unprofessional, but Murphy knew they would have left something for him, something for him to follow.

"I know these people, Georges. I may see something you don't."

He heard an audible sigh.

"Very well. There is an airport one and a half hour's drive from here, in Faro. You'll need to make a connection. London will be best. A British Air flight leaves every day in the early afternoon."

Murphy thought for a moment. He could call the office, tell them he'd caught a bug, the flu or something, and would be out for a few days. No one would know.

"I'll catch the first available flight and make the connection."

"I'll monitor arrivals."

"We shouldn't meet at the airport," Murphy said.

More silence.

"We can meet here in Luz, in a turnout overlooking the sea."

The Frenchman gave him directions then. After hanging up, Murphy hurried upstairs to pack a bag. The last item he tossed in was a passport in the name of James Carty. The occupation listed was an innocuous one, commercial sales. He had it made up when he worked at Interpol headquarters in Saint-Cloud. Another rule he'd bent.

Before leaving he scribbled a note to Liz. In it he wrote he had to go, that he had no choice and that he loved her and would be back in a few days. Friday at the latest.

***

Late the next afternoon Murphy drove past Val Verde camping. He had flown uneventfully out of New York using the Carty ID, lost a night over the Atlantic, then made the British Air connection in London and landed in Faro three hours later. He rented a car at the airport, traveled west on Route N125 through Lagos and turned off the main road as Georges instructed when he saw the sign for the camping place.

The sun immoderate in its brightness seethed overhead and heat waves shimmered in the distance. Murphy squinted in the glare. Off to his left a grove of scraggly trees clung to life, the earth below scorched, sepia-brown, and it occurred to Murphy that when he exited the plane in Faro he had left every vestige of winter behind.

A few minutes later he drove into Praia da Luz. The town had the feel of a fishing village cum resort, reminding him of a vintage Mexican beach resort, quaint in a way that offended his sensibilities. He passed a real estate agency on the left — LUZ BAY CLUB proclaimed a sign affixed to the wall. Farther along he came to the strip of shops Georges mentioned. He turned left at the next intersection and followed a cobbled lane down to the turnout overlooking the sea.

Georges was leaning against a car in the unpaved turnout, a white Ford Fiesta rental not unlike the one he rented. The Frenchman raised a hand in acknowledgement. Georges had changed little since they had worked together in Saint-Cloud: he was still tall and trim, an elegant dresser, distinguished looking with a new hint of silver at his temples. He looked like someone who would stay at a place called the Luz Bay Club.

A well-traveled Vauxhall van was parked opposite Georges' car, fast against the seawall that rimmed the turnout on three sides. The van had UK number plates and an AUS disk on the rear window, CAPE TOWN OR BUST traced in the dust. Free campers, Murphy thought as he pulled up in front of Georges' car. Young vagabonds.

Georges climbed into his rental and started the engine. Murphy got out and as he locked the car doors he took another look at the van. Makeshift curtains hung at each of the windows concealing whoever or whatever was inside. It's kids. Free spirits.

He walked around Georges' car and hopped in.

"The directions were satisfactory?"

"Perfect."

"Naturally." His friend didn't mince words — one of the things Murphy liked about him. "It isn't far."

Georges reversed at speed, differential whining, then swung around and raced up the hill. When they came to the intersection he drove straight through without slowing. French drivers, Murphy thought. As they continued up the hill they passed a block of shabby buildings, a band of ragged children chasing a soccer-ball along a dirt lane. The scene belying the quaint village atmosphere that lay behind them.

Then they were out in open country. After a short distance they came to a gathering of snow-white villas, an oasis in the otherwise parched landscape. Within the encampment walls sprinklers shot sheets of water into the air, and it occurred to Murphy that the desert-like starkness would have appealed to Karla, the sense of desolation familiar after her years in the desert, sane.

"How did you find her?"

"A rumor," Georges said, keeping his eyes on the road "You told me Kiefer was traveling on a U.S. passport, though frankly that wasn't much help. You Americans travel here without discretion. No one keeps track. So I tried another tack."

Georges paused for a moment and smiled as if sharing a private joke. "I decided to investigate her group, indirectly of course. I looked for coincidences, for rumors, for gossip. These people are like old women at times. Finally, a rumor surfaced that piqued my interest. You said there was a shooter in Vermont and the rumor had Kiefer living with a shooter."

"No. She didn't know about the shooter."

The Frenchman gazed at him for a moment, then without comment turned back to the road. They were approaching a crossroads. A clot of dingy buildings languished on the far side of the intersection; on the right a red and white road milepost — N125 — stood at the edge of the tarmac.

"At any rate," Georges said as he turned left and joined the main road, "the coincidence intrigued me so I drew up a list of possible shooters. The list was necessarily short since professional assassins don't normally associate with Kiefer's people. The one who lives here was the last on my list. That he is a shooter is only a rumor."

They were zipping along now, the landscape undulating before them.

"His name is Black, Andrew Black. Though my sources referred to him variously as Blanc, Wit, Weiss." The Frenchman smiled again. "These people … such jokers, Jim." Then more seriously: "Black is twenty-eight, average height, medium build. Brown hair, brown eyes. Absolutely ordinary. A person you would never notice. Except he lives in a villa on the Algarve."

George accelerated through a curve, tires squealing.

"He inherited the villa in 1967 after his parents died in an automobile accident. He moved here permanently in 1972 or '73, shortly after completing his university studies. He took a degree in philosophy of all things.

"At university Black had a reputation as a marksman, a biathlete. Interestingly his roommate at Stanford was a Palestinian named Khalil al-Fasani."

Murphy felt a tingle of recognition.

"Al-Fasani is clean as far as I can tell," Georges said. "He works as a financial analyst at Chase Manhattan in New York. His father was a Palestinian activist who eventually gave it up for the good life in Riyadh. Then a week ago, leafing through an Action Directe report, I found a report in which an informant of questionable character claimed Black was the shooter in Querétaro. He may have assassinated your Secretary of State."

Another tingle. Another connection, Murphy thought, another parallel. Though he sensed Black hadn't been the shooter in Vermont — that would be too improbable, too pat even for the Red Path — yet he felt certain they put Black and Karla together for a reason.

Georges was still talking. "Kiefer was definitely here. Several people saw a woman matching her description in Black's car. The first time was shortly after the shootout in Vermont," he added, seeming to read Murphy's mind. "Then, as I said, in early March they vanished. No one seems to know exactly when or why."

"Could you have spooked them?"

Georges shook his head, shifted down a gear and powered through another curve. "I didn't know about Black until ten days ago. The day before yesterday I found his car parked in a long-term lot at the Lisbon airport. No one named Black has flown out of Lisbon in the past month."

"So he's traveling on different passport."

"Or he wants us to think he is. Black is a man of discipline, of routine. One of the local people referred to him as '*um homen do ritual.*'" Georges shifted back up. "There is one other thing. Another rumor. Black may have been the shooter in El Salvador."

Murphy felt his skin prickle. There was a symmetry to it — not two weeks ago the media "discovered" the military advisor killed in San Salvador during an FPL bank robbery was a CIA operative — each revelation like harmony added to an atonal score, each seemingly timed to coax him along the intended path.

"Not sure how you dug all this up, Georges."

The Frenchman smiled. "People talk to me."

He pulled onto the verge and parked below a grove of cork oak, their trunks and lower limbs scarred where the harvesters' axes had done their work. A small house crowned the hill ahead, a dirt lane leading to it, and Murphy couldn't help but think of the day months earlier when he sat in another car, below another house. But unlike that day it wasn't cold and gray, and this time he knew Karla was gone. Fled once more.

An easy calm laced the air. The house, a compact affair, was Mediterranean in style with thick chalk-white walls that promised shelter from the summery heat. Behind it was a wash of vivid-blue sky. Silence everywhere.

"Seen enough?"

Georges had shut down the engine and sat hunched forward, arms balanced on top of the steering wheel.

"Have you been inside?"

"You asked that I be discreet."

"Let's have a look."

Georges shifted his weight on the seat, gazed straight ahead.

"What's troubling you?"

He wagged his head.

"I'm intrigued," he said finally. "I admit that. But we are out here alone when there isn't any reason for us to be alone, being discreet when there isn't any reason to be discreet. You seem obsessed by this."

Murphy remembered Georges' silences on the phone the previous day, his obvious reluctance. He had asked for his friend's trust and given nothing in return.

"I know I'm taking this personally. I'm not so obsessed that I don't recognize that. But the Red Path set me and the Bureau up in Vermont and if we are careful …"

"Why?"

"Why what?"

Georges faced him now. "Why did they set you up?"

"That's what I'm trying to find out." An edge of frustration unmistakable in his voice.

"We shouldn't be going in like this. We don't have any authority here. We aren't thieves."

"I've never known you to worry about authority."

Georges turned away, shook his head slowly. "That is what I miss about working with you, Jim. Your respect for rules."

"And protocol."

"That too."

Then his friend laughed, a laugh of surrender, and reached for the key. He restarted the engine, the sound lost among the hills, and pulled back onto the blacktop. Without slowing he turned into the dirt lane. Murphy cranked his window all the way down. The faint salt-smell of ocean in the air.

A bicycle was leaning against the house as if abandoned; dead leaves were gathered around the front stoop. Off to their right the carport stood empty. Georges swung the car around and backed in. They both got out and examined the house for several moments, checking for movement at the windows, the sound of activity, any sign of life, then walked into the sunshine and around to the back of the house as if they were expected guests. Which in a way, Murphy believed, they were. Expected.

A short flight of stairs led to the back terrace. Full-length windows flanked the glass door that served as the rear entrance, the drapes pulled shut. Georges stole up the stairs and tested the doorknob to see if it was unlocked, then produced a long narrow shiv. While he worked the lock, Murphy surveyed the hills behind the house. Oak groves rolled north to merge with pinewoods in the distance, the woods like a dark shadow along the horizon. There wasn't a single house in sight, or other type of habitation.

In the west the sun was ebbing, losing its fire, though Murphy still felt the sultry heat as if it were midday. He heard the lock give and after one last look at the hills went up the stairs. Without a word Georges slipped into the house and he followed.

Inside was cool as expected, shadowy, the air musty and still. There appeared to be only two rooms on the main floor — a kitchen and the living room. A clock, like a metronome, ticked in the kitchen. Batik prints and dark tribal masks hung on the living room walls. The furnishings were sparse and spare befitting the place. A tautly padded leather sofa claimed the center of the room; a modest wooden stereo cabinet stood against one wall, a pair of bentwood chairs flanking it. A simple console table with a telephone resting on top, a sort of still life.

Coarsely woven throw rugs were scattered on the terracotta floor, all placed with thought and care. The place possessed a certain charm, Murphy realized, though it seemed aseptic to him, like a trendy photograph in *Architectural Digest*. As if no one lived there.

Still silent they split up, Georges taking the kitchen and him the upstairs. As he mounted the stairs Murphy noticed the museum-like stillness again. There were two bedrooms on the second floor, each a monastic cell with a single iron-framed bed and a tiny window set in the wall facing the door. He paused in one of the doorways. A shaft of sunlight slanted through the window casting a golden haze over the room. A cinematic effect. Dust motes hung suspended in the air.

Georges called out to him and he retreated to the top of the stairs. "Yeah?"

"I found something." Georges' voice was muffled, seeming far away.

Murphy trotted down the stairs. As he was crossing the living room he noticed a wrinkle along the edge of one of the throw rugs. He kicked it back into place and continued toward the kitchen. Like the rest of the house the kitchen was spartan, austere. On the left a door opened onto a cellar, a light burned at the foot of the stairs.

"What'd you find?"

"You should see this," Georges called.

He went down the stairs and found Georges standing in front of a gaping hole in the cellar wall. He was holding up a handgun.

"Black is definitely a shooter. It's a Hämmerli 208. Very unique, .22-caliber."

But Murphy already knew that Black was a shooter. Because it was ironic and the people running Karla seemed to love irony. What he couldn't understand was why Black left the gun behind when he and Karla fled.

And all once it came to him. Black didn't leave the gun, the

Red Path did. It was what they had left for him. They were playing Black too.

Chapter 16

The road seemed to crawl up the hillside. Karla ran at Andrew's shoulder, short of breath, determined to keep up. On either side of the road were clusters of live oak, their leaves dull and limp in the California heat, and stubbly patches of dry-yellow grass. Not an inkling of a breeze.

Andrew held the pace as they passed a side road — a sign among the trees: WILCOX SOLAR OBSERVATORY. For nearly a month they had been running in the foothills west of Stanford. Andrew insisted on the daily workouts from the start; he never varied their route. The discipline appealed to him, Karla knew, the regularity and routine, but she felt there was something more to the runs, something about these hills, about this place.

She shot Andrew a glance. He held himself erect, loose-jawed, breathing easily, arms swinging freely at his sides. He ran as if with a purpose, as if with a mission. He'd been the same way the night of their escape, she remembered, during the long dark drive down the coast road. The wind came up before they left and drove clouds in front of the moon, and even after her eyes adjusted to the greater darkness she was barely able to make out the bundled shapes of the trees at the edge of the road. Yet Andrew drove to the Lisbon cutoff and beyond, more than twenty miles, before switching on the headlights. It was as if he had memorized the road.

Later, Karla found out he had. He'd stored away every detail, every rise and fall, every twist and turn in the road against the day he would have to flee. It was inevitable, he told her as they drove north. *I knew they would come for me some day.*

And he spoke with absolute equanimity, she recalled. Not once did his voice betray the slightest emotion, as if his house and home, his life and past, *his* history, meant nothing to him.

Karla thought of her life in the desert, of the odd innocence of her daily devotions on the Syrian ridgetop, then of Sam and Vermont and what she did. But she felt only regret, regret at the futility of it, the pointlessness, and she realized their part — hers and Sam's — was just that, a part. Pure artifice.

The waste, she thought as she continued at Andrew's side. The utter waste.

The tangle of oaks gave way to a broad expanse of open field and in places there were thistles, like leggy bouquets, along the edge of the road. A dirt single-track crept through the field on their right and blazed up a short hill, but they kept to the road. The true summit lay farther on, a few hundred yards away.

Andrew shifted up a gear and Karla stayed with him, matching him stride for stride. The sun bore down on her and her thighs began to burn. Her head pounded and her heart surged, but she forged on, focusing on the road, on the slap of their running shoes, on her own breath. Then without seeming effort her body slipped into the pace, and Karla felt the glow in her legs, a loosening in her chest, vibrance and strength. A second wind.

When they came to the summit area they continued on without a break in the pace. Grasslands, more golden each day, rolled before them in a series of shallow swells; cows dotted their flanks and there were other runners here — joggers, fartlekers, shufflers — all headed in the opposite direction, following the gray ribbon of asphalt back to the campus. Without fail she and Andrew raised a hand in silent greeting as they swept past.

Off to their left, barely visible beyond the ridgeline, was a massive radio telescope. Most days a hydraulic arm propped the huge dish upright and it loomed monstrous against the sky. But today it lay on its back, asleep, and not for the first time Karla wondered if the telescope had something to do with their presence here.

She raised an arm toward the dish.

"They study the atmosphere," Andrew said without breaking stride. "SRI operates it." Then he lapsed into silence. Since they'd arrived in Palo Alto an easy camaraderie had blossomed between them and he spoke more easily now, more openly, though with no less economy.

Time, Karla told herself. She would understand in time, why they came here. Then she could decide what part she might play.

They swung left onto a branch road before they reached the ridgeline and followed it west. A cattle grid bridged the road ahead, twin strands of barbed wire fencing stretching in both directions. They quick-stepped across the metal bars and began to wind downhill, lengthening their stride, running easily, side by side. Before long the road turned to a mix of gravel and broken-up asphalt and the freeway came into view, eight lanes of blacktop cutting through the pale-gold countryside, and even after weeks running the route Karla found the sight incongruous, out of place.

At the foot of the hill they crossed another cattle grid and into a tunnel that passed beneath the roadway, the air cool, cave-like. A car rumbled overhead, then another as they ran back into the sunshine. They powered up a short rise, the road surface hard-packed dirt now, and slipped down the backside and found themselves in a ravine, the air fresh and piquant, alive with the sound of birdsong and passing automobiles.

Soon, they left the ravine behind and came to a reservoir that lay in a depression in the landscape. Felt Lake, Andrew called it. They crossed a spillway, picking their way through a series of sinkholes left from the cows' daily treks through the mud during rainy season, and followed a dirt track along the shoreline. Flies rose around their ankles as they wove through the plops of cow dung.

At the far end of the reservoir a gigantic oak sprawled atop the embankment that formed the north shore. The oak was uncultivated, gnarled and old, and appeared half-dead. Beyond it, down a short pitch, were the town of Portola Valley and their usual route back to the campus. Today, however, when they came to the ancient oak Andrew turned them back and they retraced their steps along the shoreline and started up the southern slope of the watershed.

There wasn't a track here, not even a trail, and Karla fell in behind, careful with her step on the uneven ground. The unshorn grass dragged at her legs as she followed Andrew up the steep slope, followed him as she had across Portugal, then on to New York and California, followed him if for no other reason than her belief that if she stayed with him long enough she would learn something about herself, about what she did.

"You okay?" Andrew called over his shoulder.

"I'm fine." She huffed, blinking at the sweat in her eyes.

"Tell me if I'm pushing too hard."

She nodded, conserving her breath. She could feel the steepness in her legs, in her thighs, along the backs of her calves. On their left was a row of eucalyptus, beyond that more strands of barbed wire fence. Where was he taking her?

Andrew eased up and she pushed past him, churning up the last bit of hill, then slowed to a walk, hands on her hips, head back, sucking air.

"Good run."

Karla bobbed her head, leaned forward and rested her hands on her knees, still trying to catch her breath.

"You're getting strong," he said.

She squinted down at him. "You're trying to wear me out."

Andrew gazed at her for a few moments, then smiled and turned to face the reservoir. The back of his shirt was soaked, she noticed, his hair wet, ropey with sweat. Otherwise he seemed unfazed by the run. Composed.

Like a bombardier — she thought — peering through the sights.

She wondered about the rifle, the type he would use. It would be precise, she decided. Like him. *Exakt.*

"You shouldn't speak in German."

The sound of Andrew's voice startled her. He was still facing the reservoir, slightly downhill from her, in the bark-strewn area beneath the trees. She let her eyes wander over the scene below, the setting placid, idyllic. A series of dirt tracks converged on the lake — each offering a different approach, a different angle, a different field — and now she knew why Andrew varied their route. Below them lay the killing field.

"This is the place," she said.

Andrew acted as if he hadn't heard.

"You told the Swiss three or four weeks."

Still he remained silent.

"You brought me here for a reason. The shooting is at hand and you want me to know."

Andrew squatted down and plucked a strip of eucalyptus bark from the ground, sniffed it. "His name is Velasquez," he said finally. "Jorge Velasquez. He runs here every evening."

"Who is he?"

"The Mexican energy minister."

"Neither side wants him assassinated."

Andrew turned his head and looked up at her. "True."

Karla felt lost. "Then why?"

He smiled, a wry smile. "For that very reason. There are no sides, Karla. Plum proved that."

And with that she began to understand. The Red Path operation wasn't about the Palestinians, or even the old man. It was about power, control. And everything hung on her executing Bacchetti. Raymond was adamant, she remembered. But he suspected — no, knew — that I would try to salvage the operation so he sent the shooter ... to force my hand.

The thought stopped Karla. She went back over it in her mind, the crack of the first shot, Sam dropping, the severity of his wound. Then putting the gun to the old man's head ... *Use the handgun we discussed.* And she understood that too.

"The shooter didn't miss," she said, her voice surprisingly calm.

Andrew looked at her, perplexed.

"He was there for Sam," she said, still not believing the depth of Raymond's — and Khalil's — betrayal. "He wounded Sam intentionally so I would exact revenge."

A look of recognition: "With the Browning Hi-Power."

"Exactly. They are setting someone up."

"The FBI," Andrew said. "Khalil told me about it."

Then he stopped and Karla could see his mind working. "The shooter's rifle will lead to the CIA."

Of course, she thought. It was about betrayal ... *about power, control.*

A cow lowed in the distance. After several moments a small herd appeared in the wash below the spillway. One of the cows broke away, trotting, and lowered its head to the water.

"When did you leave the camp?" Andrew had turned back to the reservoir.

"In August."

"When in August?"

"Later in the month. Why?"

"I was just wondering when it really began," he said and paused to consider that. After a few moments he rolled his shoulders and shrugged. "It doesn't matter. No one knows ..."

Andrew turned and raced up the hill, grabbed her arm and pulled her back among the trees as a pair of runners crested the embankment at the far end of the reservoir. The runners — both were women, Karla noticed — trotted past the sprawling oak.

Beside her, Andrew remained absolutely still. Like an animal scenting the air. His hand was still on her arm and she could smell the sweat on him, feel the heat coming off his body as the women, arms extended at their sides for balance, skidded down the embankment to the dirt track. When they came to the spillway they threaded their way through the cows and started down the wash.

She felt Andrew uncoil beside her.

"They didn't see us," he said.

Then he noticed his hand on her arm and took it away, and for a moment Karla wished it was still there as impossible as that seemed, to feel his touch, to have him hold her. She felt a flash of warmth and let it go.

"I'll stand guard for you."

Andrew stepped away. "I'll be fine." He began to prowl among the trees, curls of eucalyptus bark, like ancient parchment, crackling beneath his running shoes. "I always work alone."

"But you will be exposed here."

"No," he said, still prowling, checking the angles and fields of fire.

"Then why did you bring me here? Why didn't you leave me?"

Andrew stopped, peered up at her, eyes narrowed "Let's just say I don't like to see people being used."

"Can't you believe I feel the same way?"

"No." Not — no, he didn't believe her. No, he didn't want her to get involved.

"You helped me. Now let me help you."

He was moving again. "You don't owe me anything."

But she did — she owed him this.

"I fucked up, I know that. I let Raymond use us."

"This isn't about revenge."

And all at once she realized why Andrew brought her here. He wanted her to see that taking the energy minister was a deliberate act — a statement, not mindless anger. An assault on power itself. And he was giving her the only thing he could, what he had learned.

Karla felt another flush, of gratitude this time. "I understand. This time it will be my choice. Not Raymond's, not Khalil's."

Andrew stopped again, his gaze inescapable, without a shred of pretense.

"Not even yours per se," she added.

"You watch," he said. "Watch only. If someone comes along, call out to them. A greeting. Anything. And I'll withdraw. We're not here to sacrifice ourselves."

"It's decided then."

"Yes, for now."

Then a smile drifted across Andrew's face, an ironic smile. "Perhaps I intended to use you all along."

But Karla knew that wasn't possible. His conscience wouldn't allow it.

***

Sunset — the same day.

The last rays of sunlight glinted off the surface of the reservoir and cast a rosy blush over the landscape. The sharp pungent scent of eucalyptus in the air. The trees stood motionless overhead. In the distance a dog howled.

At strangers, Karla thought. Or shadows.

It was still warm so she unzipped her sweatshirt partway and let the front blouse out as she waited. After dropping Andrew along Arastradero Road she parked the car they had rented next to the non-descript office building he showed her earlier and followed the faint path up the backside of the hill to the barbed wire fence and line of trees. He wouldn't be long, he told her. Twenty minutes at most.

That afternoon he had explained how it would go, his voice soft and gentle belying the intent of his words …

Velasquez comes shortly after sunset when no one else is around. Like most people he mistakes privacy for anonymity. It will be over before he knows it.

A flock of geese appeared, their sleek compact bodies swooping low over the watershed, dark wings extended, gliding, then back-flapping as they settled honking and splashing onto the lake. The surface rippled and tiny waves lapped at the far shore.

Then it was quiet, calm. The geese floating, drifting; the dog in the distance silent.

***

Ten minutes later Andrew ducked through the barbed wire, rifle case in hand. Karla watched him take up position among the eucalyptus thirty yards below her, set the case on the ground and squat beside it. She heard the locks click and saw his hand slip

242

into the case and pull out the olive-drab weapon. After inserting a magazine he dropped to one knee and brought the rifle to his shoulder ...

I'll take him along the track. Before he reaches the spillway.

The same soothing tone. Yet he spoke with feeling, Karla remembered, with passion, and she sensed it now as his hand went to the telescopic sight, his skin pale against the dull-green housing. He flipped up the lens covers and swung the rifle in a series of stops along the track, seeming to envision it in his mind.

Then he lowered the weapon and rested it on top of the open case and settled back on his haunches, peasant-style. Not once did he look in her direction or acknowledge her presence. As if he were alone, she thought.

A warm gust of wind swept across the slope. Andrew rose slightly and turned to face it, testing its velocity and exact direction. Then he eased back on his heels, the tall grass still, and it was as if he hadn't moved. As if time present and time past had merged, fused in a perfect weld.

Then something in the air changed and he was up on one knee again, rifle at his shoulder. Karla spotted them: four men topping the rise at the far end of the reservoir as the women had earlier that day. She watched Andrew track the men as they passed the ancient oak, as they scuff-skidded down the embankment. Track them as they trotted along the shoreline, as they approached the spillway. Karla holding her breath without realizing it, seeing Andrew completely for the first time. On his own ... alone. Nietzsche's *Übermensch*. The act itself.

The crack of the first shot shattered the calm. The geese exploded into flight, screaming, and the first man went down — *Velasquez*. Then another crack and the second man fell. Then another, Karla watching in horror-fascination.

The last man reversed direction and galloped back toward the embankment, toward the oak, as if toward some imagined sanctuary. Andrew shot him as he started up the rise. His head snapped forward, bursting, and Karla flashed on Bacchetti's head slamming against the back panel of the car … the man down there stumbling, lurching forward as if he had tripped. Then his legs gave way and his body crumbled soundlessly to the ground. Madness. He killed them all.

"Let's go," Andrew called. He had already re-packed the weapon.

Karla ran to the wire, hauled up the top strand so he could pass through and followed. She led the way down the backside of the hill.

"Slow down."

She eased up, adrenaline coursing through her, bitter in her mouth. Felt Andrew come up behind her and peel off. Still running, she twisted partway around and saw him cutting across the slope on her left, heading toward a thick stand of trees.

"Pick me up where you dropped me," he shouted. Then he was gone, among the trees. A mage.

Karla swung back around and picked up the pace, the daily runs paying off. The tall grass whipped at her legs. She felt something wet on her hand, looked down and saw the oozing wound on her palm, red rivulets of blood trailing down her fingers. A sharp stab of pain. Without slowing, she raised her hand to her mouth and sucked at the wound, the blood salty and thick, metallic.

Then she saw it all again: Andrew tracking the men, detached, alone; the great gouts of blood; the bodies crashing to the ground, thrashing wildly, like slaughtered beasts — and she realized this was Andrew's world, not hers. She may have let go of her past but she couldn't let go of herself, of who she was: she had to be *a* part of the world, not *apart*.

And it was as if she was seeing without blinders for the first time. Beyond politics, beyond illusion. Unfettered.

Alone … but not alone.

The office building came into view, their car parked in the otherwise vacant lot, then the road among the trees beyond. A lone cyclist, his head bowed low over the handlebars, flickered past. He didn't slow down.

Nor did she.

Chapter 17

Still feeling the rush of flight Andrew waited at the edge of the road in the gathering darkness. He expected it would be hours before the authorities cordoned off the area, maybe even morning before the bodies were found, the series of shots dismissed as backfires, as kids taking potshots in the watershed.

His thoughts turned to Karla. She handled herself near-perfectly and he had to admit it had been reassuring having her there, on the hillside above him as he made the shots. He had never felt so exposed, so out there, so in control. So much the renegade.

Andrew felt another rush, like an elixir flowing through his veins. In the near distance he could hear the hum of evening traffic on Page Mill Road. To the south a nimbus of light — Silicon Valley — shimmered beyond the trees, while higher up a sliver of moon was clearly visible in the darkening sky. The road before him quiet, rural, worlds away it seemed.

He heard a vehicle leave the flow of traffic and after a few moments a car came around the bend, headlight beams dull in the dusky light. Albert's courier was right on time. Andrew remained where he was, hidden among the trees, and watched the car slow and turn into the dirt lane thirty yards away, and as he did he was struck by a sense of *déjà vu*, of having seen this before.

Not forty minutes ago he watched the same car, the same man etched in the driver's side glass, turn into the lane, and now as then Albert's man looked like he belonged here, as if driving down a dirt road that led nowhere was the most natural thing in the world.

Andrew pictured the man pulling up at the stone barricade a quarter of a mile away, getting out of the car and retrieving the case from behind the pile of rocks, tossing it into the trunk, then getting back in and driving peaceably back up the lane.

The car toddled back into view and slowed further as it approached the blacktop. Then without so much as a glance in his direction the courier pulled back onto the pavement and returned the way he had come, the weapon en route to Albert. They were away clean.

Both he and Karla, Andrew thought feeling a strange and uncharacteristic euphoria. It's a remnant of the kill, he told himself, an oxygen rush. The same thing you experience after a long ride. Endorphins, nothing more.

When the car slipped from view, he stepped from the shelter of the trees and at that moment their car appeared in the opposite direction as if Karla was waiting for him to show himself. The car coasted toward him, lights off. She was driving cautiously though not obtrusively, and he could see her indistinct shape hunched over the steering wheel as she struggled to make out the road in the dim light. She gave him a fluttery wave and he raised a hand in return.

He hopped in and they drove away slowly.

"You should put on the headlights."

Karla reached forward awkwardly with one hand, steadying the wheel with her thigh, and switched on the lights, her other half-curled in her lap. There was a smear of blood on her palm, dry streaks on her fingers.

"You've hurt yourself."

"It's nothing."

"Let me see."

Karla slid her hand across her lap, away from him. He could see the line of determination along her jaw, and remembered the day she arrived at his house, pulling away when he reached for her pack. *I can handle it.* The way she cinched the strap tight on her injured shoulder. He saw the blue-black bruise the next day.

Then, as if remembering as well, Karla slid her hand across her thighs and let him take it. Her skin was icy cold. It was a minor wound, Andrew saw, a three-quarter inch-long gash that had bled a good deal, but the bleeding had slowed, the blood grainy and rust-colored where it had dried along the edges of the wound.

"It's nothing," she said again without looking at him, keeping her eyes on the road.

Andrew dug in the glove box and pulled out a wad of Kleenex. He dabbed at the wound and she winced.

"Are you all right?"

"I'll be fine," she replied, taking back her hand. "It must have happened when I spread the barbed wire. I didn't even feel it." Then she paused as if she realized she was arguing too much, denying too much. "We all have our quirks."

"And yours is pigheadedness."

"Absolutely."

Then she turned and gave him a wistful bittersweet smile, and not for the first time Andrew wondered how Khalil could have betrayed her.

***

Twenty minutes later they pulled to the curb in front of the house they had rented on Fulton Street. The house lay east of Middlefield and south of University Avenue, a neighborhood of academics and young professionals, of renovated bungalows. When prompted, Andrew told the real estate agent they were doing independent research at Stanford. It was late in the academic year and the agent accepted his explanation without comment.

They sat in silence for several minutes, surveying the street and cars parked along it, listening. Crickets chirped, the stray voice of a television. In most of the houses the lights were dimmed, drapes drawn shut, though many of the front doors were open in celebration of the early spring heat.

"There isn't anyone," Karla said.

Andrew nodded and pushed his door open and got out. He ran his eyes over the street as he waited for Karla to come around the car. She flowed past him and up the front walk, shoulders squared, her injured hand carried loosely at her side, and he was reminded of the last day at his house watching her climb the hillside, watching as much to see the way she moved as to confirm the stranger's presence. He closed his eyes for a moment, fending off the thought.

Karla stepped onto the porch, unlocked the front door and went inside. He followed silently. She marched across the living room to the hallway and bathroom beyond. The light flashed on. From the darkness of the living room Andrew watched her strip off her sweatshirt, toss it aside and step to the vanity. He could see the slope of her breasts in the mirror, her nipples hard beneath her T-shirt, thighs pressed firmly against the sink.

He turned away sharply. Craziness! Now is neither the time nor the place.

Yet Andrew felt powerless, as if whatever lay between them had reached critical mass. Was inevitable.

He retreated to the front window. It was full night now. He heard the faucet go on, Karla humming softly as she cleaned the wound, washed away the blood. Almost mercifully visions of the men in the watershed came back to him: their heads snapping, blood spraying, forming halos ...

Then he was tracking the last man, taking his time. The man wasn't a bodyguard — bodyguards didn't panic, didn't run. He was harmless, a no one. Perhaps one of Velasquez's hosts. Yet instinct demanded that he be taken, that no witnesses be left alive.

"What do you see?"

The question brought Andrew back abruptly. He could feel Karla behind him, on the far side of the room.

Outside, the light of the streetlamps reflected off the cars.

"Nothing."

He turned and saw her standing in the doorway between the living room and hall, hip cocked against the jamb, a strip of white adhesive tape on her injured hand, and even in the near darkness he could see the front of her T-shirt was wet, the sheer fabric clinging to her breasts, the dark shadow of her nipples. She made no attempt to cover herself.

Andrew turned back to the window.

Karla walked softly across the room and stopped behind him, almost on top of him. He smelled the fresh scent of soap on her skin, felt the heat radiating from her, her breath on his neck.

"How's the hand?" A diversion.

"Fine."

She put her hand on his shoulder, squeezed.

"This is insane."

"I know."

Then they were in each other's arms, feverish, kissing, mouths open, tongues searching, seeking. Unbridled lust.

Karla pulled away and in one fluid motion peeled off her T-shirt. Her breasts were pale, taut mounds. As if sensing Andrew's hunger she drew him to her, arched her back, hands in his hair, caressing him.

Andrew ran his tongue over her breast, slid his hand down her spine, stroked the curve of her buttocks. Karla shuddered.

"I'm going to come just thinking about it," she said.

Inflamed, Andrew grabbed at the waistband of her pants. Together they hurried them over her hips, down her thighs, over her calves. Karla kicked them away. Then, frantic, they were tearing at his clothes, yanking down his zipper.

When they were both naked, Karla stood on her toes and straddled his erect penis, gripping him between her thighs. They paused for a moment and kissed deeply, drawing the moment out, securing it in their minds.

Then, still on their feet, they were grinding against one another, Andrew tilting his upper body back slightly, stirring. Karla reached back and cupped the head of his penis and began to stroke lightly. He felt a spasm in his loins, a gush of heat.

"Oh yeah."

She increased the rhythm, harder, faster, his pleasure her pleasure. Andrew grabbed her hips and drove into her, over and over. Again and again. Until he gasped, "Ah …" Hands clenching her hips.

Spent, Andrew felt the blood rush to his face. "I'm sorry. It's been a long time."

Karla nipped at his ear, took his hand and led him into her room and into her bed. They held each other, quiet, bodies entwined, their fingers tracing delicate figures on each other's skin.

In time Andrew was hard again. Karla guided his hand between her thighs, to the wetness there. As he fondled her he took her breast into his mouth. She spread her legs, rocked her hips, moaning.

"I want to feel you inside me," she whispered.

Andrew pushed himself up and knelt between her legs. Half-smile on her face, Karla reached out and touched him. He entered slowly, easing deeper. She gasped. He leaned forward, arms supporting his weight, and kissed her damp forehead gently; her arms encircled him.

They went more slowly this time, exploring each other, their secret places, their little joys. Hips locked, they rocked together, finding a common rhythm.

Karla pressed her hand against the small of his back urging him deeper, deeper, until she cried out to him and he to her, bound in the moment.

A moment that was timeless, eternal.

***

Some hours later Andrew awoke. Outside, all was quiet. Light flooded through the bedroom window making Karla's silky skin glow. Like moonlight on a fresh field of snow.

He watched her sleep for a while, her lips parted slightly, chest rising and falling lightly with each breath. He knew she was gone, lost to him. He sensed it in the car earlier when she smiled — *wistful, bittersweet.* A seraphic smile. She had known too. Yet they made love — because they knew they had no future.

Andrew leaned forward and kissed her lightly on the cheek, an act of reverence. For a moment they were *simpático.* And it was agreeable. No, more than that, he thought, remembering their shared passion. Cherished.

Karla stirred. Her hand strayed to his chest. Finding him, she smiled. He snuggled closer.

"Du warst so objektiv. So konzentriert."

She was talking about the moment on the hillside, Andrew knew. And that she speaking in German was intentional, a statement. She was already gone.

He felt a surge of sadness, of loss, absorbed it. They'd had their moment, a rare moment of intimacy, a moment of pure devotion.

"When do you leave?"

Karla opened her eyes. "You know everything."

He smiled. "Not everything."

"You knew from the beginning I would leave."

"In the beginning I didn't want you to come."

"But you helped me anyway."

Andrew looked away — she was making him something he wasn't.

"You can go home now," she said.

"Maybe. Khalil won't be happy. What about you?"

"I don't know. Home eventually. *Aus Deutschland.*"

Her naiveté frightened him.

He turned back to her. "Don't go home, Karla. Don't go anywhere you have ever been. Disappear. I know Plum. And I know Khalil even better. If they think you have turned, they will kill you without a second's thought."

Karla rose onto an elbow and gazed at him, her pale-gray eyes crystal-clear. He wanted to tell her to stay — they could disappear together — but knew that was pointless. Delusion.

"You can't fight them, Karla."

"I can try. I can end the lies."

"You'll lose."

"That isn't the point."

She flung her arms around his neck. "God, it isn't fair."

"Who said it was supposed to be."

"Don't be so rational," she cried.

"Then let it go."

"I can't. I have no choice."

She kissed him long and hard on the mouth. And they began

again, knowing it was for the last time. For all time.

Chapter 18

Karla stepped off the Carey shuttle bus in midtown Manhattan, the first flush of the coming day lighting the sky. The previous evening Andrew dropped her off at the San Francisco airport and she caught the America Airlines red-eye to New York. Both of them found her departure difficult, wrenching even; she missed him already, longed for him, for his gentle touch, for his wry observations, for the simple discipline of their life together, though she knew that any happiness they might find together would be fleeting, illusory.

She had watched Andrew drive away. He didn't look back. In the end he became the old Andrew, the silent Andrew, the rational Andrew. Someone else, someone other than who he was.

Karla collected her pack from the baggage compartment and walked from the East Side Airlines Terminal to Penn Station, checking for a tail all the while. At the station she found an unoccupied seat and spent an hour watching for undue interest though to even the most practiced eye she appeared the typical young traveler in her faded blue jeans and fawn-colored corduroy jacket, a silk headscarf covering her hair.

Not far from her a woman, wasted, anorexic, sat plopped on her grim-faced partner's lap, head drooping by degrees then jerking back up, a junkie's nod. Elsewhere, another woman — a mother, she presumed — scolded a red-faced adolescent, preoccupied commuters billowing around them. At one point she noticed a businessman at one of the kiosks, feigning interest in a magazine. Another lingered at a payphone. Eventually the two men moved off.

Finally, satisfied that she was alone, Karla stowed her pack in a locker and bought a ticket to Montreal. The train was scheduled to depart at 8:55 p.m. Not wanting to wait in the station, to sit still, she went back outside and walked across town to the East River and down to the Brooklyn Bridge, still mindful of a tail, then reversed direction and wandered uptown to Lexington Avenue where she lost herself in the crowd as if rehearsing the final leg of her journey.

From Montreal she planned to take the daily Air France flight to Paris, then work a soft route across France and slip into Germany where she could disappear. She would heed Andrew's advice, however. She wouldn't go home.

Together they decided on Montreal as her exit point. They would suspect she was involved in the shootings, Andrew told her, and Plum would be looking for her. But the last thing he would expect was for her to follow the original escape plan. *Plum lacks a sense of irony. He is without a shred of humor.*

Karla felt herself smile. Andrew liked that, the thought of taunting Raymond, of tormenting him. She had to admit she liked it too, even if it did seem childish, and now she knew where she would make the call.

Destination in mind, Karla continued to press through the crush of pedestrians headed down Lexington. At the next cross-street she swung left, walked one block to Park Avenue and turned uptown again. Shafts of sunlight marked the avenue ahead, the tall buildings like great canyon walls. As she crossed each intersection she felt the draw of the morning sun, the temperature neither hot nor cold, perfect, and for the first time she sensed the promise of New York with its wide boulevards and flowering trees, the promise of a new life, of renewal.

Yet everywhere there was noise, noise as diversion: bleating horns, screeching tires, engines screaming, the occasional shriek like fingernails being drawn down a blackboard. Noise as contradiction, she thought. Trickery.

When she turned west on East 59th, the buildings closed in again, choking off the light as if she had entered a narrow gorge. She checked the reflections in the shop windows, considered doubling back. She reasoned she could make the call from anywhere, from the lobby of one of the office buildings, from the station, from any of the public phones along the way, but the phone booth at the back of the drugstore on West 63rd appealed to her sense of completeness. She was returning to where the beginning met the end.

Directly ahead, a crowd was forming at the crosswalk on Fifth Avenue, the "DON'T WALK" signal flashing red. As Karla eased into the crowd a whistle trilled. Across the way, in front of the Plaza, the stately doorman waved a cab forward with a twitch of his upraised hand. A chic couple bound down the hotel steps and into back of the waiting taxi; the doorman whipped the door shut with a flourish and the cab pulled away. Resonance.

When the signal changed, Karla let the crowd filter past then drifted across Fifth Avenue and continued along Central Park South, weaving through the fashionable citizenry exiting the hotels. Beside her, traffic moved along the avenue without deliberation; she didn't notice anyone matching her pace. Then she felt someone's eyes, like a camera tracking her, and after a few moments she spotted the man at the end of the block watching her from the other side of the street. She met his gaze and he shrank back into the park. He was interested in her body, she realized, not her.

At Sixth Avenue she crossed to the park side of street and fell in behind a group of dread-locked Jamaicans toting steel drums toward Columbus Circle. Morning entertainment. Foot traffic was more scattered on this side of the street so she lengthened her stride and passed the Jamaicans. They smelled of sweat, of ganja. She turned right at the next corner and started up traffic-clogged Central Park West. Exhaust fouled the air. A ragged street person lay asleep on a bench, head pillowed on one arm, while sunlight dappled the leaves above making them appear shiny and wet, vivid-green, though it hadn't rained.

After a couple of blocks Karla picked her way through the stalled traffic and entered the drugstore; the bell tinkled overhead. The clerk — a different man with a rosy drinker's complexion and slicked-back black hair — glanced up from the newspaper spread on the counter. As if on cue she smiled and pointed toward the phone booth in the back; the clerk nodded and returned his attention to the newspaper.

Without hesitating Karla walked down the aisle between the well-stocked shelves and stepped into the phone booth. The fluorescent light fixture buzzed when she secured the door. A fresh tag spray-painted on the wall next to the phone. Echoes everywhere.

She didn't bother with the phone book — she committed the number to memory when she was at the station. Instead she thought of Andrew, his moment alone on the hillside, and knew this was *her* moment. It wasn't about causes anymore. It was about dues, debts, what she considered her debt to existence.

Karla reached up and lifted the handset from its hook, deposited twenty-five cents and dialed the number.

"Good morning, Federal Bureau of Investigation."

Karla sat up. "James Murphy, please." She kept her words to a minimum.

"I'm sorry. SAC Murphy is away from the office today."

She had considered that. "Is there another number where he can be reached?"

"I'm afraid not."

A flutter in her chest.

"It is important that I speak with him."

"Would you care to leave your name and a number where he can contact you?"

"It isn't possible." She heard the urgency in her voice.

"I'll connect you with a member of his squad. One moment, please."

The line seemed to go dead. She imagined the call going out, pictured the agents scrambling, cars screaming onto the street, sirens wailing.

She glanced at her watch, gave herself one minute.

What if they have a car in the area? What if they already know I'm here?

She felt her pulse quicken.

They won't be that fast. Only Andrew knows I came to New York.

Karla stole another glance at her watch. Forty seconds.

The clerk had stepped from behind the counter and was sorting through a box of miscellaneous inventory. Outside, pedestrians continued past the shop door, unconcerned. The clerk lifted his head and peered at her. His gaze wasn't unfriendly.

Karla rolled her eyes as if to say: people. The clerk flashed her a Draculean grin. She shuddered. Ten seconds.

"Plum here."

Karla felt as if she had been struck in the chest. *His name is Plum.*

Get out. Run!

But she couldn't run, not anymore. Running was beneath her, a rat reflex. She had to confront Raymond, who he was, *what* he was.

"Hello?" An echo like a ripple in time.

Karla closed her eyes, emptied her mind. *Alone ... but not alone.*

She cleared her throat. "*Guten Morgen, Raymond.*"

Silence.

He knows now. Who I am. What I am.

"Karla?"

A content smile on her lips, Karla lowered the handset and folded the door open. She left the receiver hanging when she stepped from the phone booth. She wanted him to know she had been here, that she had used this telephone.

"Karla. Karla ... Karla!"

She heard the register of Raymond's voice rise from acknowledgement to despair then command as she walked toward the front of the shop. The clerk flashed her another grin. She thanked him politely, pouring it on, wanting him to remember her, her accent, her face. *Who she was.*

***

Outside, the street was bristling with taxis, testy horns. Karla shunned them and wove across the street briskly. She entered the park and took up position at the top of a knoll where she had an unobstructed view of the drugstore entrance.

She reconsidered her travel plans while she waited. The original escape plan was out, she knew. Raymond would expect that, or for her to remain in New York to exact revenge. But she also knew he couldn't afford to panic and dump endless resources onto the street, and it occurred to her that she was fleeing again. But this time, she promised herself, her flight would be more orderly, more controlled. Like Andrew.

Ten minutes later they arrived without a fuss. A powder-blue sedan pulled to the curb on West 63rd. Two dark-suited men got out and when she saw their faces Karla was astonished yet unsurprised. One was the man who followed her in Portugal, the other her rescuer in Vermont. The bearded freak with the sympathetic eyes.

The bearded man waited outside while his partner went into the drugstore. He peered down Central Park West, eyes moving slowly over the pedestrians. Karla heard the *plink-plink* of steel drums and felt her skin crawl as she saw his gaze settle on the crowd gathering at the park's southwest entrance, zeroing in …

It had been him. Her rescuer Sam's executioner.

Then — Raymond wanted me to escape, to find my way to Andrew, to …

Again resisting the urge to run, Karla moved off swiftly.

∗∗∗

Eight hours later Karla joined the queue at the departure gate at Logan Airport. After retrieving her pack from the station she returned to the East Side Airlines Terminal and bought a ticket for TWA flight 810 to Paris that evening. To quell undue curiosity she booked a roundtrip ticket, Logan to Charles de Gaulle with return in three weeks. Then she bought another ticket on a different airline for the flight to Boston. It had been simple enough — there were plenty of seats available on both flights — and she arrived in Boston in mid-afternoon.

When her turn came, she stepped to the podium and handed her boarding pass and passport to the gate agent. The passport was new and beyond reproach, because it was genuine. Shortly after she and Andrew arrived in Palo Alto, she went through the steps necessary to obtain a U.S. passport. She started at the local library with obituaries that were at least twenty years old, searching for girls whose years of birth were close to her own. Once she found several that seemed appropriate, she requested birth certificates from the various county recorders' offices and sorted through them looking for a pale-eyed child. Then she went to the California DMV and applied for a driver's license. With the license, birth certificate and several passport-sized photos in hand she completed Form DS-11 and paid an expediting fee. As far as anyone knew she was a U.S. citizen named Caroline Hall.

The agent returned the passport, boarding slip tucked neatly in its pages. "Have a nice flight, Miss Hall."

Karla mouthed the name as she walked down the jetway, securing it in her mind. The flight attendant smiled as she stepped on board, the smile bright and feckless, eyes hard as rock candy. She inclined her head in return and held out her boarding pass; the attendant pointed the way.

Her pack bumped against her thigh as she eased down the aisle. Mercifully the row to which she was assigned was unoccupied. She stowed her pack in the overhead bin and collapsed onto the seat next to the window. While waiting for the shuttle bus at the East Side Airlines Terminal she had telephoned the house in Palo Alto, but the line was already disconnected. Then she tried Andrew's house in Portugal without success and assumed he was in transit. She tried again only minutes before boarding.

She attempted to contact Murphy as well. Somewhat to her surprise Directory Assistance had a listing for James and Elizabeth Murphy on Sawmill Road in Stamford — early in the operation a television reporter had cornered Murphy in front of his house, Stamford CT emblazoned at the bottom of the screen. The first time she dialed the number no one had answered. The second time, after she arrived in Boston, a woman picked up on the second ring. Her husband wasn't home, the woman told her. When she asked when he would return, brandishing her accent as she had in the drugstore, the woman become wary. In the end she gave her name, her real name, and promised to call again the next evening at seven o'clock, praying all the while Raymond hadn't tapped the line.

The engines stirred and one of the flight attendants began to recite the safety instructions on the p.a. Karla buckled her seatbelt and sat back, pressing her spine against the seatback. As the plane was pushed back from the gate she saw the lights shining dimly in the terminal concourse. Raindrops streaked the glass, the sky above gray, leaden.

She wondered if Murphy would believe her. She imagined he would think *she* was trying to set him up, not Raymond. The passport. She would give him the passport number to gain his trust. She would give him the Caroline Hall identity.

The plane lurched to a halt at the end of the taxiway then wheeled into position. The engines rumbled, surging, and they were off, gathering speed, fuselage rattling, and as the aircraft rose from the ground Karla couldn't help but wonder about Raymond's plan, the operation's ultimate goal.

Then she remembered: *Power, control.*

Chapter 19

Murphy arrived late to his office, too unsettled to sit behind his desk. Everywhere he saw conspiracy, reflections: Black and the shooter in Vermont, Bacchetti and the dead agent in El Salvador, Karla and his lost daughter, Plum's informant and the "someone inside."

A week ago, shortly after his return from Portugal, the press had learned about the Browning Hi-Power. The AD acknowledged the disappearance of the weapon right way. A clerical error, he called it. Nothing untoward. News reports insinuated collusion. Then there had been Karla's call; she'd said his safety was involved.

Murphy sensed they were approaching the endgame, the final pieces put into play. As he pondered this, Plum stepped into his office unannounced and took possession of a chair facing his desk.

He was shaking his head, clearly annoyed. "The Red Path keeps jacking us around."

Murphy remained standing and gave his young colleague room to vent.

"Now my informant is claiming that Black, with Kiefer's assistance, was behind the Velasquez hit."

Another piece, Murphy thought. He imagined he should be sickened, outraged by the murders, the arbitrariness — one of the dead was a post-doctoral fellow, an astrophysicist accompanying Velasquez and his security team on a run. Yet he felt only a strange moral ambivalence, as if caught in some gray area between good and evil, between empathy and disgust. Between present and past.

He felt Plum's gaze. "They're still playing us. All of us. Black and Kiefer are pawns." He chose not to mention Karla's phone call. "Something more is going on, something larger."

"So what do you want me to do with the info?"

"Send it to the San Francisco office. List it as unverifiable."

"Whatever you say."

Plum got up to leave.

"What did the source say about Black?"

Plum stopped, looked at him, sapphire eyes intense, cold. "Nothing."

"How did he know Black was the shooter?"

"He didn't. He said Kiefer was there and it seemed logical."

Murphy frowned, crossed his arms. He hadn't said anything about logic; he'd said the informant told him Black was the shooter.

"You think the info is bogus?"

Murphy didn't answer directly. "Just considering all possibilities."

Plum seemed to accept that and walked out of his office. Could it be him? The "someone inside?" Plum had been with him every step of the way.

Impossible. You're imagining things. Plum's credentials are impeccable, his career without blemish, ascendant. The next thing you know you'll be finding connections to the JFK assassination.

And the absurdity of it made Murphy want to laugh outloud.

***

7:00 p.m. The sun lingered along the horizon.

Murphy held his wife's hand as they sat in the screen-enclosed porch behind their house, the telephone set on the table before them, a note pad beside it. From the house came the rising and falling melodic voice of Arvo Pärt's *Spiegel im Spiegel*. The music soothing, introspective. He could hear children playing in the next yard, hooting and screaming with delight, a football looping back and forth above the hedge separating the two plots. Back and forth, back and forth …

The telephone rang and Murphy started. He let go of Liz's hand and picked up the handset. "Hello." It was his work voice, earnest.

"Is this James Murphy?"

"Karla …"

She cut him off. "I must be quick. You have been compromised."

But Murphy wouldn't let her rush him. "Was that you in Palo Alto?"

There was a momentary silence at the other end of the line.

"I was there."

"You and Andrew Black?"

More silence, longer this time.

"I prefer not to speak about anyone else. Whoever else was there isn't important."

She was right, he knew. What mattered was between them. And she hadn't lied to him.

"Was that you then?"

The question confused him.

"In Portugal," she said, seeming to sense his confusion. "Outside the house."

"You knew I was there?"

"I saw one of your men. He followed me."

"When?"

"Six weeks ago." Before Georges knew about Black.

Liz was looking at him, a questioning look on her face. He shook his head — he'd explain later.

"What did he look like?"

"Very distinctive. He had badly scarred skin. His face was *packennarbig*. Pockmarked."

The man didn't sound familiar to him.

"I saw him again yesterday."

Murphy was lost again. "Yesterday?"

"Yes, in New York. After I telephoned your office."

"No one told me you called."

"As I've said, you have been compromised."

Her voice was quiet, confident, as if they had reversed roles, as if she were the pursuer and he the fugitive.

"Who did you talk to?"

"I must tell you in person. You won't believe me otherwise."

Murphy saw conspiracy again. Was this their final move?

"You have a choice," Karla said, seeming to read his mind. "You can hang up if you wish, even agree to meet and have me arrested. Or you can trust me as I am trusting you."

Her voice steady, calm. And it occurred to him that this wasn't about the past anymore.

"When do you want to meet?"

"This Sunday. In the morning, at eleven o'clock."

"Where?"

"In Genève. The Jet d'eau. Do you know it?"

It was a fountain, a water cannon at the end of a jetty on Lac Léman. The spot was exposed, very exposed. And very public.

"Yes, I know it."

"I will give you something. A token of my trust. Check U.S. passport number 152410582."

Murphy made a writing motion in the air. Liz handed him a pen. "Again."

Karla repeated the number slowly. "The passport was issued to Caroline Hall." Then she hung up.

Murphy set the receiver back in its cradle. "She wants to meet in Geneva."

"Go," his wife said.

"Just like that?"

"You know you're going."

"It could be a set up."

Liz smiled knowingly, the skin next to her eyes crinkling. "Then take the necessary precautions."

The telephone rang again and Murphy grabbed the receiver.

"Jim? Ben Liker here."

He put his hand over the mouthpiece and mouthed the name.

His wife made a face as if she had caught a whiff of something foul.

"I've been called to Washington. I've recently come out of a meeting at Headquarters about the Velasquez thing. It appears the Kiefer woman was involved. The shooter was someone named Andrew Black."

Plum. Goddamn Plum. The son of a bitch went over ....

Then tempering the thought; he's young, ambitious, looking out for himself.

Trust no one.

"I heard a rumor to that effect."

"We think it's connected to the Bacchetti affair. You took care of the weapons, right?"

He heard a tremor of anxiety in the AD's voice.

"Yes, I took care of them."

"I want you in Frisco immediately. You know SAC Morgan."

He and Morgan had met a few times.

"Get out there ASAP," Liker said. "You know the Kiefer woman better than anyone. Find her trail. I want this put to bed."

A man the depth of clichés.

"I'll be there. I'll call Morgan, tell him which flight I'll be on."

"Good man," the AD said, now amiable, and signed off.

Murphy hung up. "Liker wants me in San Francisco."

"But what about Geneva?"

"I'll stall Morgan. Tell him I have a hot tip. Figure it out from there."

He could see the worry on his wife's face, the lines etched along her brow. She leaned against him and he put his arm around her, kissed the top of her head and thought about the timing, the sequence of recent events: the Velasquez hit, Plum coming to him, the AD being summoned to Headquarters, Karla's call.

Trust no one.

"What's going on, Jim?" his wife's head still on his shoulder.

"They're making me choose. Either way I lose. It's ironic. Meant as a joke."

"It isn't a joke."

He loved her indignation, her vehemence, her resilience.

He took her hand again. "I need you to do something for me. I want you to take the things I stored in the shed to Mick's house in Westhampton. I'll let him know before I go."

"Find her, Jim. You have to."

And for the second time that evening Murphy realized that his wife knew him better than he knew himself.

Chapter 20

After Karla departed Andrew considered flying to Geneva, cleaning out his safe deposit box at the bank on the Route de Florissant and disappearing. In the end he rejected the notion and decided to go home, to face Khalil regardless of the consequences. He wouldn't run. He booked a flight to Boston with a TAP connection to Lisbon for the next day, then closed up the house on Fulton Street and returned the key to the property agent.

The skies were gloomy and a damp mist draped the city and airport when his flight landed at Logan so he remained in the terminal and took a mediocre meal at one of the airport restaurants. While he waited for the TAP flight, his thoughts strayed to Karla. After dropping her at the airport he had buried his feelings, buried them so deep it was as if they didn't exist; he never expected to see her again.

The next day, fifteen hours after leaving San Francisco, Andrew arrived in Lisbon. It was 6:30 a.m. local time and he began to move more slowly — discipline demanded he exercise appropriate care. For the better part of the morning he avoided his long-neglected car, observing the airport parking lot from various angles, looking for watchers and finally inspecting the car itself, but he found nothing.

Shortly before noon, the sun high in the hazy sky, he drove out of the carpark and headed east seemingly on a whim. Windows rolled down in the summer-like heat, he crossed the vast Alentejan plain to the walled city of Évora where he whiled away the afternoon strolling along the arch-cut alleyways in the older part of town, ducking into gardens, lingering over a late-afternoon *gallão* in a café, trying to recapture the mood and pace of the place. And always he was watching, vigilant.

At sunset he returned to his car and pointed it south. The land turned desolate, as if unexplored; darkness fell and every so often a car appeared in the distance, a pinpoint of light traveling steadily like a fishing boat viewed far offshore. Then the light would swell and blur and the car would rush past and it would be dark again, Andrew watching the afterglow of the taillights in the rear view mirror.

He drove for hours, cocooned in the car, as if traveling across some remote lunar landscape. He passed through the night towns and villages, their shop doors shut tight against the darkness, and continued south through the shallow hills of the Serra do Malhão until he came to the village of Loulé where he spent the night at an anonymous *pensão*. The next morning instead of turning west toward Luz and his house, and again seemingly on a whim, he continued south to the seaside city of Faro.

Months had passed since he visited Faro and it was well past noon when Andrew parked along the seawall at the far end of the harbor. He remained in the car for several minutes, watching the languorous flow of the local populace as they went about their daily tasks. Fishing skiffs, their hulls painted garish reds, greens and blues, bobbed lazily at the buoys dotting the harbor; a solitary fisherman rowed soundlessly toward the harbor entrance, oars dipping rhythmically, breaking the placid blue surface as the boat skimmed through the water. And finally Andrew felt connected. Restored — he was home.

He hopped out of his car and shut the door. A sultry breeze washed over his face as he walked toward the pedestrian zone. A motorbike whizzed past, the smell of raw petrol tainting the air.

271

Off to his right palm trees luffed in Jardim Manuel Bivar. After checking for further traffic he crossed to the pocket-sized park. A scattering of old men, their faces the color of fine leather, occupied the park benches and shifted their collective gaze as he ambled past. Young children chased one another among the trees.

Andrew sensed someone behind him. He resisted the urge to look over his shoulder and continued walking, filtering the sounds: children hooting, the rustle of the palm fronds, a stray conversation in Portuguese. The motorbike shrieked past on the other side of the park, rider hunched forward, squinting in the speed-induced vortex. Directly across the way a mix of tourists and locals lounged beneath umbrellas shading the tables in front of the Aliança café; others strolled up and down the pedestrian passage.

Andrew scanned the faces and spotted Majid standing in front of Hotel Faro. When their eyes met, the young bodyguard grinned and he tipped his head in compliment. Then he noticed Khalil sitting at one of the tables fronting the Aliança. The Palestinian was speaking with a white-shirted waiter, and in his dark glasses and crisply starched shirt he looked every bit the part of a prosperous bank officer on holiday.

Without breaking stride Andrew crossed the street. Khalil beamed and kicked out a chair as he approached.

Andrew eased into the proffered chair. "Your people are very good."

Khalil tipped his head as he had only moments ago. "You confused us this morning."

"I wasn't expecting anyone."

The Palestinian smiled. "After last time I thought it best we meet here."

The dig was subtle, a jest. Everyone was being polite.

Majid moved to the park and joined another young Arab, the one Andrew had felt following him. There would be others, he knew, stationed along the pedestrian zone, perhaps even at a window of Hotel Eva, which loomed above the harbor area. As the night in New York they left him no way out.

Khalil removed his sunglasses and set them on the table. "That was you in California." A statement.

Andrew nodded though he suspected this wasn't about the Mexican energy minister, and he didn't feel obliged to volunteer any information about Karla or her intentions.

Khalil signaled the waiter and indicated his cup. "Would you care for anything?"

The waiter stepped up to their table. There was a dark smudge on the front of his white shirt, Andrew noticed, a coffee stain.

"*Um gallão, faz favor,*" he told the waiter.

The man gave him a curt nod, a quasi-bow, and retreated.

"Of course you know why I am here." Khalil had switched to French.

Andrew settled back in the chair. "We split up," he said.

"After California?"

He let that stand for a moment, watched a seagull catwalk along the curb. He didn't feel obliged to lie either. Not unless he had to.

"I don't know where she is."

"She's in Genève."

Andrew didn't react, concentrated on not reacting.

"She contacted the authorities," Khalil said. "She telephoned Murphy and wants to meet."

He had warned her. Twice.

Khalil looked at him, waiting for a response. On the wall above his right shoulder dull-gray primer showed where the yellow topcoat had flaked away. Majid and his compatriot hadn't moved.

"She's misguided, Khalil."

"No, she's turned."

"After Vermont they will think it's a set up."

"Apparently Murphy doesn't. He's on his way."

And Andrew saw the endgame now, the final act. Karla, the German terrorist, and her alleged pursuer in his scope, proof of a conspiracy, of collusion. He couldn't deny the elegance of Red Path operation, both agencies compromised, Plum's position in the FBI likely enhanced somehow, and if he weren't involved he would have to admire the sheer audacity of Plum's plan, no matter how much its essential duplicity offended him. But he was involved. Deeply, Andrew admitted now. Inextricably.

"Murphy's the 'influential man,'" he said aloud.

Khalil bobbed his head.

"And Raymond will spin their deaths as a CIA plot."

Another bob of the head, a look of smug satisfaction on the Palestinian's face, and Andrew suspected they knew Karla would go to the authorities, to Murphy in particular, planned it; it was the reason they chose her.

"I won't do it."

Khalil hunched forward over the table. "She will tell them everything. About all of us."

"No."

"Everything!" A whispered hiss.

Andrew stole a glance at the neighboring tables: no one was showing any interest.

"You know as well as I," Khalil said, throttling back, "Raymond can't allow that. At least you will keep it clean."

Andrew knew they had him, had since he agreed to the job in

El Salvador. He felt a throb of resentment and willed it away. It was pure madness, he knew, what Karla was doing. Brave but madness all the same. And regardless she was dead. He could even justify it as a mercy killing in his mind. She wouldn't feel a thing.

"I do it my way."

"Of course."

The waiter brought their coffees and set the fresh demitasse and tumbler on the table before them. Khalil raised his cup in salute and Andrew joined him as if in accord. He took a sip — the coffee tasted bitter, sharp but pleasant — then set the glass down.

"When?"

"In two days," the Palestinian replied. "At 11:00 a.m., Sunday."

"Not much time to prepare."

"We have an air ticket for you."

"How far away will they be?"

"Two to three hundred meters. We have arranged a place for you, an apartment on Quai Gustave Ador. They are meeting at the Jet d'eau."

There was a promenade fronting the south side of the lake, Andrew remembered, a causeway leading to the fountain.

"I need to make a couple of calls."

"Of course, my friend."

Andrew felt another throb of resentment — *my friend* — and let it go. The task at hand required all of his focus, all of his discipline.

He pushed back from the table, chair legs grating on the cobblestones, and stood up. As he made his way to the café entrance he saw Majid cut through the snarl of vehicle traffic at the foot of the pedestrian zone. His cohort remained in the park.

Inside was cool, the air subterranean. Only two of the dozen tables were occupied. At the one closest to the entrance four men, three locals and what Andrew took to be a Finn with his straw-colored hair and ready smile, were discussing the benefits of foreign investment in local real estate development. At the other, well back in the room, a middle-aged couple sat in rigid silence, the woman's expression pinched, sharp.

English, Andrew thought as he moved into the adjoining room. The room smelled of bodies, of close quarters, though none of the tables were occupied. On his right, windows flanked the side entrance providing a view of more tables set up along the pedestrian passage. Majid was standing beside one of the tables; the young guard grinned once more.

Ignoring him, Andrew made his way to the payphone in the back corner near the toilets. He placed the first call; this time a different woman answered, her voice melodious, playful almost, and he asked for Albert.

"*Un moment, s'il vous plait.*"

As he waited for the shipper to come on the line he watched a waiter attend to Majid, who had taken a seat at the table. The English woman scuffled into the room, a perplexed look on her face; Andrew pointed out the toilet.

"*Allo?*"

He turned away as the woman shambled past.

"It's me, Albert. I trust the package I sent arrived." As with Khalil he spoke in French.

"Yes, it arrived a few days ago."

A roar of raucous laughter rose in the next room.

"And the items sent earlier?"

"Here as well."

"I will need to take delivery of both shipments tomorrow in Genève."

"Not a problem." Albert didn't ask why he needed the handgun.

"Where shall we make the delivery?"

Andrew thought for a moment. "The Hotel de la Paix. I haven't booked a room yet. Perhaps you can handle that? One with a view of the lake."

Albert didn't question that either, the room with a view.

"Certainly. Tomorrow, you said?"

"Yes, Saturday. I apologize for the short notice."

"Not a problem."

Andrew watched the other bodyguard approach Majid. They spoke for a few moments then the second guard retreated the way he had come.

"Will you require further shipments?"

"I'm uncertain at this point," Andrew said. "I will let you know."

"Again not a problem."

They agreed to meet the next day at 4:00 p.m. on the Pont du Mont-Blanc. Albert would have the key to the hotel room. Then they set two fallback times and locations.

After the shipper rang off Andrew placed the second call. The UBS manager was amenable though he found the request for a meeting on such short notice, and on a Saturday no less, unusual, but he agreed to make himself available in the early afternoon.

When they finished, Andrew replaced the handset. Majid was still seated at the table. The English woman exited the toilet and Andrew followed her into the next room where she rejoined her partner in mute silence.

He continued past the land speculators, a portrait of jovial health, felt the flare of heat when he stepped outside. Intense, bright. The waiter was clearing the table where he and Khalil had taken their coffee. He spotted the Palestinian standing near the stoplight that marked the entrance to the pedestrian zone, the second guard at his side.

The young Arab stepped away as he approached.

"It's arranged," Andrew said.

Khalil smiled as if he expected no less. "Let's walk." An echo.

He took Andrew's arm and they started up the pedestrian passage, two longtime associates taking a post-meal stroll. Nearly everyone had taken shelter from the afternoon heat and the smell of the waterfront faded as they moved inland. On both sides of the passageway were tourist establishments, shops, cafés, a bank — a mix of colonial whitewash and modern glass façades. And all the while Andrew sensed eyes monitoring their progress.

They passed through a construction zone: a pile of torn-up cobblestones, a building undergoing renovation, façade removed, shadowy interior exposed, the scent of sour milk. Farther on, a bone-thin dog lolled in a sliver of shade in front of a shuttered pharmacy, tail twitching as they approached.

"There is one other thing," Khalil said.

"What other thing?" Andrew said, focus disturbed.

"Raymond wants to have his man there."

He considered telling Khalil that he knew about Raymond, who he was, then thought better of it.

"I always work alone, you know that."

"Still he will insist."

Better to go along — Andrew remembered — *to act tamely*. But not too tamely.

"He observes only."

"*Bien sûr.*"

Then the Palestinian smiled, smiled as if he believed he had thought of everything.

***

Dawn — gray light.

The curtain sheers stirred in the faint breeze. The lake was flat, still, achromatic; sailboats, their masts like quills, stood motionless in marinas along the far shore. In the distance the Mont Blanc massif caught first light, a cloud-like ridge of alpenglow.

The previous evening after he entered the room Albert arranged for him at Hotel de la Paix, Andrew set the previously purchased artist's portfolio and soft canvas bag of documents on the bed next to the rifle case, then went to the terrace doors and opened them. He had arrived in Geneva on Friday night and checked into a different hotel, the Clos du Voltaire on Rue de Lyon. The following morning he went to an art supply shop and purchased the portfolio, then located a grocer and bought enough food for several days and returned to the hotel until his appointment with the banker.

After removing the IDs, credit cards and bundles of cash from his safe deposit box at the bank he met Albert at the appointed hour without incident. Then he returned to the Clos du Voltaire once again, had a meal and slept for several hours stockpiling his strength for the long night and day ahead.

At 10:00 p.m. he walked into Hotel de la Paix as if he were a guest, took the stairs to the room on the third floor and hung the DO NOT DISTURB sign on the door. Even now, standing a few paces back from the open doors, Andrew was uncertain how the shooting and aftermath would play out. He saw complication everywhere, his only confidence that afterward he would disappear, vanish.

He walked to the bed, retrieved his binoculars from the duffel bag Albert had delivered with the rifle case and panned the opposite shore, the Promenade du Lac, the Jardin Anglais with it well-tended gardens and spotless footpaths, the vacant benches. He felt certain Karla would leave it until the last moment — she wouldn't trust Murphy completely — and he pictured her gliding along the promenade, weaving through the crowd of strollers in their Sunday best, breaking free finally ...

He saw her on the hillside facing his house, the wind lifting her hat, the golden highlights in her hair, the damp sheen along the tunnel of her spine ... then lying in bed beside him, her skin silken in the glow of the streetlight.

They'll kill her anyway.

Andrew turned on his heel and returned to the bed, to where his rifle lay crosswise on the open case. The faint smell of ripe banana in the air. The previous evening he field-stripped the weapon, cleaned and oiled it, then inserted a loaded magazine. He wanted the shots to be perfect, absolutely perfect. *She wouldn't feel a thing.*

And it occurred to Andrew that was his focus, his discipline. Not feeling a thing.

***

The sky had lightened, the lake a palette of blues. There was a bit of chop and small clusters of people, like ants, were gathering on the far shore. Andrew brought the rifle to his shoulder, put his eye to the scope, adjusted the focus. An elderly gentleman in a dark business suit and homburg was making his way along the promenade, furled umbrella in hand, *tap-tap-tapping* soundlessly on the walkway.

One ... and two.

But it was rehearsal. It wasn't real.

***

Andrew glanced at the digital clock on the nightstand — 7:11. A roll of the dice. Karma. He wondered whether good or bad, then turned his attention back to the far side of the lake. After his rendezvous with Albert he had strolled past the building on Quai Gustave Ador, noted the entrance on Rue Muzy, identified lines of escape.

Hours later, after entering the room at Hotel de la Paix, he pinpointed the apartment. It was simple enough: there was a sign along the roofline, BRUEGUET etched in neon against the night sky. Top floor — Khalil told him — west corner.

At first he wasn't certain Plum's man was there, though the balcony doors were open. Then, at midnight, he saw a match flare in the dark apartment, the red glow of a cigarette. Every thirty minutes after that, like clockwork, another match flared.

He's there now. In the shadows. A reflection, Andrew thought, of me.

***

Andrew glanced at the clock again — 7:50. Indecipherable, meaningless this time. He went to the canvas bag that contained his cash and IDs, removed five twenty-franc notes from one of the bundles and shoved them into his jacket pocket, then took his High Standard handgun from the duffel bag and slipped it into the waistband of his pants at the small of his back. He shrugged his jacket into place, checked his image in the mirror to make certain the weapon didn't show, then picked up the art portfolio, rifle inside, and went to the door.

Andrew listened for several moments, eased the door open slightly and listened again. Quiet. When he stepped into the corridor, the light flicked on. A murmured conversation rose from the lobby. He closed the door, leaving the DO NOT DISTURB sign in place, and peeled off the gloves he had donned before entering the room. A minute later he left the hotel, unobserved.

***

The streets were deserted, the pavement wet, freshly scrubbed. Andrew shivered involuntarily in the morning chill and crossed to the lakeside of the street. A motor launch set off from the shore, a deep-throated rumble, white V-shaped wave rising in its wake.

After crossing the Pont du Mont-Blanc he dropped down to the paved walkway and continued along the waterfront, portfolio swinging evenly at his side. There was more activity here — people sanding hulls, others laboring over outboard engines, still others exchanging greetings as they toted provisions to the docks in preparation for a day's sail. No one seemed to take notice of him.

Moving more quickly, Andrew cut through the gardens and emerged on Quai Gustave Ador. He could see the pink-blush façade of the apartment building a few blocks away, the wrought-iron railings on the balconies on the upper floors painted black. More echoes.

Two minutes later Andrew entered the building. He pressed the heavy wooden door shut with his back and paused to let his eyes adjust to the relative darkness, noticed the warmth after his walk in the cold morning air. Natural light, like a fine mist, filtered down the central stairwell. The building still, quiet, eerie almost.

He propped the portfolio against the front door, pulled the gloves from his jacket pocket and put them on. Then he picked up the portfolio and started up the stairs, taking them two at a time, pausing to monitor each landing as he went. The familiar scent of freshly brewed coffee, a baby squalling behind a door, a radio announcing the day's weather behind another, a sputtering snore, water trickling in a toilet.

When he reached the top floor he paused again, longer this time, knowing Plum's man would expect him to exercise caution. The apartment door was near the end of the landing. He strode to it, rapped twice, then twice more and stepped back so the other man could see him clearly through the peephole.

After a few moments the door inched open and Plum's man showed himself — it was the man who followed Karla to the beach — and everything became clear. His every suspicion warranted, the depth of Khalil's betrayal revealed.

Andrew quelled the thought. *Focus. Act tamely.*

"*Je suis en avance,*" he said, his voice measured. In control.

The man gave him an uncomprehending look.

"Raymond sent me."

He nodded, eyeing the portfolio in Andrew's hand. "Sully," he said by way of introduction and opened the door the rest of the way.

Andrew stepped past him. He felt the other man's eyes follow him as he made his way across the apartment to the balcony door, taking his time. He noted the open toilet door — no one else there — the Scandinavian-style furnishings, the Winchester rifle with telescopic sight, a spindle-backed chair, the overflowing ashtray on the floor.

He felt the handgun prod his spine as he propped the portfolio against the wall and took in the view: the promenade, the causeway, the silvery plume of the fountain. Andrew confirmed the distance — *two to three hundred meters* — then located Hotel de la Paix on the far shore, the terrace on the third floor, the open doors, shadows in the room beyond. As if it were a mirror image in time.

"Which one do you want to take?"

The fullness of the other man's voice surprised Andrew.

"I'll take both," he said, eyes still on the hotel.

"I thought we'd each take one," Plum's man countered, business-like. "I'll take either the man or the woman. Don't matter to me."

Andrew turned from the view. The other shooter remained by the door, expression smug yet ambivalent, without empathy, and it made him think of Plum that night in New York, knowing now what he must do, how it must go.

"Why'd they send you to my house?"

"Just checking," the other man said, smiling, his gaze fixed on the portfolio.

"On what?"

His eyes flicked to Andrew's face. "The woman, of course. She led us a merry chase."

"More like you led her a merry chase."

Sully snorted. "Got that right."

Andrew rehearsed the moves in his mind.

"What the fuck?"

He already had the gun in his hand, pointed at Sully's head. "You gutshot Grossman."

Plum's man was staring at the gun, the smell of his fear filling the room. His tongue shot out, wetted his lower lip.

"Your ass is grass, man."

The least of my worries, Andrew thought. "How does it feel, asshole?"

"You don't know ..."

He cut Sully off — he *did* know. "I have a message to send. And you're the messenger."

Andrew shot him, once, in the center of the forehead, then again for good measure, the silenced shots abrupt, like stifled coughs, and he watched the body slide to the floor. A familiar sweet scent in the air.

On another level Andrew was listening. He heard the diesel knock of a car passing on the street below, the *bumpa-bumpa* of a motorboat idling in the marina. Then realization seeped through; nothing had changed. Karla was still dead. If not by his hand, then by someone else's. Some other Sully. And it occurred to him that having Albert secure the room at Hotel de la Paix wasn't mere caution. It was premonition, foresight. Fate.

Andrew retrieved the spent cartridges, pocketed them and picked up the portfolio. On his way out he passed the other shooter, dead eyes staring up at him, his last moment of confusion captured.

"I do it my way."

* * *

When he returned to the room at Hotel de la Paix, Andrew left the DO NOT DISTURB sign in place and went through the escape documents, sorting them by name. He took his real passport, the driver's license and credit cards in that name into the bathroom and cut them up, letting the pieces fall into the toilet. He imagined he should feel sad, his identity lost in a way. Instead he felt resolute, unbowed, and it occurred to him that to this point everything had been preparation, preparation for this moment, a moment untainted by personality, by want or desire: the ultimate gesture. He finally was the act itself, the act alone.

After the water took the last bits of the documents and credit cards, Andrew returned to the bedroom. Sunlight filtered through the open doors casting lattice-like shadows across the room. The sounds of the late-awakening city floated up from the street. He slid the desk in front of the terrace doors, then cleared one of the nightstands, hoisted it and set it on top of the desk to form a make-shift shooting platform.

Then he sat down on the bed, the rifle beside him, and willed every vestige of feeling from his soul.

***

At 10:54 Karla appeared. Andrew felt a sudden rush, a tremor in his chest. He almost missed her — she'd colored her hair. Wisely she had attached herself to a group of fellow travelers. He watched the group move across the bridge; she walked beside another woman, carriage erect, the two of them talking, laughing easily.

Andrew put his eye to the scope. Her cheeks were flushed, her skin radiant. He had never seen her so vibrant, so sure of herself, so committed, and he felt drawn in by her presence, by her energy once more.

He followed her as she and the group moved along the promenade, lost her in the scope for a few moments when they walked behind a paddle wheeler. Then she reappeared, alone now, and strolled toward another group of young people. Nice, he thought.

Andrew scanned ahead looking for Murphy. Instead he found Khalil and Plum standing together, deep in the gardens where Karla wouldn't see them, there to bear witness. He moved from one to the other, studying their expressions, registering their obvious complacence, their ignorance of what had transpired.

Khalil turned toward the building on Gustave Ador. Andrew moved the rifle back to Karla, centering on her as she continued toward the causeway, bodies flashing across the scope, unaware. A glimmer of acknowledgement — *Murphy.*

She brushed a lock of hair from her cheek. He remembered the spark in her eyes. Righteous, alive.

They'll kill her anyway.

Fuck it. Go with feeling.

He swung the rifle and took Plum with one clean shot. *At five — six hundred yards*. Then again: *insurance*.

Then he had Khalil in his scope. A look of acquiescence on the Palestinian's face, of acceptance. Of understanding. Khalil turned and walked away slowly, and contrary to his every instinct Andrew let him go.

He swung the rifle back to Karla and Murphy, chaos swirling around them, Karla pushing Murphy away as he tried to shield her. Then she faced the hotel, a look of comprehension on her face. Stillness. And he knew that she knew it had been him.

Bound once more.

EPILOGUE

September 1980 — Tuolumne Meadows.

The place couldn't be more unlike Portugal. There was a lingering crispness, a dryness in the air, and the silence was more private somehow. On the far side of Tioga Pass Road a streambed idled across the meadows, the immediacy of the sky making boulders of the scattered domes. Shreds of cloud. To the east the rising sun grazed the mountaintops seemingly without fire.

Andrew shivered as he locked the car doors, shouldered his rucksack and started up the Cathedral Lakes trail. He spent nearly four months traveling from Geneva to Tuolumne Meadows shedding identities as he went. At times the journey seemed endless, without direction, an exodus of sorts, though from the moment he encountered Khalil and his guards in Faro he knew he was coming here, where for him it all began.

During his travels he came to understand that his reasoning was flawed, misguided at best. His views simplistic, unworkable. His mistake was in believing it was possible to exist in an ether, alone. But that was a con, a sleight of hand. So he returned to the Yosemite high country to find his way anew. Without illusion.

While en route he had monitored the news each day. Murphy resigned from the FBI. Other opportunities were cited. A cliché. As for Karla, not a word though he took comfort in knowing she had escaped.

In Denver he used his last best set of ID to purchase the car, considered visiting a gun shop but reminded himself he had left that world behind, and headed west on I-70. At a small outdoor store in Grand Junction he bought a pair of trail shoes, the pack and assorted camping gear, then left the Interstate for good and continued west across the shimmering wastelands of Utah and Nevada, stopping at places along the way that stoked his interest. He was getting ready to run the mountain scree.

Andrew felt his body warm as he continued to tramp up the trail. Patches of sunlight filtered through the trees. Off to his left he heard the rush of Budd Creek, birds trilling, smelled the dusty scent of Joshua pine. Before long he located the faint users' trail that led to Budd Lake. The trail dropped down to the creek and skirted it for a while, the white-cold water tumbling over rocks in places, his heart thrumming as he gained elevation. Then the path ascended a steep gully to a series of granite benches and died out but he remembered to keep to the right, the occasional stacked duck confirming the way.

Soon, he found himself among stands of white and lodgepole pine near the base of Cathedral Peak, the trail distinct once more. The peak's scree-clogged lower slopes tempted him but he marched on.

When he was above the tree line, Andrew swung south traversing low on the saddle that connected Cathedral and Echo Peaks, the hardy alpine sod soggy, spongy underfoot. He could feel the mountain breeze, crisp and clean, as if it had traveled unimpeded for thousands of miles. When he crested the last rise he stopped to consider the view. Budd Lake, turquoise verging on aquamarine, was set in a shallow basin below him. At the far end granite peaks formed an amphitheater and soared skyward, their faces white-hot in the sunlight. Exultant, immutable. Exactly as he pictured it in his mind all these years.

Contented, Andrew set off and descended the drainage to the lake. Gnarled wind-stunted pines endured at water's edge. When he came upon an orange one-person tent pitched near the shoreline he felt a moment's disappointment — he'd thought he would have the place to himself. He scanned the area quickly working out from the tent, then peered up at the summit notch, the peaks themselves, huge cairns of broken rock. He saw no one.

He passed the tent, zipped-tight and unoccupied, and found a place to camp farther along, a sheltered spot on a granite shelf well back from the lake. He set his pack on the ground and took out the night's provisions. Tomorrow he would run.

Water bottles in hand, Andrew picked his way back down the slabs to the shore. As he refilled the bottles he gazed up at the peaks and again saw no one. He returned to his site and unpacked his bivy sack and sleeping bag. Shortly before sunset a man hooted from the summit notch, the cry echoing among the peaks, then began to half-jog, half-skid down the scree slope below the notch.

Andrew dug out his Zeiss mini-binoculars and glassed the man. He was big, burly, yet he moved with apparent grace, long shaggy hair flying. A full bushy beard laced with gray cornsilk. An old hippie from another era.

When he reached the saddle, the man followed it until he was directly above the tent. He paused and raised a hand in salute, then made his way down to his campsite. At sunset Andrew watched his campmate fetch water from the lake and as darkness fell they both settled in for the night in their separate sites. Andrew thought of Karla as he was nodding off, wondered where she was. Then pictured her pressed against the chain-link fence, facing the hotel. The stillness.

Once during the night he was awakened by the sound of rock careening down one of the faces, a sharp crack each time it struck. Andrew stuck his head out of his sleeping bag and listened, felt the night chill, the other man's tent a shadow in the moonlight. He listened for a long time but there was only the rustle of the wind, and after a while he fell asleep staring at the star-studded sky.

***

In the morning the cold woke Andrew. The other man's tent was gone. He scrunched down into the warmth of his sleeping bag and watched dawn break. In time he slipped into his clothes and crawled out. Shivering in the early morning chill he pulled on his pile jacket and jammed a wool stocking cap on his head, then sat on the rock windbreak and tied his shoes, already anticipating the day's run, the rush.

He took the sack of food from his pack, spilled some cereal into a bowl and poured water over it; he ate efficiently, the bowl balanced in one hand, the other shoved into his pocket for warmth between bites. When he finished, he went down to the lake and examined the other campsite, the dry imprint of the tent, boot marks in the loose soil. There had been another car parked at the trailhead.

The freak's presence dismissed, Andrew refilled his water bottles, packed his rucksack with the day's supplies and set off. Before long he was at the foot of the slope and he started to climb in earnest, rocks sliding, clattering beneath his trail shoes. He cut short switchbacks, never attacking the slope directly, concentrating on his footing, on his breath. He stopped once to shed his jacket and gazed down at the lake, spotted his bivy sack, the patchwork of vacant campsites. Not a soul in sight; he was alone.

He turned back to the slope. Above, the scree fan narrowed and appeared steeper, foreshortened, and topped out at a gap in the ragged ridge, a pass of sorts. Five more minutes, he thought and made directly for the notch.

When he reached the summit notch, Andrew stopped for a few minutes to catch his breath, heart thumping in the thin air. On the far side of the notch huge boulders, as if frozen mid-tumble, littered the slope below and washed across a granite basin and up against the prehistoric fin of Matthes Crest. Farther on were more mountains and he gazed upon the scene with a sort of reverence. A holy place.

Already heat rose in waves from the basin, beckoning him, but Andrew took his time luxuriating in the feeling, in the moment, all the while visualizing the run in his mind. He reached into his pack and took out a water bottle and some food. When he drank, the cold water made his teeth ache. He munched a handful of raisins, some nuts, and re-stowed it all.

Then he tightened the laces on his shoes, stood and stretched, arching his back, rotating his spine. He rolled his neck from side to side, then shouldered his pack and snugged down the straps slowly, drawing out the moment. Savoring it.

Finally he started down the rock field, jogging slowly at first, concentrating on the motion, on balance, testing the texture and contour of each rock, sliding to the edge of control, then back, toying with it. Then he picked it up a notch, running now, twisting and turning, following the terrain, his knees absorbing the shocks, gliding, and suddenly he was running full out, fluid, harmonious. He braked, skidded, straight-armed the side of a boulder, spinning off in another direction. Faster still. Flying now.

A rock tipped precariously and Andrew tottered. His ankle rolled beneath him and a sharp pain shot up his calf, a wave of nausea. He hobbled on, forcing himself to move, knowing that he had to keep moving, pushing through the pain. And then he was running again, regaining his momentum, jumping, braking, hurdling rocks, flowing through space. Everything blurring, merging. Free. Consciousness — him — gone.

The force of the shot knocked Andrew back and he tumbled down the face of a boulder. He lay wedged among the rocks, winded, shoulder on fire. Fuck. He thought of the rock cracking in the night. Then remembering: *A man in a pickup helped me escape. An old freak.* Betrayal upon betrayal, he thought. And he pictured Karla again, letting her go. The one "good" thing I ever did.

Andrew rolled onto his side, winced; white stars fired before his eyes. "Christ." He felt around the wound, his shirt wet, sticky. The bullet had entered the fleshy part of his shoulder and exited high in the back. A clean shot, through and through.

Arm clamped tightly to his side, Andrew worked himself up and peeked around the boulder. He caught a flash of light. A reflection. Idiot.

You can traverse left, rabbit your way through the warren of rocks.

That's the rat thinking. Grasping thinking.

Zen, he thought, understanding for the first time.

Andrew steadied himself against the rock. A shaft of pain. He took a breath gentling the pain, enclosing it. Absorbing the hot glow.

He remembered a line from Nietzsche: "The ultimate goodness is not to be afraid."

Then he was running, plummeting down the broken field of rock. Not away like Khalil. But straight-ahead, toward the shooter. Flying again.

And he was there. Mindful.

In the moment — in time.

CPSIA information can be obtained
at www.ICGtesting.com
Printed in the USA
FFHW022044301018
49039676-53337FF